STAR SEED

A Novel

D. C. Poyer

Northampton House Press

First edition published by Donning Starblaze in 1982; second edition revised and copyrighted 2024.
Cover image by NHP LLC from an image by Perchance.org.
Copyright 1982, 2024 by D. C. Poyer DBA David Andreissen. All rights reserved. Published by Northampton House Press, Franktown, Virginia, USA.
Trade paper edition, ISBN 978-1-950668-29-8.
Library of Congress Control Number: 2024909136
Printed in the USA
9 8 7 6 5 4 3 2

Other Books

As D. C. Poyer

Stepfather Bank * *The Shiloh Project* * *White Continent*

The Hemlock County Novels

Thunder on the Mountain * *As the Wolf Loves Winter*
Winter in the Heart * *The Dead of Winter* * *The Hill*

Tales of the Modern Navy

The Academy * *Arctic Sea* * *Violent Peace* * *Overthrow*
Deep War * *Hunter Killer* * *Onslaught* * *Tipping Point*
The Cruiser * *The Towers* * *The Crisis* * *The Weapon*
Korea Strait * *The Threat* * *The Command* * *Black Storm*
China Sea * *Tomahawk* * *The Gulf* * *The Passage*
The Med * *The Circle*

The Tiller Galloway Novels

Down to a Sunless Sea * *Louisiana Blue*
Bahamas Blue * *Hatteras Blue*

The Civil War at Sea

Fire on the Waters * *A Country of Our Own*
That Anvil of Our Souls

Non-Series Works

Writing in the Age of AI * *F-35 (with Tom Burbage et al.)*
The Whiteness of the Whale * *Heroes of Annapolis*
Happier Than This Day And Time * *Ghosting*
On War and Politics (with Arnold Punaro)
The Only Thing to Fear

STAR SEED

ONE

*S*hark," warned Deela in seatalk, pointing to her left, toward the Deep.

The high-pitched word carried clearly through the water, and Darrin "Dinker" Cross slowed the sweep of his fins. He breathed out and sank toward the grayish, rocky floor of the Caribbean.

His gaze followed her pointing arm, and as he settled toward the bottom he reached back to his support pack for the stinger. He turned in a circle, holding the weapon ready for use.

They hovered in the center of a vast blue bowl. Two hundred feet below the surface, the sun seemed light-years away. A feeble bluish glow, faintly tinted with a wash of white, arched over their heads, deepening to cobalt and then to navy as the sea met the sandy, rock-strewn plain.

He finished his sweep and looked back toward Deela.

She'd swum ahead a few feet, bare legs scissoring slowly, dropping to the very lip of the Deep. He glanced down at the stinger, a meter-long shaft of black-chromed steel tipped with an ultrasound head, checking that the safety ring was set on Off. He took a dry breath of argon-oxygen, craned around again, then swam downward to follow her.

From above she was hard to see. Both of the Kids had been designed with the countershading typical of most large marine animals, and the darker skin of her back and legs blended with the bottom in the dim blue light. The small five-liter oxygen tank, all she wore, was slung across her back. She glanced at him as he approached. Her mouthpiece hung free, and she vented a small stream of bubbles. *"Careful, Dinker. Couple of them. Over the edge."*

He nodded, touched down lightly on one hand, and peered over the edge into the Deep.

From Hispaniola and Puerto Rico and the Virgin Islands, the Continental Shelf slanted slowly down, dropping as the land was left behind. It rose briefly in a last barrier of submerged plateaus and reefs; the Caicos, Silver Bank, Navidad Bank. Then, very suddenly, fell away. Here, fifty kilometers out, was the true edge of the continent. Beyond it lay the Atlantic abyss.

Though he was weightless in the sea, Cross clutched at the rock as he looked down. He couldn't see far; light was swallowed up below them in a night far darker and more profound than any midnight. Inky, vast, the deep ocean lay below them, as mysterious as space, and as unexplored.

And now, he thought bitterly, *it will stay that way. Forever.*

Deela gripped his arm through his wetsuit at the same moment a flicker of motion from below drew his eye. A grayish shadow detached from the gloom, moving slowly upward along the projecting rocks and fissures of the face of the cliff. He barely had time to swallow before a second shadow appeared behind and below the first, long thin tail sculling unhurriedly. Also, like the first, heading up.

He glanced at Deela. Her eyes were vast and dark, pupils wider in the dimness than Human Surface Norm; but something else, very human, showed in the way small white teeth gripped her lower lip. He smiled tightly behind his mask at her. It wasn't often one of the Kids looked their actual age. But just then, she really did look only sixteen. He reached a gloved hand to squeeze her shoulder reassuringly, and turned his attention back to the sharks.

From up here at the edge of the drop, the slowly approaching predators looked like tadpoles seen in a creek, the same thick body tapering to a sinuous whip of a tail. But they were already growing larger, and his jaws tightened as he realized how close they were. He had to correct for the distortion of the water (*unlike Deela*, he thought), but still the sharks could not be more than fifty meters away, and still rising deliberately along the edge of the shelf.

By the same token, they were *big*. From the long pectoral fins, the tips of which he could now see as they rose, and the grayish color, carcharhinids. If that identification was accurate, he and Deela were in for trouble. He frowned, puzzled. There was something wrong about them, something he couldn't quite put his finger on, but that smelled fishy.

Right, Dinker, he thought wryly. *The end of the world and you're cracking puns.* He clicked the stinger's safety ring to Ready, wincing at the sound.

The lead shark swung leisurely toward them.

"Cover," he squeaked at Deela, articulating the high-pitched seaspeech with difficulty. It hurt his throat; replacing fricatives and sibilants with high-pitched, clicking consonants had a price. She nodded and they back-pedaled from the edge toward a low jumble of rocks a few feet away. He dropped to swim below her. In the dim light the girl's paler underside seemed to glow, outlining small breasts and streamlined, hairless groin. That always jarred, that neither Kid had body hair.

The sharks were at least three meters long. They could be duskies, blacktips, or reef sharks, all genus carcharhinids, all dangerous. Too big to be smalltails, a number of which he'd killed around the Station in the last two years. It was hard to tell one kind of shark from another, from above.

He and Deela reached the rocks, a pile of tan flat boulders, as Cross's support pack began beeping. He reached back to toggle the alarm off. The Mark 39 closed-circuit rebreather was a fine air supply, versatile, tough, and efficient. Had to be, for the Navy to make it standard; but it was cumbered with too many gadgets for his taste. The alarm that had just gone off was a warning his oxygen usage was above normal.

Of course it is, stupid machine, he thought, reversing the stinger to hold it out butt-first as the lead shark sailed over the edge. His breath whistled in and out. He glanced around to see Deela, mouthpiece in her teeth, working furiously to dig a rock out of the sand.

When he looked back, he knew they were in for it. These weren't duskies or reef sharks; dangerous, but not killers. The first view of their silhouette told him that. The dorsal was broad, rounded, like the rudder of a World War I fighter. As the leader turned to circle them he noted light patches where the tips of the grayish-brown fins and tail seemed to have been dipped in chalk.

Whitetips.

No time to wonder what they were doing here, these open-ocean killers. Their element was the deep, the endless sea without bottom or boundary to hem them in. *Every rule has an exception, I know,* Cross thought, watching the second whitetip, a bit smaller, coloring more brownish and irregular, follow the first into the lazy circle. *But why here? Why now, after everything else?*

Deela had stopped digging, resting her hands on the loosened rock. Her mouthpiece was out again, hanging against her chest. She was ready for ten minutes of all-out effort before she'd need another breath. The Kids used oxygen much more efficiently than the poorly 'designed' Human Surface Norm.

Like her, Cross was frozen into immobility, his back to a large rock, the metal rod held diagonally out butt-first like a medieval quarterstaff. Motionless, he should be almost invisible to the sharks. The closed-circuit Mark 39 absorbed his carbon dioxide and monitored his blood and enriched the argon demand-flow gas stream with oxygen from an integral tank. There were no bubbles. His dark suit blended with the seabed. Seldom a bottom feeder, they should have lost sight of him, lost interest, moved away.

These didn't. The leader's tiny dark eye was expressionless, fixed. Fixed, Cross saw, on him. It circled closer, the slightly smaller companion trailing. He made out clearly the ugly, slightly-parted gash of a mouth, the gill slits like parallel knife cuts in the rounded powerful body, the long, tapering, slightly curved pectoral, trailing edges a little ragged, as if it had been gnawed by rats.

Carcharhinus longimanus, he thought. The gray shark with the long hands.

It turned suddenly, wheeling with a single powerful thrust of its tail, and came directly for him. He crouched and parried easily; in a career of underwater work he'd met scores of sharks, mastered them all, and eaten well of many. The butt of the stinger grated audibly on the shark's rough skin, shoving it away, so that it passed overhead. He could easily have killed it had he struck it with the rod's business end. But it was a long way back to the Station, over a klick, too far to tow a large carcass.

And after so much dying, thought Dinker Cross, looking after it, *There's no thrill in killing. No thrill at all.*

The big whitetip circled, tail flicking side to side. It seemed annoyed, appeared to be studying him, but he dismissed that thought. He knew enough marine biology to realize the futility of attributing human emotions to fish. Or even to the porpoises, civilized though they'd become as a result of the Station's work.

And a shark was far below any mammal in intelligence, by any measure. *Pure instinct,* he reminded himself as the leader came in again. *Frustrate it a few times and it'll go away.* He poised the rod, ready for the thing's mindless rush.

It did not come in as fast as the first time. But at the last possible instant it swerved, and the open jaws narrowly missed his exposed left arm.

Son of a bitch. Cross's spine prickled under his wet suit. *This joker don't wanna play by the rules.*

"Dinker!" Deela's voice, high-pitched both in seaspeech and alarm. And he remembered, belatedly: *The other shark.*

He turned, to see her trying to fend off its attack with the too-large chunk of rock. It scraped against the thing's nose and was torn from her hands. A thin black mist bloomed around her hand, blood, dark in the dim blue light.

He twisted his neck to search. The mask narrowed his

vision, obscured by the burned-out and no longer functioning heads-up displays. Then found the bigger whitetip overhead, its light belly melting into the bluish whiteness. He constricted his larynx to the seaspeech. *"Over here. By this boulder."*

He pulled her beside him against it, to the left; he was right-handed. Then reversed the stinger to hold it point-first and turned the ring to On. A thin whine drilled into his ears as it built up charge, while he eyed the sharks.

The sense of wrongness was overpowering now. There were no whitetips around the Station. Had never been. Whitetips did not come in from the open ocean. They did not attack targets that blended with the bottom, that did not move, that did not present high contrast. And he remembered now what had seemed so eerie at first. Most of all . . . they didn't school.

Sharks met only to mate, or when the same stimuli attracted them, like blood, or chum. They were loners, independent predators, abiding the presence of their fellows only when they were too large to be eaten; or for mating.

Yet these were both males. He could see the claspers behind the pelvic fins. And he and Deela had been swimming quietly; there'd been nothing, so far as he knew, that would attract more than one shark to their area.

He was diverted from his thoughts by the smaller shark, which darted in low over the bottom, between two hillocks of rock and sand, straight for them, like an immense arrow. Cross reared up, drawing its attention, then dropped at the last second, whipping the tip of the humming stinger up to its belly.

The sound smashed not at his ears but into the top of his head, a sharp blow that came close to blacking him out. He looked back, blinking, in time to catch the shark's last convulsions as momentum carried the relaxing body on in a shallow glide down to the bottom, where it slid to rest on the sand. The stinger's millisecond-long burst of 100-kilohertz ultrasound had ruptured every cell membrane in the forward half of the fish, leaving it a skinful of homogenized protoplasm.

The rod hummed again, recharging from its integral battery. He glanced quickly around, looking for the larger shark.

Deela punched him. *"There it is."*

He followed her pointing finger. It was some distance out, still circling, and obviously had seen the whole action. It passed near its dead companion, but made no move either to investigate or eat.

It seems so deliberate, he thought, taking a fresh grip on the rod. *So calm, so slow. As if it has all the time in the world, as if we're being served up on a plate. Well, next time it tries it'll find out differently.*

As if on cue, it turned inward again, the fins making it a fat bodied star seen from head on. He lost it for a second behind an outcropping. When it reappeared, from an unexpected quarter, it was very close and coming in very fast and he was turned the wrong way to hit it with the rod. He hurried to shift the stinger's tip as the shark veered farther left, so he had to hold the stinger out at arm's length to reach it.

And the long, stiff pectoral came up as the shark rolled, knocking the humming weapon out of his hands. The stinger tumbled over the rocks and sailed gracefully down, over the Edge.

The humming faded. It was gone.

He watched it disappear, stunned. When he was quite sure it was out of reach forever he shifted his gaze to the shark. *"Watch it,"* he squeaked to Deela. *"If we lose it now, we're toast."*

"Okay, Dinker. I see it, behind you."

He craned around, cursing. It was behind them, the cold dark eye staring unwinkingly, unfathomable, unreachable. Deela pressed against him. He reached down to feel for her tank harness and pulled. She struggled for a moment as they left the semishelter of the rocks, then twisted free and swam beside him toward the edge of the Deep.

He pumped hard, sucking his breather for all it could deliver. The dry air tasted of cardboard, or maybe it was fear. He glanced back as they neared the edge. The whitetip was overtaking them, but slowly; either it had learned caution from the fate of the smaller one, or did not yet understand what Cross was trying to do.

He no longer doubted that, somehow, it *could* understand. All too well.

They reached the edge and started over, still at full speed. Head downward, swimming hard, he had a dreamlike sensation of falling into a nightmare. Below him the dimly-lit cliff merged into misty blue-blackness, then into midnight. They were falling, dropping fast into something endless and without light.

He risked another glance back to see the shark come over the edge above them, bank, then spiral out away from the side of the cliff as it too turned downward, but farther out. When it began to close again he stopped. He pulled Deela with him against the cliff. A slow beat of his fins sufficed to keep them pinned against it, protected by the protruding rocks, though in air they would have tumbled endlessly down into the dark.

The shark approached, sheered off, and turned again, sliding by so close he could have reached out to touch it. As he watched it circle away after the second approach he nodded slightly. It was working; the shark, slightly heavier than water, could not stop, or it would begin to sink. Nor could it get at them against the craggy face of the dropoff. They had plenty of air; his pack held LOX enough for a day, and Deela could make a five-liter last for hours. At a pinch, they could buddy-breathe, sharing air as long as either's equipment held a sip of oxygen.

The whitetip circled higher. It was swimming faster now. Finally giving up, he guessed, craning his neck upward to follow it. *Good work, Dink. Thought you'd bought it there for a moment, you and Didi both.*

The shark passed over them, just at the lip of the cliff, swimming hard, whipping the big gray tail in short powerful strokes. Puffs of sand and mud clouded the water. Small rocks came sliding down, falling slowly, as in a dream, down the face of the drop.

He watched them come, unbelieving, as they gathered

speed. One hit Deela's tank, making a hollow bong like the toll of a cathedral bell.

The whitetip emerged from the cloud, slowed, turned, and swam back, a trifle closer to the cliff this time. The cloud grew denser, and the wash of water from the tail rocked several larger stones poised just at the lip, directly above Cross and Deela.

He sighed into his mask. *It was bound to come*, he thought. *For us, like all the rest.* He glanced upward, at the feeble blue glow that was all that remained, at eighty meters, of the Sun he had not seen for two years. He remembered in that split second the days, years before, when he'd walked with the Pats in its splendor, had breathed the open air without fear.

The days before the Dying had cancelled it all. Cancelled his life, cancelled humans and all their grandiose and pitiable dreams.

He bent to tug his knife from the sheath on his leg. A puny weapon against hundreds of kilos of shark, but there was a minuscule chance he could occupy its attention long enough for Deela to get away.

He pushed off from the cliff as the first really big rock came tumbling down, and turned to say goodbye.

She was smiling.

He drifted slowly upward, following her look, and saw, silhouetted against the shifting light above, the shapes of two human beings and a large dolphin. And also that of the shark, disappearing slowly, in the opposite direction, into the bright blue haze that lay in the direction of the open sea.

TWO

Twenty years before, the Navidad Bank Subsea Research Center had been built as a permanent base for aquaculture and delphinology. After the Kids, known at first as the Subsea Adaptation Program, were conceived, it had been expanded. Thirty 20-meter graphullerene-impregnated concrete cylinders were sited on a level brown sand plain, average depth seventy meters. From a distance, provided visibility was good, they resembled a small city, a daisy chain of low buildings. Later, as the Kids grew, the pressure in the Station had been gradually increased, the atmosphere replaced by an argon-oxygen mixture, and the squat pressure-resistant concrete tubes supplemented by light plastron bubbles.

At its peak, just before the Dying, the Station had been home, office, and laboratory for over three hundred scientists, engineers, divers, and delphinologists, who worked at the nearby Annex.

Now it was all but empty.

A red light burned over the concrete overhang that shielded Lock III, the main entrance. Cross ducked under it and swam upward. Inside the lock, sea pressure and the Station's atmospheric pressure balanced, and he broke through the surface, into air.

Behind him, splashing up one by one, came Deela and the two other divers.

Treading water, Dinker jerked his mask off. Hauling himself onto the concrete platform that covered half the cylinder's interior, he tripped his gear belt. Carefully extracting the blood gas analyzer from his upper arm, he plugged it into the keeper socket, then shrugged the pack off and placed it in a wall mount, plugging in power and gas connections to recharge it. He stripped off the wet suit and carried it into the shower. He washed himself and his gear with three liters of fresh water, hung everything to dry, and stood in front of a hot-air blast.

The others came in, headed for the showers. He took a small bottle from his locker, squirted disinfectant into both ears, and shook his head to clear them. He broke out a pair of submarine-issue khaki shorts, pulled them on, and slammed the locker closed.

The automatic door slid open, and he stepped into a short, rather low-ceilinged corridor. Steel gratings rang underfoot; looking down, he could see the dark water that filled the lower half of the tube. The next door did not open automatically. He waited for a second, then pulled it open, and walked into another, larger cylinder, most of which was taken up by a colorfully-furnished dining area, with seats for at least a hundred.

Deela was already at one of the corner tables. Her left arm – brown above, white below – was stretched out under the stern gaze of Dr. Matthew Oursler. The old man, scowl framed by gray hair and short white chin beard, glared up as Cross padded wearily in. "Commander. I suppose you're responsible for this?"

"That's right." Cross lowered himself gingerly onto a chair. He touched his arms where bruises were beginning to show blue. "I tortured those poor whitetips till they had no alternative but self-defense."

"Whitetips?" Oursler's bushy eyebrows kneaded. "No. *Carcharhinus longimanus* is a pelagic species. Probably they were only – "

"Dinker's right, Matt," said a short, dark-skinned younger man, pausing at the door of the lounge. He mopped moisture from the dense curly hair on his chest with a green towel and grinned at Cross. "I'd have doubted it too if I hadn't of been there. Two of 'em, big mothers. Eight to ten-footers. Dinker, you got one, right? It was lying dead near the Edge. Aquaman here was getting ready to feed himself to the other one when we showed up. Sheila and me and Engines."

"Aah," said Deela softly. Cross looked at her. She was hugging herself with her free arm, and tears had gathered in the corners of her eyes.

"Almost done, Didi," said Oursler reassuringly. "Remember, when you run out of first aid spray, iodine will do, or even alcohol." He covered the raw red scrape on her hand, where the rough skin of the shark had abraded her, with a sterile dressing and taped it quickly and professionally. "Just like that. Keep it clean afterward."

"And what will they do when they run out of dressings?" said Cross.

The professor glared down at the girl's arm. "That, sir, is beyond our power, or our knowledge. Ian and Deela will have to discover solutions for themselves. Their future, Humanity's future now, lies under the sea. All we can do is give them as good a start as we can."

Cross shook his head, but said nothing. A world dead up above, gone over two years now, yet Oursler had never wavered in his belief in the future of the Kids.

Future. What did that mean, in a world empty of people, yet still deadly to them? A world where a new Red Death rode the wind above deserted cities, seethed in the soil around the piles of bodies that were by now becoming only junk-heaps of bone?

The old dinosaur story, Cross thought. *Only it happened so fast, and to us.* Humans had been reaching for the planets, beginning to modify themselves for new worlds, preparing for the leap outward. The unholy triptych of World Wars finally past, the Coordinate given the grudging consent of the great powers, humankind at last united, at least provisionally, and ready for the new Age of Expansion.

Then the Dying had begun. And barely a year later it was over. The virus had penetrated everywhere, air-carried, virulent. Those who breathed air, died.

That, at the end, had left alive only the skeleton crew at the Station, along with the two Kids. Oursler thought they could survive, rebuild a society underwater with the dolphins' help, and someday carry the torch back into the open air.

"What's the trouble, Dinker?"

"Sheila." He looked up, then pulled out a chair next to him. He registered the soft press of her hip as Sheila Klassen curled into it. He rubbed his face to erase whatever expression had interested her – she'd been the Station's psychologist, primarily concerned with the dolphins, though humans, too, came within her purview. "No trouble. A little shaky, I suppose. I thought we were about done for."

"You were," she said, mock-sternly. She shook her head, tossing thick waves of dark damp hair and setting her breasts rolling. Like most of the Station crew, she wore only shorts. He caught himself staring and looked away, missing her amused glance. "What the hell were you doing? Where was your stinger?"

As he explained Oursler and Graham listened, exchanging glances when he described the way the sharks had varied their attacks.

"You saw all this, Ken?" said Oursler to Graham.

"Well, no. Only the last part, at the cliff-edge."

"I know what I saw, Doctor," said Cross. "Granted, I'm not a scientist. But I still know sharks."

"I never understood that," said Oursler. "How your submarine could be sent on a scientific expedition without a single qualified person aboard. But I intended no imputation. It's just so unexpected." The old man shook his head. "Well, I'm glad you both escaped intact. Though I can't help feeling you must have annoyed or attracted them in some way. At any rate, it's over."

"One thing puzzles me, Ken," said Cross. "How'd you happen to come by just then? Your party was scheduled to hunt to the northeast today, wasn't it?"

"I can answer that," came a high whistle in seaspeech. Cross jerked his head up, grinned, and left his seat to walk to the edge

of the room. Water lapped there, part of the canal system that threaded its way through the entire Station. As he approached a grayish rounded bulk lifted itself, and he knelt and rubbed it affectionately between liquid brown eyes.

"Hi, Engines. You 'heard' us, eh?"

"We can 'hear' fright from far away," piped the dolphin, narrowing its eyes in a smile.

"I'll bet every dolphin in the station could hear me today," said Cross, smiling down at her. 'Engines' was a contraction of her formal name, 'Sound of Ship Going Over,' which like all dolphins she'd chosen for herself at puberty. She was a New Dolphin; new not physically, but culturally. Interaction with human beings, the evolution of a shared speech, training in a thousand human concepts and ideas – culture – had changed the once wild *Delphinus delphis*. Making them valuable partners in the sea, with remarkable talents of their own.

"We were almost to the hunting area," said Sheila, kneeling beside him to stroke the animal's back. "When she 'heard' something. It's a wonderful gift. For a long time we thought the cetaceans hadn't any speech, because we couldn't break their code. But they did: telepathy. Apparently it works, at least occasionally, between all the higher animals, especially those capable of sympathy with one another. Even between dolphin and human. Ian and Deela have been learning from them. Engines probably picked up Deela's fright, Dinker, not yours."

Cross glanced over. Her love for the dolphin she was touching had softened her face, and he remembered, almost against his will, the times it had softened for him . . . "Well, I'm glad she did," he said. Then, to Engines, *"Hey, want a fish? I owe you for that rescue."*

"Thank you, no," squeaked the dolphin. *"Hunting was good today; the Herd is well fed. Many fish are moving in from the Deep."*

"How about a bite yourself, Dink?" Graham stood to stretch. "It's lunchtime."

"Thanks, no. Got to get with my guys and check out the boat today. I'll skip lunch."

"Your stomach, your funeral."

Graham, Oursler, and Klassen left for the kitchen. Cross, still scratching Engines' head, looked around. Deela was sitting at the table, bandaged hand cradled on her lap, watching him. He was suddenly touched; she looked so young. *Was* so young, though she and Ian had grown fast and matured early. But her expression was so lost, so helpless, he had to say something. "It'll heal, Didi. Won't hurt for long."

"It's not that." She used the standard English that she and Ian called 'airtalk.' "I'm just . . . scared. I thought . . . ."

"Well, it's all right now." He gave Engines a last pat and stood. "I've got to go out to the boat. Better get some lunch with the rest. Right?"

"Well . . . okay." She slid off the chair and padded off on bare feet.

He crossed to the status board that covered one wall, and stood studying it.

Once it had tracked three hundred people and five anthropic 'bots through the Station's five kilometers of corridors and thirty departments and five berthing areas, as well as the satellite research camps at Fifty-Meter, One-Sixty Meter, and the massively-walled glass-steel sphere at 790-Meter. Now the rows of names were dark. Only a few glowed here and there, standing out like fading beacons on a forgotten shoreline. Under the heading SCIENTIFIC STAFF, he read:

Chief, HSO Project:　　　Dr. Matthew Oursler

HSO, thought Cross. Homo Sapiens Oceanus. *The Kids.*

Head, Dept of Marine Biology, Mammalian:
Dr. Kenneth Graham
Chief Psychologist, Director, Delphinus delphi project:
Dr. Sheila Klassen
Interns:
Roger Comiskey, Heather Johnson

His gaze dropped, to rows of unlit names. They'd answered the call topside, to Atlanta and Cambridge and L.A., when the Coordinate had needed researchers to combat *Carsonella*.

They'd failed . . . and died.

Next was a blank section, hand-lettered in red grease pencil:

MISCELLANEOUS ADDITIONAL
Crew, DSRVN-3, Research Vessel "Pilgrim"
Commanding officer   Lcdr. Dinker L. CROSS
Chief of Boat   DSCS Joseph C. SVEC
DS1 Paula S. WELCH
MF1 Lewis PARRISH

His crew; his ship.

The message, OP IMMEDIATE via a very-low-frequency covered satellite link, had reached them a thousand feet down, drifting slowly south along the coast of Africa with the equatorial current. Their three-month cruise had been extended. And extended. They'd not known why until, hearing nothing at last, they'd surfaced. Fortunately, they hadn't cracked the hatch before the Chief found one of the last active radio stations. They'd dived again at once, and headed west. Two weeks later they'd beached *Pilgrim* and joined the few left at the Station.

The next lighted section of the board held only two names:

RESIDENT CHILDREN
 Deela HUNTER
Ian SILENT

Like the dolphins, the Kids had picked their own last names at puberty. Though, he mused, it was getting harder to think of them as 'kids.'

And after that, in a separate blue-lighted section of the

board, was a roster of the Station's dolphin colony. Cross knew several, having been out hunting in mixed parties many times over the last two years, but the only ones he really considered friends were Engines and a large male friend of hers named Swimming Fast. Graham and Klassen, who'd been working on the Delphinus project since long before the Dying began, knew them all by sight.

He looked back up at the 'crew' section, and saw, by the locater code glowing next to Svec's name, that the Chief was already out at the boat.

From a hundred yards away, the DSRVN-3 was a sixty-meter slaty-gray whale stretched comfortably out on the brown sand of the bottom. Fore and aft, Cross noted as he swam closer, the blue subsea running lights were on, meaning Svec was aboard and already checking out the electrical system.

He finned steadily on, above a heavily-insulated wrist-thick black cable that stretched from the Station to the sub, and ran his eyes over his ship. She sat square on two long bilge keels, squatting in the sand, and he could see she was well ballasted down and would not move. Forward, below the swelling bow, the control cabin was visible between the keels, with lighting and extensible manipulators folded in just forward of it. Astern, the hull was long, a little out of proportion to the rest of the stubby sub, as if added in an afterthought. Four shrouded rotatable motor/plane combinations along the hull supplemented the big main screw centerlined aft; and atop the hull, where the conning tower or sail would have been on a conventional submarine, there was only a low protrusion, capped by the stubby forms of several retracted antennae.

Reaching the sub's blunt bow, he punched the valve that operated the forward airlock.

When he crawled into the control room Svec was absorbed in a hydraulics check. The Chief, lanky and relaxed in faded khaki shorts, was seated in front of the diving console, his normal station during operational watches. The red overhead lights gleamed off his bald head and narrow, sharp, good-humored face, and Cross had a sudden feeling of being home.

"Hi, Cap'n."

"Hello, Chief. How's the distilling business?"

"Makin' progress," said Svec. "Found a coil; took one out of a reefer in one of the empty berthin' spaces. Mash is got maybe a week to go."

"What are you using?"

"Kelp. The light green stuff. Sugar. And cookin' yeast."

Cross chuckled. "The moonshiner's coming out in you. Well, good luck; we need a source of volatiles."

"Need a source of drinkin' whisky, too."

"Amen. Where's the rest of the crew?"

"I don't know, Cap'n," said Svec. "I reminded them both to be here for the weekly tests. They know the sched. But I guess they're figuring it don't matter anymore whether the old girl's ready for sea or not."

"It ought to." Cross dropped into the conning officer's chair and peered forward, through the thick quartz porthole. Nothing but the brown sand bottom, dotted here and there with broken shells. "Our plant's providing the power to keep the Station going, now shore power's gone. Parrish should be here, at least. I know it's a simple thermionic pile, but anything that starts with the word nuclear, I want it checked regularly."

"Right. Couldn't agree more."

"I saw the lights on outside. We finished electrical checks?"

"Right. "

"Freq sweep?"

"Not yet. Cyclin' hydraulics now."

"I'll take it, then." Reaching for the comm panel, Cross flipped the switch that extended the antenna and turned on the receiver. "Tune across bands," he told it. As usual, it paused occasionally at bursts of noise, but they always turned out to be random static.

"Anything new?"

"Nothing." The spectrum covered, Cross tuned manually to a Sharpie mark on the dial. On the third sweep he found it, faint against the crackling hiss of daylight static. He turned up the gain and the humming, steady drone, with the monotonous four-second beat that sounded like a huge, slow heart, filled the control room. "But there she is. Still."

"Almost sounds like a time signal."

"Isn't. Welch timed the beats at 4.23 seconds. It's manmade, though."

"Gonna call?"

"I don't think so," said Cross, turning the set off. "I must have tried a hundred times since we first heard it a year ago. We may just not have the power to punch through. Well . . . done with hydraulics yet?"

"Yep. Permission to blow to 100 positive?"

"Do it." Cross watched Svec's long fingers flicker across the diving panel. His left hand flashed red fire; a massive ruby, set in a deep-cut silver chief's ring. The fingers paused. A roar came from astern as the pile flashed sea water into steam, forcing water out of the midships ballast tanks. The Chief's hook-nosed profile hung above the dials. The sub rumbled and creaked as her weight shifted from the keel to the sea, and finally a shudder crept through her and she swung slightly.

A scraping came from below. Svec cut the pumps and tapped his ring against the depth gauge; a meaningless ritual, but a submarine tradition. "A meter off the bottom. Cable's holding us down."

"Right." Cross muttered orders to the panel. Motors hummed and the sea floor outside the port began to move to his right. He cut the thruster after a moment and started another. The sea floor slowed, then gathered speed to port. He tested the other motors, moving the sub about on her tether, and then rotated each motor pod on its axis twice.

"Looks good, Cap'n. Pile's supplying all we need, along with the Station drain."

"Give me twenty tons negative to hold her down. Drop easy till the keel sets."

The sub met the bottom again with a slight thud. Cross snapped on outside monitors and checked the lay of the cable. It was free of the keel, leading fair and straight toward the domes of the Station, barely visible even in the crystalline water of the Caribbean.

"Pumps secured. Securing propulsion."

"Thanks, Chief. That's it, then, until next week. And what about Parrish?"

"I'll have a talk with him, Cap'n. But he's been actin' up. Depressed, who isn't? But it's gettin' to him."

"Has Dr. Klassen seen him?" *Stupid question,* Cross thought. How could they avoid each other?

"Not, uh, professionally."

"I'll talk to her about it. I don't know if we can do anything for him, but we ought to try."

Svec nodded, completed shutting down and left, crawling forward to the lock. Cross heard him cursing as he suited up for the swim back. *Pilgrim* hadn't been designed for easy diver access, especially for six-footers. But finally the hatch clanged, a light changed from red to green on Cross's board, and silence returned to the boat.

He leaned back in the chair and rubbed his face wearily with his hands.

After a few minutes he opened his eyes, looked around the inside of the control room, then reached for a small locker. He spun the dial right, left, left, right and opened it. Inside it were a cardboard box, a Navy-issue nine-millimeter pistol and box of cartridges, a hologram cube, a sealed, foil-wrapped envelope, a commander's manual, and a flat green clothbound book. He took out the book, leaving the locker open, and turned to his last entry in the log of the *Pilgrim,* dated one week before.

June 14

On the bottom as before at Navidad Bank Subsea Research Center. Depth 210 feet/70 meters. All present except Parrish for weekly muster and tests. All equipment operational, ready for sea.

He looked at the page a moment longer, then took a waterproof pen from his pocket.

June 21
Bottomed as before. Parrish and Welch both absent today. Weekly tests carried out. All equipment operational, ready for sea. Today makes two years since the Dying ended.

He hesitated, holding the pen. Should something more be said? In all likelihood this would be the only record of life at the Station, the final history of humankind after the Dying. The page seemed to call for more, for comment, drama, description, for a paean of hope or a scream of despair.

But for whom? he thought. *Who will ever read it?*

He turned to the locker and took out the cardboard box. He selected a metal-capped tube from a small number of similar tubes. He unscrewed the cap and shook the fat green cigar out. He stuck it in his mouth and sighed. Couldn't light it; the air scrubbers would go nuts. Still, it tasted familiar, a treat. There were so many small things the senses missed. He shoved the box back in the locker, slumped in the chair, and gazed at the log again.

Yes, for whom, he asked himself again.

Not for people as he knew them. Not for himself, or his children, or Oursler's or Graham's or Klassen's or Welch's, or Heather's or Roger's. They could never go back.

Human beings would never stand upon the land again. Carsonella had made sure of that.

Cross rolled the cigar between his teeth, reviewing what he knew about that tiny organism that had changed so much.

It had first appeared in the early summer. Accounts of its origin had differed. Some said Patient Zero had been diagnosed in late May, west of Bahia Blanca, in Argentina. Almost simultaneous outbreaks had been reported in Capetown and Auckland. Its extreme virulence – most victims went into coma within eighteen hours after exposure and were dead within twenty-four – and its multiple modes of transmission earned it immediate attention.

He shifted in the chair. That much he'd overheard during those terrible months when the world topside was dying. But he'd also learned from Ken Graham, who was still devoting hours every day in the microbiology lab to work with sealed cultures, hoping to find a cure.

Graham had once described Carsonella, or Oxyphilus Virus X, as it was also called, as "the perfect friend, gone mad." It seemed to be related in some way to common toroviruses, ubiquitous symbiotes that lived in every human gut on the planet. The infection, too, festered in the gut for a brief period; long enough to defeat the body's immune response and invade the blood stream. From there it spread to the blood-rich lungs, choking off oxygen to the brain and causing the 18-hour coma.

The symptoms varied, but the end results were the same. Carsonella's vicious hunger for oxygen starved the host tissues, turning the skin a characteristic bright cherry red. Antibiotics were useless. Antivirals and even phage therapies failed. The virus splintered into a hundred variants. Victims coughed, trying to gasp in oxygen their blood could no longer use, but succeeded only in filling the air of homes and hospitals with the virus. They died and were buried, and Oxyphilus, infecting E. coli, migrated into the worms and the soil, where it continued to bind oxygen, though at a lower rate. It seethed in the water table and contaminated the fields. Dogs, rats, livestock, birds, all airbreathing creatures, all became carriers and then died. It followed the panic-stricken 'vackies as they fled new outbreaks.

The end had come very quickly.

And, thought Cross, glancing upward, *it's still up there, waiting.*

Fortunately, some unnamed and now long dead bureaucrat had clamped a strict quarantine on the Station, a piece of farsightedness those responsible for the settlements on the Moon and Antarctica had not emulated in time. The Lunar base had died early, wiped out after a shipment of live plants from Baikonur was unloaded. Antarctica and the scattered

Arctic bases had followed shortly after.

The Station had been luckier. The high halogen content of sea water killed the virus. But if human or dolphin dared even take one breath of the air that still whirled sweetly above the waves, blown down over the still-green hills of Haiti and Inagua, they'd die.

Cross thought how much like a Biblical curse it sounded. He blinked, seeing the page again. Despite Graham's hope he might eventually find a cure, the human comedy was over, Closed down in the middle of the performance, actors gone, scenery struck, footlights out. Finis.

What about the Kids? They breathed air, true, but with significant differences. *H. sapiens oceanus* had been the first attempt at a human subspecies, one designed for a wholly new environment: the sea.

Some of the genetic material, the DNA, had been borrowed from the cetaceans, mammals that had readapted to the sea naturally. Oh, the Kids were human. That much was evident at first glance. But there were some external differences from mainstream human. The two-tone skin. A sleeker shape, the result of a thicker layer of subcutaneous fat for insulation. No body hair, except – and Cross was glad of the exception – on the head. Larger, flatter feet, not like fins, but better adapted for swimming than the narrow pedal extremities City Man had considered normal. The eyes larger, pupils wider, since sunlight attenuated quickly as it slid downward through water.

But more fundamental were the unseen differences. Those larger eyes could focus in either air or water; for the Kids, masks were unnecessary. They were also four times more sensitive to blue light than the mainstream human eye, with some loss in the red. The flattened ears heard well to 20 kilohertz, with an expanded lower-end response down to two hertz. Ian and Deela had more tumor suppressor genes, and other modifications; they'd both probably live to well over 150. But it was in the lungs, spleen, and the system of oxygen utilization, that the changes, both genetic and induced, were greatest.

The Kids' lungs had been larger like a normal child's even at birth. And patient conditioning had made them far more muscular, and the rib cage more flexible. When a mainstream teen took a deep breath, they renewed perhaps a quarter of the air. The Kids could replace almost all of it.

That alone meant they could last for four times as long on a single breath; and improved blood chemistry, adapted from the dolphins, made their use of the air thus breathed far more efficient. They extracted over 80% of the oxygen. Their exhalation, when they breathed pure oxygen on a dive, was almost pure carbon dioxide. They couldn't breathe water, of course; no mammal could ever do that. Even if one could be "built" with gills, there wasn't enough dissolved air to sustain a mammal's metabolism. But one breath would last Ian or Deela a long time, and the ability to dispense with a diluting gas and breathe pure oxygen eliminated any question of the bends.

At the same time, the Kids would have been perfectly comfortable walking around on the streets of New York City, breathing the complex mixture of 77% nitrogen, 20% oxygen, 1% inert gases, and the rest a witch's brew of hydrocarbons, ozone, fluorocarbons, etc., etc. which made up the atmosphere.

Perhaps "comfortable" was an overstatement, Cross thought, remembering New New York as he'd last seen it, but they could have tolerated it as well as any mainstreamer. They just wouldn't have needed to breathe as often.

Keep it for the Kids, then? For the descendants of Deela and Ian, who would make their home in the sea?

Again Cross shook his head. Oursler, yes, the old man thought so. But the Kids had been his life's work; he'd conceived them, in the form of an AI-assisted genome model. Had directed the unimaginably delicate gene splicing, the long suspense of gestation after implant of the resulting eggs in artificial wombs, and finally, attended at those virgin births. If Ian and Deela had a father, he was Dr. Matthew Oursler.

But Cross didn't think the Kids would make it either. *Two people aren't a new race,* he told himself, taking the cigar out of his mouth and eyeing it critically. Suppose Ian, exploring some cave, lost his balls to a moray? Anything could happen; the margins for error were too small, the chances against it too great.

It all added up to a futility that anchored his gut as if he'd swallowed a rock. Rolling the cigar in his fingers, Cross examined his feelings. At first he'd been angry. *Angry? You mean mad rage, Dinker,* he thought, recalling the metal partition he'd torn apart with his bare hands when he'd realized he would never see the three Pats again.

The Pats. He reached for the locker again, stood the hologram cube on the open log in front of him, and looked into their eyes.

Pat's eyes had been green. His first wife, and . . . but he couldn't say that; he'd loved them all. Patricia, brown-eyed, had joined them later, the older woman completing that strongest of all family structures in a man-short postwar world, the family triangle. She'd been past childbearing, but their relationship hadn't been platonic. For a moment Cross could close his eyes and be with them all again in the big king bed on a rainy Saturday morning, Pat warm against and around him, her legs wound tightly into his, Patricia already satisfied and cuddled spoon-fashion against his back.

And young Patty, the laughing one, so attached to Daddy and to peanut-butter kisses. She would be . . . he paused in the daydream . . . seven? Yes, seven now. Born just after Christmas.

He opened his eyes. Theirs, green, brown, clear childish blue, smiled back from the hologram, taken in their home just before *Pilgrim* deployed on what was to have been his last cruise prior to some richly-deserved shore duty.

His teeth met through the cigar and he tore it from his mouth and threw it across the compartment, but it was futile, it did nothing. *I should feel cheated,* he thought, *I should feel bitter . . . I should feel* something.

But he didn't. He missed them, but by now it was the kind of feeling he had for his classmates who'd gone drinking with him and slept in classes with him and had died in the Last War. He felt regret, loss, but so many had died that individuals could hardly be remembered, much less mourned. A sense of. . . .

"Emptiness," he said aloud.

"What?"

He whirled in the chair. Deela sat in the entrance to the control room, legs modestly tucked beneath her, wet hair twisted into a knot atop her head. "Oh, Dinker, I didn't mean to interrupt. Are you busy? I'll go, I – "

"No, that's all right. I was just thinking. I didn't even notice the hatch light come on." She'd covered the bandage on her hand with a plastic sack and rubber band, sealing it. "How's the fin, kiddo?"

"It doesn't hurt. I put some oil on it."

"Oil?"

"From a fish liver. Ian's always trying things like that. New ideas he has. I-I's quiet, but I think he's smarter than I am."

"Does Dr. Oursler know about this, um, oil?"

"No. But it's all right, really. It stopped hurting." She looked down. "Really, I'm okay."

He saw she didn't want to discuss it anymore and turned back to the log.

After a moment she asked, "What are you writing?"

"Just keeping the ship's log up to date."

"What's a log?"

"Like a diary. A sort of ship's history."

"Can I see it?"

"Sure." He held it open and she came to look over his shoulder. She was so close he could feel the heat from her body and smell the fish oil and something else, something sweet and half-familiar. After a moment he identified it as vanilla extract, from the Station's kitchen.

"Who are they?" she said, inspecting the cube.

"My family. They were topside."

She did not say "oh", or even "I'm sorry", as someone older would have. Instead she simply looked at him, with such sadness in her eyes that he was touched. He reached up to pat her shoulder. "I know."

"You know. What do you know?"

"How you feel. And I appreciate it."

Her eyes changed, grew wide. "You do?"

The next second she was bending over him, and he found himself being kissed with great enthusiasm and no skill. "I knew. I knew!"

"Deela!" he said. "Get off me! What in hell are you trying to do?"

"I love you, Dinker. I didn't know when I was little what it was I felt. But then Sheila told Ian and me about, you know. And I knew then why I liked to hunt with you. And you saved us out with those sharks today, I was scared, and you were going to kill it with your knife, weren't you? I'm sorry about your family, they look sweet, especially the little girl, and that's your mother, isn't it? But you can love me too, can't you? And even if you like Sheila or Paula or Heather, oh, don't push me away – "

"You just stay there," said Cross.

She sat again and stared at him, twisting her hands together.

"I don't know where you got this idea," he began, searching for the right words. He didn't want to be cruel, but this was ridiculous. "Because although I like you, Deela – "

"I knew you did. When you – "

"But I don't love you."

She said nothing.

"Look, let's face facts. All right? First, you're just a child. You're only sixteen."

"Sixteen *and a half*. But Dr. Oursler said we mature quicker than the Land People."

"All right, sure, but to me you're still a kid. It wouldn't feel right. All those hunting trips, our checker games . . . "

She frowned. "A *kid?* I'm an adult now."

"Well . . . you don't understand. I'm talking about feelings." Briefly he wondered about Ian and Deela. Growing up together, would they feel an incest taboo? *That's Sheila's problem*, he thought. "You should be thinking this way about Ian. He's a Sea People. I'm a Land People. We're different kinds."

"Don't I make you think about it?" she said, face carefully bland. *She's clever,* he thought. *Or maybe I'm more transparent than I think.*

"That's beside the point. You're very attractive. You'll grow up to be a lovely woman and you'll have babies, I'm sure, if you want. *Ian's* babies."

"And yours."

"No." He shook his head. "Not gonna happen."

She sniffed and looked around the control room. "Don't you do it with Sheila?" she said, in a small voice. "Paula and Lewis do it together. And Dr. Oursler and Ken, even if they're both guys. Heather and Roger? Maybe. Aren't you lonely too?"

Cross sighed. It seemed so meaningless. A few small lives in a microcosm, the last human beings on a dead planet. A pointless postscript to the great lost library of Man. "Look. I'm going to try to tell you something. Even though I don't think you'll understand."

"Try me."

"You won't, because you've grown up here and the way things are now seems natural. But we're not going to survive like this, Deela. Human beings are finished on Earth."

To his surprise, she sat silent, thinking it over. Finally she looked up. "I was trying to see it the way you do, and maybe I do, a little. You see everyone you used to know, and love, dead. Everywhere you used to go is gone, or at least you can't go back. You don't act sad, but maybe that's too big a thing to be sad enough about. Anyway, since it's all over, trying to keep what there is left going is silly. Right?"

"You seem to think this is all in my head," said Cross, getting irritated. "Our situation here's more precarious than you realize. If Pilgrim's pile fails we couldn't make oxygen to breathe any longer. Ken tried to grow plants, but he didn't have the right lights. Our spare part situation's critical: compressors, filters, air scrubbers, the compressor to store the oxygen, they could go any time. We can't jury-rig repairs forever. Half the auto-doors are crapped out and we can't fix them; if we had a leak most of the Station would flood. Food's no problem, lots of fish, kelp, shellfish; but we could die of thirst right here, underwater, if the desal plant breaks down. We're crowded into the last corner, and we can't go on forever.

"It's hard to face, but if you think you're old enough to, um, think about sex, well, you're old enough to know how it really is."

It hadn't touched her, he saw. She couldn't understand; with the serene conservatism of the very young she knew what was had always been and would not change. The Station was her home. She could not imagine it flooded, dark, its air stale, machines silent, inhabitants dead.

"Is that final?" She scowled, and her tone said now she hated him.

"Yeah," said Cross.

She left. He stared after her for several seconds, then roused himself, closed the log, and put it and the hologram and the cigar box back in the locker. He was about to close it when his gaze fell on the envelope. He smiled tightly as he remembered what it held: the key to the true mission of *USS Pilgrim*.

And that, too, now seemed silly and useless.

He was starting back for the airlock when the signal chirped for the internal phone.

"Cross here," he said. "What is it?"

"This is Ken, Dinker." Graham's voice was too controlled. "Can you come back? We've got one of your crew here. Welch."

"Paula? About time. Ask her why she missed weekly muster."

"I'm afraid I can't do that, Dinker."

"Why not?"

"Because she's dead."

THREE

"N o. Not you, Paula," he whispered, staring down at the shattered thing on the deck of the lock.

Someone had laid her body on a blue tarp, but the precaution had hardly been necessary; there was no blood left. The noncommissioned officer's face, strangely calm and untouched, was the color of bleached coral, with a waxy translucence that made her even paler than years beneath the sea had.

The rest was savagely mangled. One arm was gone, sliced off just above the elbow; shreds of black rubber and red flesh lay intermingled. The wet suit was open at the chest, showing a gaping circular wound that exposed entrails and ribs. Long slashes in the right side and lower abdomen had closed up, showing only neat cuts in the rubber, as if an exceedingly sharp razor had been drawn quickly across the trunk. Part of the left calf and thigh had been taken and the stripped tendons lay white against the blue plastic.

Svec, looking grim, came in with a gray Navy blanket. He shook it out over the body and tucked it in neatly and stood back. He shook his bald head angrily. "I warned her before, Skipper. Not to dive alone."

"I know, Chief. But still, she had a stinger, didn't she?"

"She had one, all right," said Graham, who'd been standing quietly against the lock's wall. He held the rod out for Cross's inspection. Its shaft was bent through a thirty-degree angle and the mylar-titanium spark transducer at its head was half burned away. "It's completely discharged. She must have killed with it till it failed, then used the butt to fend them off until one of them got hold of it."

"Where's Parrish?" said Cross suddenly, remembering their attachment. "They usually dive together. Was he out there too?"

"No, we saw him at lunch," said Graham. "I think he and Paula had some sort of tiff; they haven't been sitting together the last couple days. He's probably in his rack now, or working on the air gear."

Dr. Oursler came in, followed by Deela and Ian. He bent and flipped back the blanket without a word. There was no effort to hide it from the Kids; they knew the sea, knew how quickly it could kill. The professor, expression grim, probed the terrible gash in the abdomen, then stood. In his open hand he held a whitish object, some two inches long and roughly triangular in shape, with tiny saw edges on two sides. Graham stepped over to look. The two scientists exchanged glances.

"That's it," said Graham. "*Longimanus.*"

Oursler, rubbing the tooth, looked puzzled. "Where'd you find her, Ian? Tell us what you saw."

The boy was thinner than Deela, quieter, dark-haired, but with the same wide intense eyes. He spoke without any childish shyness. "We were going out for shellfish today, toward shallow water. Paula talked to me about it at dinner last night. Said she wanted to show me a wreck she'd found our on the south reefs. This morning I decided not to go, I wanted to read, and . . . well, I decided not to." His voice was calm, without regret. "I . . . felt something, later, and went out to try to find her. She was in shallow water, about two klicks southeast, in a shellfish bed. Her bag was half full."

"Did you see sharks?"

"No, I didn't. There were a lot of," and here he paused, gulping before continuing. "A lot of the reef fishes there, feeding on . . . what was left."

"I see." The old man tossed the tooth up and caught it. He looked around. "No one dives alone from now on, under any circumstances. That was the rule before. Now make each other obey it. And no one goes out without a stinger."

They all nodded, and Oursler turned as if to leave.

"Is that all?" said Cross, grabbing his arm.

Oursler halted. "What more do you want, Commander? She's dead. I'm sorry. Do you want to hold a service?"

"I do, but that's not the point. I'm talking about preventing it from happening again. Of course, we can buddy-system and carry stingers. But that's not enough. Not now."

"I fail to see what you mean," said Oursler coldly. "Two divers with stingers can hold off any shark, even" – he held up the tooth – "Longimanus."

Cross looked at Deela, who was staring at the body, but spoke to Oursler. "There were two of us out there, Deela and me. But the shark outmaneuvered us. I had a stinger, but it outthought me and removed that advantage."

"Let's not be anthropomorphic, Commander. That shark may have appeared to 'think' to you, but I assure you, it – "

"Matt, wait," interrupted Graham. "I'm not sure Dinker's right, but the whitetip we saw attacking him was acting atypically." Glancing around, he added, "Look. Let's go into the lounge and talk there. Maybe we should have this out, the three of us."

They took a corner table and Cross brought over a carafe of fresh water. Graham poured and Oursler, obviously making an effort, unbent so far as to grimace when his cup was filled. "Ah, water. Remember, Ken, those three-martini luncheons at the symposia? Remember the party, right here, it was – "

"For the Nobel, when the Kids were born," Graham laid his hand on the older man's. "But water's not so bad. And it's thanks to Dinker we even have that."

"Can't take credit. Svec and Parrish set up the desal plant," said Cross.

Graham pulled an old pipe from his pocket. He fiddled with it, but there hadn't been any tobacco since the final supply sub, and his experiments with seaweed had been disasters. "Dinker, let me see if I can moderate between you and the Doctor. Now, you're convinced the whitetips that attacked you were different from species-typical, in that they seemed to plan their attacks in a rational way. That about it?"

"Same thing must have happened to Paula. Only she wasn't lucky enough to have someone else arrive in time."

"But you don't have a background in biology. From what I know, you had an engineering education at Annapolis West, sub duty in the war, then that drift-cruise business after the Services were dissolved. So you may not understand just how impossible a conclusion like that looks to us.

"The Selachii – the shark order – has been studied pretty extensively since the middle of the last century. There's no reason, I suppose, why someday a shark might not evolve intelligence; but none ever has. In all the research conducted on the elasmobranchs, nothing above instinctive reactions has been reported. They show no pattern of co-operative attack in the wild. Unlike porpoises, orcas, and seals, which hunt in packs.

"That goes for the whitetip as well. Now, I didn't want to get into a pissing contest, 'cause I know how goddamned stubborn you can be, but I agree with Matt. You didn't see what you thought you saw, because it isn't possible."

Cross tried to check his temper, but didn't quite succeed. "That's a nice way of saying I'm making it up, and – "

"No, it isn't. I didn't mean that. Anyone can misinterpret what they see. Even a scientist. But if what we think we saw's impossible, then we look for another interpretation of the data. Like the UFO scares just before the Dying."

"I don't care about 'interpretations', dammit. The big one watched me kill the little one. It figured out how I did it, and used that to disarm me. That's what happened, and you can think what you like."

"Now he *is* being stubborn," said Oursler loftily. "A desirable quality in a military man, I suppose, but not too relevant here. Let's drop it, Ken. Shall we?"

"I don't know," said Graham. He tucked the pipe away. "Dinker obviously saw something, even if it doesn't mean what he thinks. And we did lose Paula. To a whitetip, apparently. It could bear investigation, Matt."

"Investigation? Why?"

"To find out why the sharks are acting up. Whitetips shouldn't even come up on Navidad Bank. Could save somebody else's life."

Cross looked from Oursler to Graham. "That's all I really want. Just to have someone look into it. Doctor, I'll admit, maybe I'm wrong in my conclusions, but there was something weird going on there."

Oursler looked undecided. Graham refilled the older man's cup with distilled water. "An experiment. I'll organize it. Purpose, to attract some whitetips, observe their behavior, and possibly to bring one back for dissection. And dinner." He looked at Cross. "Agreed?"

"Count me in."

"Matt?"

"I still consider it a waste of time, but I suppose we have plenty of that. I may even come along. But one caveat." Oursler paused. "Be careful."

"Of course," said Graham. "And just for an extra safety factor, Dinker, mind drafting a couple of our friends to come along?"

"Friends?"

"Dolphins."

"Well, I'll be glad to talk to them, but . . . aren't they sort of your preserve? And Sheila's?"

"I'm trying to wean them," said Graham, smiling a little. "They need us, and we need them, if either race is to make it under the sea. We've got to stop this thinking of human and dolphin as separate and get used to working with them, thinking like them, like the Kids are doing. So, if you wouldn't mind – "

"When do you want to go?"

"Let's leave tomorrow morning, and plan to stay out all day."

"Right," said Cross, getting up. "I've got a couple of things to get out of the way before then, so, if you'll excuse me."

Graham and Oursler nodded. He could hear them discussing the route in low voices as he walked out of the lounge.

Deela stood in the passageway, attending to one of the arrangements of dried sponges and shells she'd set up here and there around the Station. And, no doubt, eavesdropping. "Hi," he said, but she stalked away without a word or look. He went on, shaking his head, but it didn't help his mood. She was an adolescent, sure, but it was annoying, all the same.

Sheila Klassen looked up as he pushed the nearly-frozen autodoor to the next cylinder open. She lowered her tablet. "Dinker . . . I heard. I just couldn't go and look. I'm sorry. You knew each other a long time."

"Only a year, but just the four of us? You get to know your crew pretty well under those conditions. Have you seen Parrish?"

"Lewis? Everyone's looking for him – the Chief came through just now." She shivered. "It's so horrible. You know, it sounds strange, with everyone dead up Above, but that's the first time anyone's . . . really been killed, violently, whom I knew."

"Maybe we can find out why." He explained Graham's idea, and finished, "But I have to see Lewis first. I don't think anyone's told him yet, and it's probably my place to do so."

"He's not wearing his location tag, Dinker. But he's been getting slack about that lately."

"That, and other things. I'll look in his quarters, then. See you later."

"Dinker. . . . "

He looked away. "It's finished," he said, in a low voice. "Don't try to revive it, Sheila. We'll both regret it."

"Revive? It never really started, Dink. You never let it."

"What did you want? Don't you think it's a little late for all that?"

She put her hand on his. "Too late? Not yet. After we're dead. That's when it'll be too late."

He shook his head. "I have to find Parrish."

He watched the canal as he walked the rest of the way around the ring of the Station, but the dark surface lay still. The canal linked to the sea outside at each Lock, and was always open to the dolphins, but apparently none were around.

Halfway to the quarters he stopped at a half-open side door. Stooping, he peered into the translucent plastron dome that housed Parrish's pet, the jury-rigged air plant.

He wasn't there, but out of habit Cross ran his eye over a heterogenous mass of machinery, pipes, wires, and control linkages, obviously cobbled together in haste and without regard for appearances. A half-disassembled 'bot lay in a corner like a severed torso, spilling multicolored wires. They'd all gone dead when the AIs topside had shut down. Low on the concrete floor squatted a twenty-horsepower water pump, cannibalized from the mariculture labs. It pumped seawater through strainers and filters and finally into a crudely-welded metal box about three meters on a side. The box contained an experimental gill, which they'd found in a storeroom, abandoned after whatever project that ordered it had folded. Inside, thousands of square meters of synthetic permeable membrane were wound in a tight spiral. With seawater on one side at pressure and a near-vacuum from a makeshift air ejector on the other, dissolved gases came out readily. A Worthington water-lubricated diving compressor stored the freed gas in banks of six-foot aluminum cylinders, stacked around the edge of the dome.

Cross, looking at it, remembered the weeks they'd sweated to get it working. It had been a race; their bottled air had been nearly gone, the absorbent canisters nearly exhausted, and the resupply subs from San Juan would never sail again.

He checked gauges, put his hand on the compressor to check its temperature; everything seemed normal. He looked at the clipboard that hung from one wall. It had been due for a check at 1200, but the space left for Parrish's initials was blank.

He initialed it himself and hung the board up again. Lewis Parrish, MF1, was piling up quite a bit of explaining to do. Still, he was bringing bad news. Go easy? He'd try.

He walked on into the living quarters and rapped sharply on the closed door of Parrish's cubicle. No one answered, and he knocked again, harder.

"Uh, c'mon in."

"Afternoon, Parrish."

"Skipper."

The tall, thin young man glanced up from his bunk. He brushed thin sandy hair out of his eyes as Cross took in the cubicle; the soiled, unmade bunk; books, wrappers, damp clothes drifted up in corners; a stench that flashed him back to a dog kennel; chess pieces set out in an endgame on a small littered table. He pushed some of the detritus off a chair. "Lew. I've got some bad news."

"News!" Parrish sat up. "What is it?"

"I'm sorry about this as I can be. Believe me. Paula was just brought in. Sharks. She, well, she didn't make it."

Parrish seemed dazed. "You wouldn't be joking, would you, Captain? No, I suppose you wouldn't." Then the thin face crumpled and he began to sway on the bunk. "This was my fault. I should have been with her out there."

"You can't look at it that way. Any of us could say that."

Parrish shook his head angrily. "You know that isn't true, Captain."

"Yes, it is. I knew her as long as you did. There's not the same kind of emotional attachment – "

But Parrish had begun to sob. Cross sat awkwardly silent. At last he reached out to squeeze his shoulder.

Finally the petty officer sniffled and sat up. "Thanks," he said, clearing his throat. "I guess I . . . haven't been much good lately."

Cross was about to reply when he saw it: a loop of wire dangling from under the dirty pillow. He reached and pulled. Parrish grabbed for the little box as it slid out.

He missed, and it shattered on the floor, pieces of plastic skittering across the floor. He glared up. "Why'd you do that? It wasn't hurting anyone!"

"Frying your head with that?" said Cross. "You'd better get up, Lewis, get busy again. You'll feel better."

But instead the younger man curled back into the bunk. Hugged himself and rocked back and forth. "Paula said that too . . . said I was freaking out. That was why she left . . . so I killed her, I – "

Cross gripped him by a shoulder. "Don't torture yourself. You don't need the stimulator. You can't break down now. We need you."

"For what? I'm done, count me out." His voice rose. "It's no use prolonging it! We're all going to die. Let me do it now." His hand groped for a small bottle near the chessboard but Cross pocketed it. He brought his face close to Parrish's.

"Look. Frankly, I don't care if you sauté your brain on your time off. But we've all got duties and yours are just about the most important around. Without that air plant we don't breathe. So I want you back on the job, right now."

"You're kidding yourself, Skip." Parrish laughed. "If you think we'll get out of this alive, you're crazy as old Oursler."

"Nobody lives forever," said Cross. "No. I don't think we'll get back to land, and, yes, we'll probably all die here. But, by God, it won't be for a long time. And it won't be for lack of trying."

Parrish wiped at his nose with the back of a hand and scowled at the floor. His eyes narrowed. "I'm not under your command anymore. That's over. So why don't you just – "

Cross slapped him, careful not to make it too hard. Parrish folded and lay groaning on the littered floor, holding his face.

Cross stood. "Get up, Lewis." He gave him a hand up and looked at his watch. "Now listen. Next check on the plant's due at 1800. I did the 1200 round. I want your initials there before dinner. Sorry I had to hit you. We'll have a service for Paula later, out at the Edge."

Parrish said nothing. Cross looked around the room, picked up the broken subcranial stimulator, then left, closing the door gently behind him. He headed back toward the lounge, pausing only to mash the stim box to a flat wreck in a trash compactor. *He hates me now too*, he thought. *But if it steadies him up to hate me, I can stand it. He might be a mechanical genius, but the Kids have twice his emotional maturity.*

No one else was around as he suited up, but as he stepped into Lock III he saw the blanketed shape, and was abruptly reminded he'd told both Oursler and now Parrish he'd hold a service. It would have to be in the morning, when they left. He puzzled briefly over how to do it, then dismissed it for the moment, pulling on his wet suit and gear.

He checked the gas levels in his Mark 39. Tested it with a breath, strapped it on, and plunged with a long stride into the water, holding his mask on with one hand. The sea was cool against his skin and the Mark 39 adjusted him to neutral buoyancy. He finned out of the lock and turned south.

The day was ending and the shimmering blue overhead was darker than it had been. Rays of sunlight, limned by tiny lifeforms and debris, slanted yellow downward from his right. Looking upward, he began to climb. As he neared the surface he felt the gas expanding in his chest. He breathed faster; if he locked his throat his lungs would rupture as the pressure lessened.

Moment by moment as he climbed the sea around him grew brighter, yellower, more golden and joyous. He lifted his mask to the sun that shimmered and danced through the silver mirror above his head.

Halting his ascent a meter beneath the surface, he hung there, looking up.

It was calm up there, the mirror ruffled slightly by the light summer trades. Cat's-paws chased each other, looking oddly rounded from below. In their troughs he could catch glimpses of the sun.

This far offshore, could it be safe to go up? To look for a moment on the sea from above? He could stay on the pack, not breathe the free air.

But he couldn't risk it. That was as irresponsible as Parrish's escapism. *We're all going nuts down here*, he thought, *with the possible exception of Deela and Ian.*

The vicious thing about it was, they had no alternative.

He made a slow circle just below the surface, scanning the seascape below for moving objects, then finned downward again in a shallow glide, heading for the long inverted rain gutters of the Annex. His thoughts moved on to the dolphins. *They're in the same fix we are*, he thought. *I wonder how they're taking it?*

For the dolphins, and the other cetaceans, had been just as vulnerable to Carsonella as men. Anything that breathed infected air died the Red Death. The whales, the seals, the blues, pilots and rights and grays, were all gone, along with the wild dolphins. Only the few "cultured" dolphins – "Delphinus sapiens," as the educated *Delphinus delphis* had been unscientifically but popularly tagged – had been able to realize the danger. And to act, in concert with the people remaining at the Station, to survive.

As he swam closer he examined the long semicircular concrete vaults of the Annex. They'd been built as the nexus of a city, a subsea education and living area where man and dolphin could interact in an environment congenial to both.

Every scientist since Pliny had known the brain of the dolphin was special. It was bigger than the human brain; even the cerebral cortex, seat of the "higher" functions, was larger.

That much gray matter had to have a function. But early efforts to communicate had come to nothing. Years of recording whistles, clicks, and squeaks had been tantalizing, but in the end left investigators little farther toward real communication. Cetacean and man simply had no common symbols, no common experience. Except, perhaps, the harpoon.

The breakthrough had arrived, as so many discoveries had, by way of a crackpot.

Cross had met Dr. John Leafe briefly, before the War, at a party in D.C. The man had not mellowed with the years. From being a brilliant eccentric he'd evolved into a zealous nut, approaching the narrow line of genius with enough drive to achieve psychological escape velocity.

But his early work had opened a new world to two hitherto estranged races.

Leafe, clinging precariously to a position at the Virginia Marine Labs in Norfolk, had conceived the idea of mating the yogic disciplines he'd explored in an erratic youth to the new transformative semiotics. The year before Dinant and Guthrie had published *Mathematical Models of Extra-Sensory Phenomena*, and Leafe had decided to try to apply the controversial Equation VII on a dolphin. In his case, it was a female *Tursiops truncatus* named (by the humans) Nikki.

To communicate, Leafe reasoned, one first had to share the conceptual framework within which communication could take place. To do this, he spent hours each day in the murky waters of Hampton Roads, navigating by sonar with a waterproof VR headset. At the same time he tried to increase the value of the coefficient Dinant and Guthrie called *theta* by establishing a personal rapport with Nikki, playing with her in her tank, stroking her, even substituting a crooked elbow for the muscular penis of the male dolphin when she was in heat.

When he felt ready he began the experiment. Night after night he reached for *kaivalya* in lotus position beside her tank.

Sometimes he felt her mind near him, but she could not seem to understand him, nor he her.

Leafe, oddly, enough, had been idly watching a dachshund identify a bush (the dog's upraised leg ranked in scientific myth with Newton's apple and Archimedes' tub) when the insight came. The dog, he saw, was a nose with legs. The human, an eye. The dolphin was an ear.

But hearing was different from the other senses in that it did not persist in time.

Cetaceans, he'd realized, did not perceive the world as a collection of nouns. Sound existed only when something was happening. Even groping around in the muddy harbor his primate mind had interpreted the sonic returns as *objects*; pier; boat; maybe-fish.

But the world of the deep sea was not of *things*, but of *sounds*. Not of being, but of action.

The dolphin lived in a world of nearly pure verbs.

That insight, the Leafe Corollary to Equation VII, led him ultimately into communication. The Delphinidae, he discovered, used sound only as their secondary means of "speech." Their primary medium, evolutionarily advantageous in a vast and opaque sea, was telepathy.

The vastness of his discovery had been dimmed but not extinguished by Nikki's murder of Leafe's wife as she realized her "lover" was married.

The New Delphinology had grown out of Leafe's work, though he'd left the field after the tragedy. The marine biologists and anthropologists and semanticists had gone down to the sea in subs. Once communication had been opened, a common seaspeech had been devised for both species to use in the ocean. The dolphin learned from man, and man from the dolphin.

A sleek swift form, white below, black and gray above, with the tooth-ringed grin of the common dolphin, joined up to his left as he approached the Annex.

"Good you have guards out," piped Cross.

"Hello to you," said the dolphin, swimming around him, tubbily graceful. *"You are called Cross, am-I-right?"*

"Yes. You are."

"Moving Fast through the Water. Speedy for short."

"Oh, yes. Engines' friend."

The male dolphin frisked about. Culture had not much modified some of the dolphins' attitudes. They were still deeply familial, and religious in their strange way. They still rejected whole areas of human knowledge like economics and politics as frivolous insanity. And they still loved to play.

"Let me check your air," said Cross as they came up on the first long finger of the Annex. He located the power cable again, to his left now, that stretched from the Station, and dove down to check its connections under the inverted trough that was the basic structure of the Annex. The exposed anode bubbled merrily, venting electrolytically separated oxygen up into the trough. The cathode, venting hydrogen at twice that rate, was outside the building, venting straight up to the surface.

"I see you're keeping it clean."

"We take turns polishing the bubble-makers. To breathe air is good."

Cross searched for something to say beyond the banal, and failed. He swam under the lip of the trough and surfaced into the air inside it and tossed his mask up onto the shelf on the inside and looked around.

The interior was shoaled with black backs, curved fins, small and large. The intermittent pop-*whoosh* of their breathing filled the narrow tunnel with a steamy warm animal smell. A splash to the rear told of a guard returning for a quick breath before returning to the sea. Cross wasn't psi-sensitive himself. At least, he'd never had an experience that led him to believe himself a Talent. But he felt strangely elated and confused but very welcome, and knew he was sensing the murmurings of the minds that moved in these fishlike bodies.

The two interns, Heather Johnson and Roger Comiskey, rose from where they'd been sitting and strolled over. Twentysomethings, older than the Kids but younger than the degreed scientists, they'd lingered here when the Dying had begun, and been immured with the rest. Comiskey wore faded

Speedos and Johnson the bottom half of a bikini. Both looked extremely fit, and not for the first time, Cross wondered if they really spent all their time together studying.

"Hello, Commander. What brings you here?"

"Hi Rog, Heather. Holding everything together? Need anything?"

"Just working on our dissertations." Johnson shrugged. "Yeah, I know, why bother?"

"But hell, why not," said Comiskey, adjusting the waistband of his briefs.

"Afraid I have bad news," Cross said. He told them about Welch's death. They exchanged sobered looks. "I liked Paula," Johnson said at last. "Um . . . will there be a funeral?"

"Who's this? Who's this?" A high squeaking reverberated from the curved overhead.

"Engines!" For once he recognized her. *"Good to hear you. –* Yeah, I'll take care of it, Heather. – *Engines, I'm here to ask a favor."*

"What? We're all listening."

"Yes, we're listening," piped up several voices. A slow drift began down the tunnel in his direction, the black wet bodies crowding in to hear. The dolphins began popping their blowholes. Comiskey imitated the sound with his lips, but Cross wasn't sure why.

"Go ahead," said Engines.

"I'm asking for help." He took a deep breath for the next sentences; his throat was starting to hurt from the seaspeech. *"One of us was killed by sharks today. We're going out to investigate at first light tomorrow. We need two volunteers."*

The squeaking began as soon as he finished. He looked from one set of excited brown eyes to another. There was a splashing commotion in the rear. *'Engines. They talk too fast for me. What are they saying?"*

"We too have noticed strange activity among the sharks. The (here she used a term Cross did not know) *have attacked dolphins, though none have yet been killed. That's why our guards are out. Cross,*

we sorrow for your friend. Yes, we're willing to help. You'll have killing machines?"

"Of different kinds. But we'll depend on you for listening."

"And you for seeing," said the dolphin politely, though her eyesight was as good as any man's. *"Moving-fast and I will come with you."*

Several others broke in, apparently disputing her arrogation of his request. But was it an argument? They were talking appallingly fast, and all together, and seemed to be leaving far too many words out to possibly make sense. Finally she stuck her face out of the water again and piped, *"It's settled. First light, then. The sea-children, will they come?"*

"Maybe. Maybe not."

"I hope so. They like to play. Your land-people do not play so much."

"No, hardly ever," said Cross grimly. His voice was used up and he had to croak to get the last sentence out. *"My speech is tired. I must go back."*

"You are welcome to stay," said Engines. *"We have new stories to tell and dances to do."*

"And fish to eat," whistled another.

A baby, not more than three feet long, twined itself in his legs and rose to the surface in his lap. The others crowded closer, rubbing their soft fine skin against his wet suit, rolling over to be scratched. Cross smiled and put in a few minutes with his fingernails. A dead grouper rose, clutched in a long-toothed beak. He tucked it under his arm.

"We'll take him back," sang several of the smaller dolphins.

He asked the interns if they wanted to go back too, but they said they'd rather stay with their charges. As he emerged from the Annex his escorts took up station above and below and ahead of him. They swam rigidly, as if on parade, making fun of land-peoples' slowness and pedestrian finning along. Cross grinned around his mouthpiece, squeaked to attract their attention, and turned a tight triple somersault. They broke into joyous imitation, after which he did a barrel roll and a frog kick, and the play was on.

"You look exhausted," said Graham, helping him strip off his suit. "Wrestling octopi again, Commander Nemo?"

"Trying to keep up with five calves. Well, the dolphins are in. Engines and Speedy'll be here at sunup."

"Then we're ready."

"Almost. Ken, I wanted to take something along a little more potent than the stingers. I know Doc thinks that's sufficient, but I'd like extra insurance."

"Like what?"

"Boomers. And something that'll reach out farther, maybe not immediately lethal, but some sort of wide-area deterrent. And we need a place to retreat to. A sort of, oh, a stronghold. In case things get really bad."

"We could use the cage that film crew left," mused Graham, "If it hasn't rusted away; it's been sitting out back of Lock I for, oh, years now. But, say, Dink, sounds like you're getting ready for a battle. It's not going to be that. Just a research trip."

"That's what Custer said. We have our ideas. The whitetips may think different."

"Okay, okay. Take what you want; just let me know what it is in the morning, before we leave. Breakfast at five."

"I'll be with Svec and Parrish tonight. We'll try to work something up."

"Oh, and what about. . . ." The biologist's gaze slid toward the blanketed body.

"We'll hold a service on the way."

"On the way? What do you plan to do?"

"She was my shipmate, Ken," said Cross. "We spent a long time together, most of it at sea. Don't worry. All we have to do is stop near the edge of the Deep."

Graham nodded. "Okay then, Dinker, tomorrow."

"Tomorrow," Cross agreed.

FOUR

Cross woke at 0400.

He knew the time before he checked his watch. Two hours of sleep didn't satisfy, but whatever subconscious mechanism was responsible for such things had pulled him up from a dreamless abyss into the dim light of his cabin. He got up and padded down the corridor, rapping on Graham's and Parrish's doors as he passed.

Svec's was already ajar, and he found the Chief busy in the head. "Les. Get any sleep?"

"Didn't get to it, Cap'n. Took a dip to check out the barrier on the cage. Seems to be working."

Cross nodded. Svec was invaluable. Quiet, competent, steady, his touch of "Kaintuck" backwoods only underlining the keen mind and sense of personal responsibility for what he considered his: his crew, his equipment, his ship. *He's been a steadying influence,* Dinker thought, looking at the narrow age-wrinkled face as Svec toweled himself down. *He takes care of the rest of us like his own family . . . the one he lost topside.* He'd even had a grandchild. Before.

Turning to the mirror, Cross pulled his microdepilator from its socket on the bulkhead and ran it over his face, burning away the whiskers. *You look tired,* he thought, noting the darkness beneath the gray eyes, the wrinkles gathering there and at the corners of his mouth. *Or am I just getting old too?*

He washed the ashes off with a splash of fresh water and padded back to his room. His khaki shorts were still damp but he pulled them on anyway. In an hour he'd be in the water.

He sat on the bed for a moment. Absently, he rubbed at his arms, feeling the smooth curve of muscle under ultraviolet-darkened skin. The time at the Station had done his body good: swimming, hunting, and a monotonous but protein rich diet had trimmed off the sedentary fat a sub-driver too easily picked up. The challenges of survival had sharpened his mind and even, he suspected, made him more than a little wiser.

It was a good way to face death: fit and strong. And with that thought he was surprised to note it didn't frighten him.

He remembered other mornings, before the other challenges of his life. Fights, as a boy growing up in pre-war California; tests; the state boxing finals, which he'd won after three rounds by a TKO; the day he'd arrived at Annapolis West in San Diego. His marriages, challenges not to his prowess, but to his tenderness. And the times he'd gone into battle in the little three-man Scalare-class minisubs, before the Treaty and the AI Coordinate and the dissolution of the Navy.

Why wasn't he afraid now? *Maybe that's part of wisdom*, he thought, sitting quietly. That wisdom meant simply acceptance; and that if he were to lose his life today, ripped apart by something fast and large and hungry, it was part of the skein of things he'd dimly glimpsed raveling throughout his life.

So how did his attitude differ from the mechanic's?

They were all going to die. Wasn't that what he'd babbled? Well, he was right. There was no reason for Dinker Cross to cling to air and warmth when the rest of his kind was gone. Humanity was a dead end, along with the thousands of species of land animals and birds it had struggled with and triumphed over and finally, with great difficulty, learned to share the fragile blue spaceship with.

A dead end, courtesy of a random mutation in a common virus.

A hundred million years from now, he thought, *the sea will try again to populate the land*. Life would go on. Without him.

He stood and stretched. As long as he was alive, a good breakfast would be welcome.

"Morning, Dinker." Graham pulled out a chair. Oursler, already at the table, was sipping at a mug of a strangely familiar-smelling black liquid.

"Coffee's on, Commander," he said. "Made a pot. Brew it too long and it'll spoil."

"I thought we were out," said Cross. "Look, the dolphins gave me a grouper yesterday. If nobody's started breakfast yet?"

The scientists nodded. Svec ambled in, said "Howdy," to the room at large, and headed for the galley that adjoined the lounge. Cross sent him back out to brief Graham and Oursler on his preparations for the dive. "And make sure Parrish is up," he added.

The grouper, scaled and filleted the night before, had stayed fresh in the reefer. Cross laid the two big chunks in a shallow baking pan. Sea salt, scraped from *Pilgrim's* flash coils, was sprinkled on with a generous hand. He investigated the reefer again. The dolphins supplied thick fatty milk that almost churned itself; the butter was oily, rich, rather like lard. He slathered it over the delicate flesh, added a dash of pepper and a garnish of sloke, and slid the dish into the microwave. Two minutes later he carried it out and set it on the table.

Parrish, the last member of the party, had arrived, looking sleepy and sullen. The five busied themselves eating for a few minutes. Cross remembered the coffee and drew himself a cup. Svec looked interested. "Grab a mug, Chief. You and Lewis deserve some. They've been up all night working," he explained to Graham and Oursler.

Parrish glanced up, but didn't respond to the implied compliment. The scientists nodded and reached for more fish.

Cross sipped gingerly at the steaming coffee. It had been months since his last cup and the liquid tasted acrid and bitter. Only at the third mouthful did his tongue remember it. The fish, on the other hand, was familiar, and he relished the delicate white flesh, steaming with butter and salt.

In the first few months after the deliveries from Topside had stopped, they'd discussed food endlessly, perhaps to divert their minds from what they'd really lost. Sheila had ravened after chocolate; Graham had missed steaks; Welch, beer. Oursler had confined himself to reminiscing about fresh croissants. The Station had been famous for its fresh and lavish cuisine, but that had the disadvantage that when supplies were cut off only a few staples had been on hand, along with the few common plants in the greenhouse. They hadn't yet touched the irradiated and freeze-dried stores, saving them for an emergency.

For food itself was no problem; the massive reefs of Navidad Bank were rich with pompano, jacks, groupers, bluefish, morays, croaker, crabs, shellfish, the strange spiny lobster called langousta, all kinds of rays and shark and skates, a plethora of sea plants – and all had found their way into the kitchen as the humans, coached by their mammalian compadres the dolphins, grew skilled in hunting with net and spear. In the shallow reef areas, some of which were only ten or twelve feet deep at low tide, they gathered mussels, clams, sea-lettuce, and other edible sea plants. There was plenty to eat, and Cross no longer dreamed of hot turkey with stuffing or corn pudding or the crisp outer shell of fresh cake doughnuts.

"How's the Carsonella work coming along, Ken?"

Cross tuned in to Oursler's question and Graham's reply. "Not great. Tough to do much without lab animals."

"Pity no one here kept a pet."

"That's a nice thing to say, Matt. What good would one cat do me? But I discovered one interesting fact, though I'm sure the people at Atlanta found it too before they . . . stopped work."

"What's that?" said Cross.

"Temperature effect. Generally viruses are pretty durable pathogens, but Carsonella doesn't tolerate low temperatures well. Instead it . . . disintegrates. The capsid, that's what protects the genome from nucleases, and snaps the virion into the receptors on the host cell, the proteins break down. Critical temp's about minus thirty Celsius. Minus, oh, about twenty Fahrenheit."

"Interesting," said Oursler.

"Couldn't that be used to kill it? To prevent infection?" said Cross.

Graham shrugged. "How? Say you've got it. If we cool you to minus thirty you might not have Red Death, but you're frozen solid. It's an interesting phenomenon, but there's no application I can think of."

They were silent until Parrish slurped at his coffee. "Well, I checked the cage and the barrier, charged the batteries, and refilled the buoyancy cylinders," he said suddenly. "It's ready."

"All right, good," said Graham.

"Just silly, if you ask me," said Oursler, glaring first at Parrish and then at Cross. "Stingers, boomers, a cage! All we really need on a collecting trip is Kenneth's dart, and shark billies to shove 'em away if they're curious. You're arming us like some punitive expedition. I warn you, I won't stand for indiscriminate killing. I authorized nothing like this!"

Cross briefly debated challenging Oursler's right to "authorize" anything, but decided a status clash wasn't what the Station needed. "If we don't need them, Doctor, I assure you we won't use them. But I'd like to be ready for the worst, all the same."

Oursler drummed fingers on the table. "I can't convince you that is unrealistic, can I, Commander?"

"Nope." Cross smiled to take the edge off it.

"The animals of the sea are overwhelmingly peaceable. If we attack them, of course they'll defend themselves. The aggressiveness of marine species has always been overrated." He turned to Graham. "Don't you agree, Ken?"

"Well. . . . "

"Man has always been the great predator. Our lust for killing leads us to see it reflected in the eye of every creature with teeth. The point is, we should try to understand, not to vanquish. When we tried to understand the cetaceans, instead of hunting them, a new world opened for us."

"We couldn't understand Carsonella," said Cross.

Oursler didn't bother to answer, just rolled his eyes. Graham fumbled for his pipe, looking embarrassed.

The Kids came in, followed by Sheila. Ian was naked; Deela had draped a sheet around her in a faintly Grecian style. The end of the sheet dragged on the floor. Sheila was yawning, haltered today and with her hair tied back. She narrowed her eyes as she caught Cross's glance at the girl.

"We're going," Ian announced calmly. "What's to eat?"

"No way," said Cross. "You two'll hold the fort today. Along with Sheila and Roger and Sara. Already been decided."

"That's silly." Deela pouted. "We're better in the water than you are. Why can't we go?"

"You can go hunting around the Station," said Graham. "This'll probably be pretty dull, anyway."

"You're hunting the shark that killed Paula?"

Oursler shook his head. "Not quite, Ian. It's long gone by now. We're just going to look around. Quite unnecessary, I think."

"Then why can't we come?" said Deela.

"Now, look," said Sheila, putting her hands on their shoulders. "Remember what I told you about sociobiology? Basically, they want to protect you two. And me . . . I *think*. It's instinct, like the way dolphins protect their young. All right?"

"We're not that small," said Ian. "And we're growing fast. In a year I'll be as big as Dinker. You keep treating us like Land People and we aren't. We have qualities you can't even appreciate."

"Now, Ian, Didi," said Oursler, chiding like an indulgent father, "Sheila's right. You two're essential to our future. And if you're mature enough to go, then you're mature enough to understand. You *will* stay, because I'm asking you to." Not waiting for a reply, he turned back to the table. Ian looked angry, but turned and left the lounge without arguing.

Deela sighed. She sat down at the table, by Oursler, as far away from Cross as she could get.

"Still some coffee left," said Graham.

"Oh, it's awful tasting. I hate it." She gave an exaggerated shiver of revulsion.

"What's the itinerary?" said Sheila, sitting down too.

"Motor northeast, to the Tongue area. Set up a beacon and observe," said Oursler. "We should be back well before nightfall, and we'll have two dolphins with us, so we can 'call' back if we need to. So have the Kids close at hand."

"We'll stay," Deela said. She looked sideways at Cross. "I'm not worried. Come back whenever you want."

He lowered his eyes to his cup, trying to look solemn. Everything she did was so obvious. Well, what did he expect?

Svec got up. "Yeah, guess it's time," said Graham, rising too. Cross tossed off the dregs of his coffee, rinsed his mug, and left it in the sink. Wondering, as he did so, if he'd ever be back for it.

The porpoises were waiting as promised. Engines Cross recognized immediately; the second he identified a moment later. Adjusting his mask, he swam out from under the lock as Graham plunged through the surface.

"Moving Fast?"

"Yes. You're Cross, the one who came yesterday."

"Aye. Good to hear you."

Svec tapped his shoulder from behind. The Chief's arms were full of gear, which he began handing out in the dim gray light that was all that penetrated of the morning. The dolphins got five-liter tanks with specially-designed mouthpieces. Cross got a stinger, an extra shaft with power pack, an old-fashioned boomer with three cartridges, and (furtively slipped to him by Svec) a flat brown-wrapped package that he tucked inside his wet suit. The shafts of the stingers and the boomer he slid into the quiver on his support pack. Svec kept as much and passed a stinger apiece to Graham and Parrish. Oursler swam over, but shook his head when Svec offered him a weapon.

Cross nodded in satisfaction as Svec led them to where the cage rested on current-swept sand. The "cage" — actually a collapsible wire basket – measured two meters by three by two high when expanded. Collapsed, as it was now, it looked like a box spring, with a streamlined ovoid in the center – the power pack from one of the disabled 'bots. Hollow cylinders along its edges permitted its buoyancy to be adjusted with a compressed gas tank. Paula Welch's corpse, wrapped in the blanket, was strapped amidships. As a finishing touch, Svec and Parrish had added a magnetohydrodynamic motor from a wrecked scooter and a crude aluminum rudder.

"All aboard?" said Svec, looking round. Bubbles burst from the pontoons as he twisted a valve, and the improvised vehicle began to rise. Parrish and Oursler joined him on top of the thing, and Graham and Cross found handholds on its trailing edge.

The Chief looked back, winked at Cross solemnly behind his mask, and started the motor. The motley assemblage of parts and people slowly accelerated. *She's no speedster, but it'll do three knots or so,* Cross thought, watching the bottom move past below. *Twice as fast as we can swim. We should have thought of this before.*

The slipstream tugged at his mask and mouthpiece. He swept his gaze around. Except for the dolphins, frisking about the slowly-moving sled, nothing interrupted the tremendous blue that surrounded them. Already, early as it was, he could see for a hundred feet or more in every direction.

He saw not a single fish. That was odd. The shoals of spadefish and porgy, even the curious barracuda that always trailed divers in these waters, had disappeared.

The soundless engine pushed them along through the early morning sea. The bottom, sloping down in a series of gentle rills and hillocks, gradually changed. The uniform sand of the plain gave way as they descended to rocky upthrusts that had become encrusted over the eons by benthic corals. The sand, smoother and whiter now, lay in drifts between the upthrusts like paths in a Zen garden. Among these coral heads, he knew, the big game fish lurked, tautog and seabass and gap-mouthed grouper. As they continued to descend the light imperceptibly but steadily dimmed, objects around them losing the last traces of green, leaving a world painted in washes of gray.

They reached the Edge. Svec allowed the sled to pass over the dropoff and, maintaining the same depth, made a shallow turn out over the immense darkness. For a moment Cross lost sight of the cliff behind, hanging suspended in infinite space, with only blue above, and endless black below.

The cliff reappeared ahead. Svec switched off the motor and let the sled hover as the divers left it, then ballasted it to settle to the top of a coral head just at the edge of the Deep.

The service was short. The dolphins, sensing the solemnity of the occasion, patrolled at the edge of visibility. At the end the divers lifted the shrouded form from the sled, and swam outward.

"We now commit her body to the Deep," concluded Cross.

Welch's body began dropping. Tilted downward. Cross had put a weight belt at her feet and the body sank faster and faster, corkscrewing slightly, growing smaller and dimmer until their straining eyes lost it in the midnight of the abyss.

They swam back to the sled in silence. Cross moved up beside Oursler as Svec started the motor again. "Where to, Doctor?"

"A klick north of here," said Oursler in fluent seaspeech, *"A tongue of shelf juts out. Setting up at the tip of that will put sound into deep water on three sides of us. Anything that's there will hear us."* His eyes rolled behind the mask as he peered at Cross. *"Including, Commander, any atypical pelagic sharks."*

Dinker nodded, glanced around as they rose from the seafloor. Still no fish. He wondered if the scientists had noticed.

The Tongue was naked rock, lower than the shelf behind it by more than a hundred feet. Cross checked his depth gauge. A hundred and forty meters. Deep by any standard, though the Mark 39 could theoretically get him much deeper. He let go the sled as Svec dropped it, stirring up a thin murky layer of sediment from the bottom, and finned around, searching.

It was a world of shadows. Though technically only blue light remained, the human eye perceived it as gray; night vision had taken over. Almost at his feet, he looked down into the sea and its eternal darkness. The sun, far above, was little more than a memory this deep. He breathed out to lose buoyancy and sank to the floor of the Tongue, fins puffing up thin clouds of silt from the rock.

A water-muffled clank came from the sled and he turned to see Graham unloading the sonic generator, a foot-wide sphere with a flattened bottom and a wire leading to a power and control box. Moving gracefully despite the thick wet suit, the biologist unreeled the sphere, which floated upward on its cable, and set the box on the rock. Nearby, Parrish peered through an underwater videocamera. Oursler waited a short distance away, observing. The trip must have tired the old man, Cross thought. Well, he was over seventy. Not an advanced age for his generation, but certainly beyond too-strenuous activity for very long.

The first pulse chattered his teeth against each other and drummed in his ears. Graham glanced around, then adjusted the control. The chattering lessened but the volume increased, changing pitch, diving downward along the sonic spectrum until Cross's stomach rumbled and his skin crawled uncomfortably to and fro. The sea began to vibrate irregularly in a cacophony of drummings and deep bass boomings that squeezed at his ears and sinuses.

Low frequencies travelled farthest in water. He visualized the call spreading outward, reflected between thermoclines, refracted downward to the floor three thousand fathoms below. Graham changed frequencies, and the sphere uttered abrupt high-pitched jarring sounds that struck at Cross's lowermost vertebrae and travelled up his backbone to rattle inside his skull. He drew the stinger and checked it. No shark in the sea could ignore calls like they were broadcasting.

The first three appeared nearly at once, swimming jerkily in from the north. Cross closed with Graham, shook his shoulder, and pointed. Graham's mask turned in their direction, and the hellish noise stopped.

Cross shook his head to clear it. His sinuses still throbbed. Something shoved between him and Graham and he flinched, but it was only Engines. The dolphins had rejoined the humans at the first sight of the whitetips.

The sharks had seen them, though, and their sight took over from their keen hearing. The divers drew together. Dinker, stinger held out butt-first, tracked the three as they circled.

"Fend them off," Oursler said. *"We don't kill unless necessary."*

Cross glanced around. Svec and Parrish were unfolding the cage, erecting the walls. *"Whitetips, all right,"* Graham confirmed.

Their second orbit was closer, some thirty meters away. The big dirty-gray bodies moved deliberately, the rear half and tail sculling powerfully. A flash of movement accompanying them caught his eye; tiny striped pilot fish, minor henchmen of these deep-sea killers.

Oursler craned around, checking, Cross supposed, that weapons were reversed for fending off. Svec set the top of the cage in place with a clank and joined the others, drawing his own stinger. They squatted, knelt, and stood in a rough circle around the silent generator, watching. The Record light of Parrish's camera winked on.

The sharks turned lazily and made directly for them. The lead one headed for Parrish. He fended it off, using the bulk of the camera to push away its closed mouth. The others followed in its wake, calm flat black eyes sweeping over the little party. When the last had passed they wheeled deliberately.

"Over there," came someone's voice, hard to identify in seaspeech. Cross glanced up to see the pale flashes of more – several more – approaching from above, from the east, the open waters of the Atlantic. He looked back for the first three, couldn't find them, then picked them up coming for him, two

almost abreast. The third had split off, circling in an arc that would bring it directly to Graham from the side.

Cross brought up his rod to guard his right, glanced to his left, and felt relieved as he saw Svec was flanking him.

The sharks struck, jaws open. He rolled left, but was brushed by one of the sharks and spun half around. His mask tore half off and flooded. He cleared it and searched the rock for his stinger, which had been wrenched out of his hands.

The new arrivals must have seen the pass the first three had made, because they skipped the checking-out process. They went directly on the attack. Cross, spinning to meet a rush from behind, counted seven whitetips circling them now. One snapped at his probing stinger, caught it, and left the haft dangling in his gloves, bitten through.

He groped in his quiver and came up with the old-fashioned boomer. On contact, the shaped-charge powerhead would blow a foot-wide hole through the largest shark. But he hesitated. The whitetips were still deliberate, unhurried, but they needed only to scent blood and offal in the water to go into frenzy.

There'd be no stopping them then.

He used the butt of the boomer to parry another pass, and felt something bump his back. He craned round; Graham. He was pulling Parrish in and Cross, grasping his intent, pulled Svec into the knot too. They clung together, back to back.

Cross found Oursler on his right. He couldn't resist it. *"Observations, Professor?"*

"Fairly typical responses," said Oursler. *"Though this attack in groups is odd. Carcharhinids seldom do that. Probably just coincidence."*

"Here they come!" said Parrish.

They came in twos this time, the second just behind the first. Like fighter UAVs in echelon, he thought. The leader cannoned into the knot, bowling divers in all directions. The second focused on Parrish, hitting him from the rear. Its speed and razorlike teeth sliced the backpack neatly away from his body. Eyes wide, he pulled his facemask off and blinked at the dangling end of his air hose.

Cross was suddenly glad for the multiplicity of gadgets on the Mark 39. One was a small backup mouthpiece, to be used if a main full-face mask failed, or a buddy needed to breathe. He reached to detach it from its clip, but was beaten to Parrish by Graham, who popped his own spare into Lewis's mouth.

When he turned back a second pair was almost on them. He slammed the leader hard on its nose with the safetied boomer as Svec, from his left, went for the eye of the second. They swerved upward.

A tone had droned in his ears for seconds but only now did Cross hear the breather's overload alarm. He punched it off and swam back toward the cage to re-form the defensive circle.

"Still think it's typical, Doctor?" he panted to Oursler.

The sharks – there were more now, a score, of varied sizes from three to eleven feet long – circled in an ominous carrousel. *"No,"* said Oursler, head following the deadly whirligig. *"Not that coordinated attack. They don't do that."*

"You just saw it."

"So I did." A flash of anger. Or was it fear?

The moving ring tightened, and changed shape. It became an oval, its centroid shifting from the divers, though he didn't see why.

"They're headin' in again," Svec warned.

They did so in twos, but now each pair, as the circle whirled, was followed by two more. They hit Svec and Cross, knocked them tumbling into the rocky floor. He cursed in his head, scrambling to right himself in the water, which was growing murky as the long tails whipped up mud. *To hell with this,* he thought. *If we can't see them, we're toast.* He reversed the boomstick and clicked the safety to Off.

"Don't," said Oursler, in an unnatural voice.

"They'll kill us. They're out of control."

"Didn't you see that? They're changing behavior, modifying their tactics. They're strategizing!"

"Great. Why don't we start? Move back here, in front of the cage. That'll cover our backs."

The others shifted to follow him, re-forming the knot with backs to the cage. The dolphins, excited, swam back and forth jerkily in front of them. *"Engines. Moving-Fast. Stay out from in front,"* called Graham. *"Get in here behind us. They'll pick off anyone who strays from the group."*

Cross, near Oursler, heard him say, *"Ken, I don't like this. Dinker was right. It does look as if they're coordinating their attacks."*

"That would mean second-order, Matt. Which we know the Selachii, as a class, don't have."

A pause, during which one of the larger whitetips swam slowly by as if inspecting their new formation.

Oursler muttered, *"Maybe we're seeing a mutation."*

"Oh, come on, Matt. You know that doesn't happen in one step."

"How long have they been out there? Maybe it's a subspecies, recently evolved. With this behavior, it would become dominant very quickly."

"This is all very interesting," Cross broke in, *"But I count over thirty sharks out there now. If they hit us all together we're finished. Shouldn't we get in the cage?"*

"Won't hold us all," said Oursler briefly.

Cross mentally damned the old man's rigidly logical mind. *"Well, let's some of us get in, then."*

"Look, Dinker, that cage is nothing but wire," explained Graham. *"It's the electric field it generates that keeps sharks away. So whoever's left outside gets shocked."*

"Will this help?" said Svec, emerging from the cage with one end of a cable.

Graham seemed relieved at the sight of it. *"A barrier wire! Wonderful. Moving-Fast!"* The male dolphin jerked around. *"Open your mouth. Here. Run this around us about ten meters out."*

The dolphin circled them while Svec and Cross paid out more of the bare copper. *"Turn it on,"* said Graham. *"Oh – wait! Not till – "*

The dolphin squeaked, dropped the wire, and barreled back toward the humans. *"Sorry,"* Svec said. *"Didn't mean to get you, Speedy."*

They fell silent, watching the whitetips circle, obviously preparing for another attack. *"Ken, can you tranquilize one from here?"* asked Oursler.

"I'll try," said Graham. He cocked his speargun and fitted a fat-bodied projectile to it.

The first shark to hit the barrier arched suddenly upward as it passed above the wire, shook itself viciously, and bolted away. Two others hit almost simultaneously; one went into convulsions, smashing itself into the rocks. The other shuddered before turning for the shelter of the deep.

The next wave came in higher over the wire and were obviously less affected; they only veered upward, showing pale ventrals. Graham, leading a small one like a duck hunter would a passing mallard, placed the hypodermic dart just behind its pectoral. The little shark wavered, but kept on, and there was no time to follow it.

The rest of the throng didn't follow the first few, but came in from all points of the compass. As each sensed the electric field it angled upward, passing over the crouching humans. Watching, Cross felt his skin crawl.

They were systematically testing the extent of the barrier.

Oursler realized it too. *"My God,"* he said, in a barely audible voice. *"Problem-solving behavior. Lewis, get pictures."*

"Who for?" Parrish said, but pivoted, following the sharks with his lens.

"Engines, Speedy," said Graham, *"You guys hear anything? Are they communicating with each other?"*

"No," squeaked the dolphin. *"No sound, and no thoughts we can 'hear'."*

"Can they break this barrier, Ken?" asked Cross.

"I don't see how. No, we're safe here," said Graham.

"The battery in that pack's good for hours yet," added Svec.

A medium-sized whitetip came low over their heads. Cross saw it had approached directly over the cage, behind them, and a suspicion began to form. *"Ken. Chief. When that wire's deployed, is the cage itself still charged?"*

They looked at him, hesitated. *"Don't know? Wait. I'll try it."* He swam toward the cage, stripped off a glove, and reached out. It was uncharged.

"Look out!" He shielded his head with an arm as the next shark slammed into the cage, tipping the fragile basket over on him. Another followed, and another, each striking at the cage with teeth and tail, dragging it along, tearing it apart. Grinding, smashing sounds filled the water. Shards of metal fluttered down around him.

The water grew dense, murky, and he pulled at the wire blindly. Graham: *"The barrier's down. Gather round me here, back to back. Use your weapons!"* He heard Oursler faintly, disagreeing, arguing.

"Hold still," came Svec's voice. Cross felt the weight of the cage lift, and they swam together toward the voices.

The cloud dimmed. They emerged to see Graham struggling with Oursler. Beyond them the whitetips were moving with less deliberation, beginning the jerky, violent motion characteristic of a frenzy.

The old man broke free and began swimming upward. *"Ken! They're intelligent! Like your dolphins! They can understand!"*

"Come back, Matt!" shouted Graham. *"Don't!"*

Oursler rose, long awkward arms and legs jerking against the blue radiance overhead. They looked up at him helplessly. He spread his arms and turned to face the approaching sharks. Hanging suspended, motionless, awaiting their approach. Inviting them to come up and look at him eye to eye and respond to his offer of himself.

To communicate.

The first one hit his chest, jerking the old man round like a puppet hit by a bullet. The jaws closed, the shark twisted violently, and continued on. Oursler clutched at his chest as a cloud of black blood erupted. The next struck at his legs and dragged him through the water before he disappeared under a knot of twisting bodies.

"My God," said Graham, starting upward after him. Cross and Svec grabbed his arms, holding him back. He fought for a moment, then sagged. *"You were right,"* he muttered. *"Matt. Matt! You goddamned fool!"*

"He's gone, Ken. I'm sorry, but . . . let's just see if the rest of us can get out of this alive." Dinker pulled the last stinger out of his quiver and handed it to him.

The behavior of the sharks had changed. The deliberation was gone. Now they were fighting one another for food. From the cloud of blood that marked where Oursler had been they turned downward, and Cross prepared to fight on the lonely seafloor, in the dim gray light.

The boomer recoiled in his gloves at the same instant he heard Svec's go off too. The smack of the stingers triggering merged into the roar of the power heads. A white-tipped body swam past, headless, floods of dark blood pouring out as the still-jerking tail propelled it on. He fumbled to replace the charge.

Another flashed by, mouth open, and he struck at it but missed; Graham, with Parrish still umbilicaled behind him, got it with his stinger; it died instantly. More bored in, inches above the rock, mouths gaping darkly, teeth extended like the blades of power shovels.

He had to squint; the light was growing dim, blood and debris mixing in the water in dark clouds.

A black eye showed for an instant and he thrust the boomer against its flank. The concussion blew him backward, ears ringing. Only the directional blast of the shaped charges kept them from concussing the diver as well as the target.

The shark disappeared. Reload. He dropped the empty and froze as a whitetip materialized directly in front of him. He raised one arm reflexively to protect his face, then blinked as a slate-and-white form crashed into the shark's side, deflecting it. Speedy? The dolphins would never live through this. He twisted the new charge in place; his last.

Something solid and muscular brushed him from below. A massive whitetip slid by, the tail of a smaller one protruding from its viciously-snapping jaws. He set the boomer on top of the whitetip's head and triggered it. The big fish canted gently to the right and slid away under him like a damaged bomber going down. Something tugged at his leg and he turned and clubbed at a small shark's gills. It held on for a moment, teeth mining his flesh, then let go as he jammed the shaft into its eyes.

He swam toward a diver dimly visible ahead. Svec, with two dead shark convulsing at his feet. As they neared each other Cross zipped his wetsuit open. He pulled out the flat packet and waved it to catch Svec's eye.

The Chief hesitated, then nodded, twice. Cross tore the packet open and waved it in the water, scattering the chemical. Svec, he saw, was doing the same thing with another. The whitish clouds spread in the eddying water. His exposed skin and lips burned as the enzyme began to attack them.

He saw the shark too late. Already dying – most of its stomach was gone, entrails streaming grotesquely from a wound that could have come only from the bite of another shark – it plunged at him through the spreading cloud, mouth open. He could count every one of the wicked triangular teeth. It slammed into his waist, knocking the breath from his lungs. Then sank away, jaws locked open, to settle to the mud by his flippers.

He sucked at the mouthpiece, fighting to regain his breath. The water burned where it touched flesh as if he'd been plunged in acid. His lips went numb. He peered around. Svec, a few feet away, gave him a thumbs-up.

The water seemed to be clearing. There were no more sharks about, except the dead and dying littering the Tongue around them. Cross peered cautiously round again, checking every quarter for threats. Then swam upward, hoping to see better once he was off the bottom.

As he cleared the whitish cloud another diver appeared, swimming above the murk, apparently searching for something. No; two divers. Graham and Parrish. He waved. One waved back and sank toward him.

"You all right, sir?" It was Parrish.

"Yeah. Chief's okay too. You?"

"Bruised, but alive. That was the K enzyme you used."

"Uh-huh," said Cross, with difficulty; the numbness had spread to his tongue and he could not hear well either; someone was clanging a bell in his ears.

Svec finned up from below. He craned round, discovered them, and swam closer. His legs jerked, as if he was beginning to lose control over them.

"You're hurt, Skipper. Your leg?"

He remembered and glanced down. The rubber of the suit showed little, but dark blood oozed from long gashes in the lower thigh, around the knee, continuing down on either side of the calf. "Mmf," he said. Then, with difficulty, *"Speargun."*

"What?"

Cross scanned the sea floor. The slow drift of the Gulf Stream was gradually clearing the silt and blood, revealing the carnage. Dead sharks lay everywhere, whole and in unidentifiable portions. He spotted the speargun Graham had discarded and swam down to it. His legs felt numb. White flashes pulsed on the edge of his visual field. Reaching the gun, he stripped off the rubber thongs and tied them around his leg as tightly as he dared.

"We better head back." Graham, settling to the bottom beside him. *"This stuff's dispersing. I'll look for Matt —"*

"He went over the Edge," Parrish said. *"I saw him go. Um, what was left."*

Graham closed his eyes behind the tempered glass of his mask. *"Okay . . . okay. But we've got to get you two out of those suits and decontaminated."*

Cross nodded; he didn't trust his voice.

The biologist, looking around the sea floor, suddenly tensed. *"Oh, no!"*

Near the twisted wreckage of the cage lay one of the dolphins, on its side, round holes showing on its belly where bites had been taken. Another dolphin — Engines, Cross thought fuzzily — was nuzzling it, as if to push it toward the surface far above. He swam after Graham as the biologist made for the dolphins.

"It is over, Kenneth," piped the female, as they approached. *"He has swum to the sun."*

Wordless, Graham put his arms around her. She, too, was wounded, Cross saw, trailing blood from a series of parallel gashes near her muscular tail. The strap of her oxygen tank had been cut, and the cylinder banged against her flank as she rolled.

"I'm sorry, Sound-of-Ship-Going-Over. He fought well; he is surely safe in the sun now," said Graham. *"I loved him."*

"I too."

"Let us treasure his memory till we too rise to the greater sea."

Cross, fascinated by the scene – they'd begun what Klassen called the Dolphin Requiem – felt a hand on his shoulder. He turned to see Parrish. *"What are we hanging around for? Those bastards will be back. I'm leaving, Skip."*

"Come on. Let's go," said Graham, straightening from blowing the ritual last breath into the dead dolphin's blowhole.

They rose together. Graham retrieved Svec, who'd begun to wander off in the wrong direction, and pointed them all southwest, after the slowly swimming Engines. Dinker was feeling increasingly fuzzy. He could no longer move his neck, but was able to keep a lookout of sorts by twisting his upper body. When he saw the shark he tried to speak, but failed. He flailed instead at Graham's flippers. The scientist turned. *"What, Dinker?"*

He pointed. The small whitetip lay between two rocky outcroppings, motionless on the clean white sand. The shaft of a dart was visible under its pectoral.

"The one I shot," said Graham. *"That hypo's good for a while. We should take it back. Engines, do you think – "*

"Tow it?"

"If you can. I know you're hurt, but it could be important."

"I'll try." The dolphin approached the motionless shark warily, nipped at its dorsal, then seized it firmly. She lifted, arching her body, and got the fish clear of the bottom. Once up, it was easier for the dolphin to drag it along.

They labored on, staying low in case the whitetips, or other sharks attracted by the explosions and blood-scents, should sight them.

Cross was finding the going increasingly hard, though all pain had been displaced by the growing numbness. He reached back clumsily to turn up the oxygen enrichment, but couldn't feel his fingers on the knob. His vision was going. The white flashes were more frequent. He could make out only vague blurs. His legs were dead sticks, like oars, that he tried to flail clumsily behind him.

The deadly enzyme was in his bloodstream, and even the infinitesimal amounts that infiltrated human skin were capable of killing. Even in a small concentration, it killed sharks in seconds, striking through their gills. But it was almost as deadly to the diver who used it, and as such, a measure to be used only when the alternative was certain death.

Svec, Graham, Parrish, and Engines were far ahead; he was falling behind. The dimness around him grew lighter, grew bright. The sun had pierced the veil of the sea and was flooding his brain with incandescence. He stopped swimming and sank slowly toward the bottom. The sea was cool on his skin. He ceased to think, and opened his mind to the all-encompassing, joyous light.

FIVE

Patricia, he thought. It had to be Patricia. The elder, the gentle, the brown-eyed.

Pat? Her hands, too, had been soft. But there was something hurried about her. She'd not yet learned patience. But these, stroking his face, were slow, gentle.

He tried to open his eyes, but the pressure of the sea held them closed. He slid backward, down, into the darkness, giving up to sleep.

Some time later his eyelids snapped open. The curved overhead of sick bay came as no surprise. Now he knew where he was, and that the Pats were gone.

Cross wished he'd left with them.

He stared at the overhead, trying to make sense of his body. Some parts responded; others were uncertain of their allegiance; a few he could not contact at all. Finally, summoning all his strength, he turned his head toward the door. His ear tingled. A tone sounded in the corridor.

Graham came in, dark homely face brightening a little as he saw Cross was awake. "Dinker. Figured you'd wake up when no one was around." He bent to unclip the monitor from his ear, and drew a chair up beside the bunk. "How you feeling? Can you talk?"

"Pretty weak," Cross said, in a hoarse whisper. "How's Chief?"

Graham looked haggard. "Next door. Apparently he got a heavier dose than you. I'm afraid there might be permanent effects. But at least he's alive, which none of us would be if you hadn't used the enzyme. Why didn't you tell us about it before we started?"

"Would Matt have let us take it along?"

"Hm. I see your point." Graham sat glumly for a moment, lost in thought. "To lose both Matt and Moving-Fast, and with the Chief hurt . . . I want you back on your feet, Dink."

"Do my best." Another thought struck him: the hands. Whose had they been? "How long have I been out?"

"Oh, about a day. It's noon. Hungry?"

"I could eat something, yeah."

"I'll tell your nurse."

"Nurse?"

"Didi appointed herself. To take care of you. We cleaned your leg up. You've got eight fairly deep puncture wounds and some tearing of the muscle. The enzyme penetrated the wound, apparently. That's why the leg's numb. I don't know how much feeling you'll recover, but we cleaned things up, shot you full of omnicillin, and glued up the gashes."

"Thanks. And, about the Professor . . . He meant a lot to all of us. In different ways, I know, but still, a lot."

"Well." He seemed to deliberate an answer, then just stood. He turned to leave, then paused. "By the way, Sheila and I are getting some interesting results on that shark we captured. We can talk later."

"I'll be here."

Graham nodded and left. Minutes later the door slid open and Deela came in, carrying a thermos. When she saw him watching she stopped, started to smile, then blushed. She was wearing a variation on the draped sheet of the day before. She looked chaste and simple, a Grecian priestess, and Cross was charmed despite himself.

"Are you finally up?"

"Yeah, back from the land of Nod."

She frowned. "Nod?"

"Sleepyland. What's in the jug?"

She sat down, abruptly businesslike. "Chowder. I made it. Ken said you felt like eating."

"Sure do. But I'm pretty weak."

"I'll feed you." And she did, holding the spoon to his mouth and wiping away the spillage with a corner of her toga. Between spoonfuls she talked. "We all feel awful, Dinker. Doctor Oursler was . . . our father. I-i and I."

"We needed him," Cross said. "Sometimes we didn't get along, but I respected him. The way he died . . . practicing what he believed in . . . he was brave."

"He cared." She blinked away tears.

"What's everybody doing today?" he said, to change the subject.

"Ken and Sheila and Heather are working with the shark. Ian's out hunting, close to the Station. Joe's in the next room. I'm taking care of him, too."

"Where's Parrish?"

"Lewis hasn't been around much. I guess, taking care of the air machinery, or whatever. He's awful depressed. About Paula. And maybe other things. He spends a lot of time in his room."

Aha, he thought. *Maybe I can solve two problems at once.* Aloud, he said, "Yeah, he's probably lonely. Maybe you should stop by and see how he's doing. Or check on Roger, over at the Annex."

"Maybe." Then she looked closely at him. "You think you're so much smarter than I am. Don't you?"

"What do you mean?" He tried to smile.

"You know what I mean," she said, anger barely concealed. "Are you really gonna get better?"

"Well, I hope so," he said, puzzled. "I might be up in a couple of days."

"Then take this, you bastard." She jumped up, emptied the rest of the thermos on his head, and stormed out, slamming the door so hard the bulkhead vibrated.

Cross sighed, wiping chowder from his eyes. "Maybe I shouldn't try to be subtle," he muttered.

* * *

Two days later he was able to get out of bed. The numbness had gradually disappeared. *A mixed blessing*, he thought, wincing as he limped along the corridor, supporting his bandaged leg with a stinger, the only substitute for a cane he could find.

"It walks, it talks!" said Klassen as he entered the white walled delphinology lab. "Welcome to the charnel house. We're about to start."

Graham glanced up from a tray of instruments, nodded. Cross rested on his cane and took in the scene.

The motionless whitetip sprawled over the dissection table. Bright lights burned above it. The biologist, in coveralls and with latex gloves covering his arms to the shoulder, was laying out saws, scalpels, and shears. Klassen, in shorts and halter, was perched on a chair, her tablet and a small pile of reference books stacked beside her. Heather Johnson was rattling through shelves of chemicals in the back storeroom.

"Have a seat, Dink," said Graham. "This could be interesting."

Cross eased himself onto a chair. "What've you got so far?"

"Not a lot more than you guessed," said Sheila, keyboarding her tablet. "Before we euthanized it, I ran several standard intelligence tests, those that I could adapt to an animal without hands. It's capable of learned behavior, and can distinguish among crosses, circles, squares and triangles, which no one ever got a shark to do before. Unfortunately, we can't make it run a maze. I trained it to perform simple tricks in response to sound in the water – turn left, turn right, snap – but since it doesn't communicate, there's no way to 'talk' to it.

"That leaves us more or less at a dead end. All I can conclude is that it's, oh, about at the level of intelligence of a rat."

"That's pretty high."

"Higher than any other creature in the sea, except, of course, the cetaceans. This level of behavior's never been observed in a non-mammal before. Other than, maybe, octopi."

"So, we decided to have a look," said Graham. He stretched. "Okay, it's dead now, let's start."

A power-driven knife whined down the shark's upturned belly, dividing the tough hide into flaps. Graham laid the tool down and peeled the rough skin back, working under it with a curved knife. Paunch, liver, and tubular intestine came into view. A pungent, ammonaical odor filled the room.

Graham hosed the abdominal cavity down with a stream of water, pulled out a mass of tissue, sliced it off. "Pancreas," he said, tossing it onto a scale.

"Three kilos?" said Sheila, from behind a book. "How big is the shark?"

"Two meters. Six feet."

"Close enough."

Heather Johnson came in, so completely and rivetingly nude Cross had to tear his gaze away. The intern leaned against the bulkhead and crossed her arms, observing.

Graham plunged his arms in up to the elbows, pulling out armfuls of bloody red-white flesh. "Stomach, spleen, intestines normal." He made a quick cut. "Spiral valve." Three more slices freed the mass and he rolled the guts down the chute that led from the table to a waste holder.

He burrowed deeper. "Liver."

Its weight was normal. The knife whirred again through tough cartilage. Graham worked silently for several more seconds, then lifted out two long strips of white meat and laid them aside. "For dinner." Another second and the rear two-thirds slid down the chute.

"Nothing abnormal so far," he said to Sheila.

Johnson leaned in, blond hair swinging forward. "Did you expect there to be?"

"Not really."

The heart came out next. Graham sectioned it and compared it with the color plate in a screen Klassen held out. "Normal," he said. Down the chute. He cut away ruthlessly. The lower jaw slid away, followed by the gills.

Now only the upper part of the head remained, a reddish mass of raw flesh, oozing watery blood. Graham rinsed it down, turned it over to expose the top, sprayed it down again. He used a tape measure to locate the centerline, and the saw buzzed again. "Hand me that other blade, there, Dink?"

Cross leaned in as Graham sliced skillfully through layers of tough cartilage – sharks were, he remembered, boneless fishes – to reveal a small, grayish, convoluted lump of tissue.

"Show me the brain, Sheila."

Klassen swiped and held the screen out again.

The biologist whistled. "This ain't no shark. Or not one anybody's ever seen before."

"What?" said Heather. "Why not?"

"Look." He worked his fingers carefully around the mass, lifted it from its bed, and laid it reverently on the scale, where it slumped resignedly, like melting wax.

"Three times normal weight," said Sheila. "It's phenomenal." She closed the book and came around the table to stare down. "And check out the structure, Ken."

"I am." Graham turned the brain over with the edge of a knife, then split it down the middle. "It's not only bigger. It's different. Look, here's the 'typical' brain. Clearly defined. The fore portion here" – he pointed it out to Cross, then to the intern – "is olfactory. Down here's the brain proper."

Dinker said, "Well, it all looks pretty much the same to me. What's the rest of it, above where you're pointing?"

"That's the question," said Sheila. "That's not supposed to be there. That's new tissue."

"New?" said Johnson, leaning in so close Cross had to look away again. He caught Klassen's amused smirk and rolled his eyes.

"Not recorded before in sharks," said Graham.

"So how'd it get there?"

Sheila shrugged. They looked back at Cross. "You tell us," said Graham.

"You don't know? How about what Dr. Oursler said, just before he . . . Something about a mutation."

Graham set the knife down. "Dinker, evolution proceeds very slowly. It seems to go fastest in warm-blooded animals, mammals, and in them it took something like, oh, a hundred million years to evolve a brain equivalent to this. It goes so slowly because the brain's so complex. No one mutation – no *thousand* random mutations in a C. Longimanus genome – could produce this."

"Oh." Cross looked at the brain. "Another of those things that can't happen. So I guess there's only one thing to do."

"What's that?" Johnson asked.

"Let's all go have some lunch."

Halfway to the lounge the clatter of running feet echoed from ahead. Instinctively they flattened against the walls. Parrish flashed into view, eyes wild, sprinting for all he was worth.

"Lewis!" said Cross.

The mechanic halted, looking from one to the next as if searching for something written on their faces.

"What's wrong?" Sheila grabbed his arm. "Is it the air plant?"

"No. No, that's fine. It's the sharks. They're outside."

"Outside? What do you mean?"

"Come to the control room."

They trooped after him. Through the big pressure-resistant window the dark torpedo forms were clearly visible, patrolling slowly. "Is everyone here?" said Cross. "Ian! Was he outside?"

Sheila glanced at the tally board. "According to this, he's back."

"Good. – Control, give me the PA. – *Attention. There are sharks around the Station. Don't go out. Meeting in the lounge, right now. Announcement ended.*" He turned to Graham. "How much food do we have, Ken? All told?"

"Maybe a month's worth."

"We may be about to undergo a siege."

When they reached the lounge Deela and Ian were already there, sitting together. They looked up as the others arrived. "I saw them," said Ian. "I was just getting back. They chased me but I made it back to the Lock. Are those the kind you fought?"

"Right," said Graham, taking a seat with them. He asked Deela, "Is Joe well enough to come?"

"No. He can't move his legs, and he's dizzy. I'm worried about him."

Cross frowned. Confined to bed, Svec seemed to be aging rapidly. The enzyme, so selective in its effects on individuals, was evidently attacking his nervous system.

Parrish, trembling, slid into a seat. "You lured them here. With that damned expedition of yours. We should have left them alone!"

"Spilled milk," said Graham. "Pull yourself together, Lew. We depend on you."

He looked around, as if for Oursler; then seemed to realize someone else had to step up. He cleared his throat. "Okay. Everybody. Let's look at our situation.

"Sonar from Control shows scores of large fish, most likely whitetips, around us on the shelf. Now, that's not normal territory for a deep-sea shark; but these aren't typical sharks." He summarized Sheila's tests and of the dissection. "So, this is a new species we're dealing with. Sheila and I are calling it Carcharhinus ourslerii, after Matt. Its distinguishing characteristic is the larger brain. We've seen they can observe, learn, and act cooperatively. That, I'm afraid, makes them a match for us in the sea."

Cross nodded. There was a certain twisted rightness to it. Human beings, the Kings of Beasts, had ruled through ruthlessness and brains. That history was at an end, and they were meeting their inheritors. A large-brained shark – the perfect combination of savagery and cunning.

Ian raised a hand, as if in class. "What'll this do to the rest of the fish?"

Graham raised his eyebrows. "Good question, Ian. How would you answer it?"

"Well, from what I know, these guys are going to be, well, eaters of everything else. Smarts were about all they didn't have before, and they were still real successful."

Graham nodded. "And that's probably what's driving them out of the Deep. They're already masters there. Now breeding pressure's sending them inshore. They'll make short work of the other predators. Take over the sea as we once took over the land."

"How about us?" broke in Parrish. "We can't go out any more. We're trapped in here!"

"Let's dial it back a notch, Lewis, okay?" said Cross. He didn't like the way the crewman was acting. Even during the drift cruises, he'd been nervous, anxious, hard to get along with. Several times, Cross had considered requesting a relief, but had always been deterred by Parrish's undeniable mechanical genius. That meant a lot when their lives had depended on fixing some pump or motor or software glitch.

But now, he had to admit, Lew was losing it. He was overly imaginative, and Paula's death, and Oursler's, and the strain of waiting for his own day after day was too much. As his sweating face and clenched fists were telling everyone in the lounge.

"Dial it back, he says, and we're dying here like bugs! First Paula, then the Doctor, now the Chief!" He pointed to the bulkhead. "Now they're out there, just waiting. We're all as good as dead."

"What do you suggest, Lewis?" Sheila moved to stand behind him, sliding an injector from a wallet she carried in her shorts.

Parrish stared at Graham, then at the Kids. He seemed to have trouble breathing. "I say . . . we end it. Take poison.

Whatever. Go out with a little . . . a little dignity." His voice rose. "And do it now. No more waiting!"

He jumped to his feet, but Klassen touched the tube to his neck. He stared around, and toppled.

Graham caught him, easing the limp body into a chair. "He's tired," he said to the wide-eyed Kids. "And maybe a little sick, too. Needs a long sleep."

"I think he's just scared," said Ian.

"That's enough, Ian," said Sheila. "We're all under serious stress, here."

When Cross and Graham came back from carrying the tech to his bunk Ian was outlining his own plan. "We should swim out and just start killing them. You killed a lot, didn't you?"

"Not a *lot*," said Cross. "Ten, maybe. For one of us. Considering how many of them there must be, that's not good odds."

"But if we kill some maybe they'll go away. They're supposed to be smart, right? Wouldn't that be smart?"

"I'm not sure," said Sheila. "We might reason that way. But would they? Even with a bigger brain, they're still sharks."

"If I was one," Deela said, "I wouldn't care about the others. If they got killed I'd just eat them."

Graham nodded. "Don't forget, they're not here voluntarily. Ourslerii probably still prefers deep water. There are more fish here than in the Deeps. That's what they're after. At least, I hope so."

"I'd hate to think they were after us personally," said Sheila.

"Doesn't alter the basic problem," said Cross. "So what do we do?"

They thought about it for a time. Cross got up and limped back and forth, using the stinger to support his weak leg.

"We can stay inside for a month," said Graham. "So there's no immediate crisis. We've got air, thank God that's no problem. And water."

"So we wait?" said Cross. "For what?"

"For them to go away."

"Why should they?" asked Ian.

"When their food supply's exhausted, they'll leave."

"And what'll we eat then?" said Deela. "We only have that little patch of sick lettuce left. Since the grow lights burned out."

"Go out, and. . . . ." Graham's voice trailed off. "I see your point. They'll strip the whole Bank clean."

"They must have some natural enemies," said Klassen. "Every species does. Don't they?"

"Only us," said Cross. "And the dolphins. And we're both just about done for."

This has, he thought some days later, *been an extraordinarily boring week*. In those seven days, the atmosphere of gloom and tension had become almost unbearable. The Kids took it best, but missed their several-times-daily swims, and took it out in bickering over the limited choice of preserved food.

In mid-week the tedium had been broken by Engines, who surfaced in the Lock, then raced madly through the Station's canals, pursued by a three-meter female whitetip that had followed her in. A hastily-improvised barrier of bunk springs had penned the shark, to be dispatched and butchered. The meat had been a welcome change from canned pork and freeze-dried instameals. But Engines was afraid to go out again, and now considered herself one of the party of beleaguered humans.

Cross, his healing leg stretched comfortably across a chair, was sitting at the control station, looking across the sea floor through the big windows. A hundred meters away, undisturbed, lay the familiar guppy shape of *Pilgrim*.

Between him and his ship were, at the moment, three sharks. Two were small, no more than a meter long, but perfectly capable of taking off the better part of a hand or foot. The third, which the smaller sharks steered clear of, was twice their size. *Longimanus, or ourslerii?* he wondered. Graham thought the root species might already be extinct, first victim of whatever leap had thrust ourslerii into the ranks of thinking predators.

As if on cue, the biologist came in, scowling. Cross nodded. "Ken. What's on your mind?"

"This whole damned operation." He glared through the quartz, jabbed a finger at the patient gray shadows. "Those bastards. Dinker, we're all worried about staying alive. Except Parrish; between you and me, I think he's determined on suicide, and Sheila can't keep him sedated forever. But that honestly is not what's disturbing my sleep."

"So what's your worry?"

"How, damn it. *How* did they get a larger brain?" Graham struck his forehead with his fist. "I could almost die happy, if I understood."

Cross squinted at the overhead. "I've got a theory," he said at last.

"It would be a hypothesis, not a theory. But be my guest."

"They were made."

Graham stared. "What?"

"If it's such a radical change, it had to be artificially induced. Like Matt and his team did with the Kids. Right?"

"Well, it sounds logical," said Graham. "But I happen to know – it's my field – no such experiments were going on. Not with sharks. And even if they were, the brain, any vertebrate brain, is just too complex to manipulate genetically. That's why the Kids were straight human as far as their nervous system goes; Matt didn't dare touch that part of the genome. That state of the art is – was – a century away, maybe more."

Dinker nodded. "All right. But let me try another thought on you. Carsonella. How did *it* evolve?"

"Far as I know, they never found out."

"You've been culturing it. What do you think it evolved from?"

"I honestly can't guess. There's never been anything that fixes oxygen like that."

"Never?" He waited, watching Graham's face change. "You see?"

"A coincidence?"

"I thought nature, evolution, worked according to certain rules."

"Which it does, in general."

"Yet here the rules were broken, pretty violently I hear, twice in the same couple of years. It took our ourslerii years to grow to their present size. So . . . doesn't the timing strike you as suspicious?'

"Let me think this out." Graham looked interested now. "A virus appears suddenly, fixes oxygen, highly virulent – tailored, almost, to kill people. Which it does, along with all the other land animals. Carcharhinus ourslerii appears more or less simultaneously, and quickly achieves marine dominance. Tailored, almost, to kill – "

"Us," Cross supplied. "And the other sea animals."

"But why?"

He shrugged. "That's as far as I've gotten, Ken. Just that hint that excites my naturally suspicious nature."

"But, leaving aside who had such an advanced capability, who *would?* What would they gain?"

"Maybe they thought they could stop the infection when it got to the borders of their alliance, or their country. The Coordinate didn't dissolve boundaries. Only put them in the deepfreeze after the War. But whoever thought they could, miscalculated. They're dead." For a moment he thought of the radio signal, that distant humming beat. Could it be related too?

"Assume you're right, carsonella's some kind of gain-of-function, artificially-mutated death bug. Then how do the sharks fit in? Even a victor would still want the fish in the sea."

"I don't know." He sighed. With what was out there waiting, it all began to sound like an exercise in ratiocinative futility.

An orange light winked on by his elbow. He raised his arm to read the legend above it. "Say, Ken. Is this operational?"

"Far's I know."

"The outer door of Lock I seems to be opening."

"What? That's the big cargo lock. We haven't used that since shipments stopped."

"Well, it's opening."

The two looked at each other, then jumped to their feet, Cross grabbing for his makeshift cane.

Still hampered by the leg, he fell behind as they ran around the ring, through the lounge, Lock III, into the diving area, setting the metal gratings of the corridors rattling with the pounding of their feet. Cross stopped for a moment, leaning on the stinger. Then, panting, began running again. At last they burst into the Lock I caisson.

"Stop right there, Captain," said Parrish.

The first thing Cross noticed was that he was in full uniform – the preTreaty US Navy submarine service coveralls. The second, that he was standing in front of the big door, beside the dolphin canal that led out the now-closed cargo lock. The third was that his hand rested on the bulkhead next to the switch that controlled the inner door.

"What is this?" Graham was saying. "You planning some damnfool kind of gesture? Doesn't work like that, Lew. You can't open the inner door if the outer one's open. There's a safety interlock."

"Yes, I know that, Ken," said Parrish, sounding reasonable. "I know all about safety interlocks. Including how to short them out."

"He can do it. Believe him," said Cross. "So. Lewis. What do you want? What's this for?"

"This is to die," said Parrish. "Ready?" He began to pull down the switch.

"Hold it right there," Dinker snapped. At the tone of command his subordinate's hand halted momentarily. Cross searched for something to say. Sweat prickled along his back. "You said, when this first came up, we should go out with dignity. Dignity, Lewis, right?"

"A fitting end," said Dr. Graham, picking up the thread. "Is this fitting? The end of how-many million years of evolution and ten thousand years of history? Come on, Lew. If we're going to do this, let's do it right, with everybody here, and some kind of prayer."

"Prayer?" Parrish made a face.

"Or speech. Why don't you give us a sendoff? I'll get everyone together. Okay? Now just hold on till we get back."

Graham left. Cross looked after him. Clever, he reflected. Now, at least, the others could be in breathing gear when the wave of water hit.

"Lewis, I didn't expect this of you," he said.

The crewman shook his head. "Sorry to disappoint, Skipper. You were a good CO. But you know – what happened to Paula made me realize this isn't really living. We've been dead for a while now, and the Station's just a kind of Limbo. It's time to accept it."

"Maybe you're right. It's tough to say you're not, okay? But wouldn't it be fairer to well, vote on it? The Kids might disagree. And Rog and Heather. They're young. They might want to live their lives out to their natural ends."

"They don't understand, Skipper. If they really did, they'd agree with me." His tone held such calm finality Cross fell silent, feeling himself outargued. *And don't I feel this way myself?* he thought. *When it's all said and done.*

But he had to keep trying. "Look, we could still get out of this. We could take Pilgrim and – "

"Stow it, Skipper. Or I'll pull this switch right now!"

Steps rattled in the corridor. Sheila and Deela, Ian and Graham came in. The Kids looked scared; Graham, angry; Sheila, disbelieving. Her two assistants followed her, looking confused. "Lewis!" she said firmly. "This is not a rational act. You're not responsible. Let's go back to your room." She walked toward him.

"Stop, Dr. Klassen," said Parrish. He tugged at the switch. The motors began to hum. The door started up.

"For God's sake, Sheila!" Cross pulled her back. "That door doesn't care if he's sane or not. Lewis, stop!"

The door halted. Water began bubbling in from a hairline gap at its bottom. "Where's Chief?" said Parrish, looking past them.

"In his bunk. Asleep," said Deela.

"Leave him," said Graham. "He can't walk yet anyway."

"All right," said Parrish solemnly. "Friends – and I want you to know you're all my friends, maybe the best I've ever had – in a moment I'm going to open this door. We'll die without pain or fear or more suffering."

Deela began to sob, trying to stifle it with her fists.

"We're doomed here, whatever happens; machines wear out, we'll run out of food or have a breakout of disease. So let's face facts, and go gracefully."

He stepped back, to the edge of the canal. "Doctor Graham suggested . . . a moment of silence. To remember all we accomplished. Conquering the earth; ending war; opening the sea and space. We weren't meant to go farther. So here we end."

"Now, wait," said Comiskey. "Nobody asked Heather or me what we thought."

Parrish gave Roger an icy look, and shrugged. "Who cares what you two think?"

"Just a damn minute here," said Heather. "Who made you judge and jury?"

Parrish ignored them both. He bowed his head, but kept his gaze on them all. The bare interior of the lock was silent, except for the bubbling of the incoming water and Deela's muffled sobs.

Cross tensed, watching Parrish's hand. But it was too far away. If he made a move it would flash to the switch, and the whine of the motors would be the last sound they heard.

If only he could buy a second, half a second, before that hand reached for the switch. . . . .

"Amen." Parrish lifted his head. He reached for the control.

"Now," said Heather, in seaspeech.

A black shape cannoned up into Parrish from behind. It knocked him down in a shower of seawater before sailing on in a short parabola across the room. Engines crashed onto the floor and skidded, leaving a scarlet smear as the concrete peeled away her skin. Graham lunged as Parrish scrambled up. They grappled, then the biologist went spinning away. Parrish, free, reached for the switch again.

"Lewis, no!" screamed Sheila.

Cross limped forward and brought up his cane.

The lethal crack wasn't as loud in air as it was underwater, but was still deafening in the confined space. Parrish, astonished, groped for the head of the stinger where it met his side. He sank to his knees, then to the wet floor. "Captain," he said in a hoarse whisper.

"I didn't want to, Lewis." Cross's hands were shaking so violently he could barely turn the stinger back to Safe. He limped to the canal and knelt. "I wish you'd left me a choice, shipmate. I really do."

"It's done, anyway," said Parrish, with difficulty. His breathing was ragged, his cheeks pale. He clutched his stomach. "Just . . . take a little longer, that's all."

"What?" Graham bent over him. "What do you mean? Speak up."

"I . . . fixed things," he murmured hoarsely. His eyelids sank closed.

Dinker shook him, but he didn't respond.

"Dead," said Graham, checking his pulse, then straightening. "But what did he mean?"

The thought struck them both at once. *"The air plant,"* Cross said.

It was, as they expected when they got to that dome, a shambles. The gleaming machinery had been stripped apart, bearings and compressor blades mangled with a hammer, lines cut, computer controls and mixing valves spread smashed on the floor. A multivoiced hissing came from the banks of cylinders against the bulkheads. Cross went from one to the next, twisting valves closed again, but the dials were low.

"Can we rebuild it?' Johnson stared at the wreckage, hands twisting spasmodically.

"Not a chance, Heather. He knew what we couldn't replace."

"How much oxygen do we have left?"

Cross studied the gauges. "A couple of weeks," he said. "No more. And maybe not even that."

SIX

So how we feeling, Chief?"

"Oh, fair to middlin'." Svec's blue eyes were dulled, fingers plucking at the gray wool blanket that covered him, making the ruby ring flash and glow. "Except for my legs. Can't get 'em to move."

Cross, sitting by the bed, felt anger. Anger at a universe that, not content to kill fine people like Welch and Oursler, had to break Parrish's nerve. Svec's health. Rolling over the bodies of men and women as if they were clods of dirt or the small creatures that had once lain casually smashed along the highways. And rage at himself, for being unable to alter any of it.

"Heard about Lew?"

"Deela told me. He always was out of tune with the rest of us. You did right, Cap'n."

"And the air plant?"

"Says you can't fix it. Soon's I get up – "

"It's beyond all of us. It's down for good."

Svec relaxed. Closed his eyes. "Damn. She's all over, then. And I didn't even get to taste my first run of Old Seaweed."

"Yeah, it's over. For here."

Svec caught the qualifier and his eyes opened again. "The boat, you mean?"

"Maybe."

"Where to?"

"Not sure. Maybe follow that signal south, see what's putting it out."

"Why not? It's root, little pig, or lose your acorns now. Think there's anybody left down there?"

"If there were, they'd have answered our calls last year. So they're probably dead. If there was anyone there to begin with."

"Then why go?"

"Because then we're at least doing something. I was half agreeing with Parrish – we can't just sit and wait to die. Going somewhere, there might be some hope. Here, we haven't got a chance at all."

"All right. Count me in." Svec glanced down at his legs, and his mouth set. "If you can use me like this."

"Can't run the boat without you, Chief," said Cross briskly. "I'll put it up to the others, then."

He found Klassen and Graham in the lounge. A pint of medicinal brandy stood open, and glasses were set out, but any atmosphere of cheer was definitely absent. Sheila looked up as he entered. "C'mon in, Dinker. Drink?"

"Yeah, thanks."

The brandy was sweet, raw, violent; redolent of lost things – love in shabby cafes, dark alleys, Europe before the War, open sky and green mold on fat ripe grapes. The first sip made him choke. "That's good. Where are the Kids?"

Neither bothered to answer. He looked at grim faces and decided to come to the point. "I think it's time to leave," he said bluntly. "Pull out of here and go."

"Where to?" Sheila asked. He explained. "Down south?" she repeated, dubiously. "Ken, what do you think?"

Graham sipped the brandy and shuddered. He lifted his eyebrows listlessly. "It's no better anywhere else than it is here."

"But carsonella – "

"Is everywhere. Remember what we listened to while the Dying went on? Everyone went – the Ukrainian station in the Black Sea, everyone who had the slightest contact. Even the

Moon colony at Mare Tranquillitatis – they got it from a shipment of potato plants or something. Besides" – he looked at Sheila – "We couldn't take the dolphins."

"Oh." Her mouth twisted and she looked down. "No, I suppose we couldn't."

"Well, what do you plan to do?" said Cross. "Sit here and drink? Breathe bad air and wait to croak sometime next week? Hell, we should've let Parrish open the lock."

"Circumstances are a little different," said Graham. He finished the glass and reached for the bottle again.

"How about the Kids?"

The biologist shrugged. "Up to them."

"Sheila?"

"I don't know. About myself, that is. Roger and Heather will probably want to stay with their, um, friends. But the Kids – maybe they should go with you."

"So you *do* think there's a chance."

"I don't know," she said. "Like you say."

He got up. "Well, I'll ask them. But I hope you'll decide to come – both of you."

He mulled it over as he walked toward the Kids' rooms. The two interns were most likely null in the equation, but if Graham and Klassen didn't come there'd be little chance of survival, even if they found favorable conditions. He wasn't a scientist. The only way he could even detect carsonella was by dying of it.

Their rooms were empty. He walked on, around the ring. As he approached the delphinology lab he heard voices. His own name caught his ear and he stopped, listening.

"Hold still, Engines. You keep rubbing this stuff off and you're not going to heal. What were you saying about Dinker?"

"He just makes me so mad." Deela's voice. "He treats me like a child."

"Which you are."

"Shut up, I-i."

"Well, you keep on bothering him. If he won't do it with you, how about Ken? Roger? Joe?"

"Ken's nice. But he's not interested. And I don't like Roger or Joe the same way."

"Then there's me," said Ian. "I'm here, too."

"Uh huh," said Deela noncommittally.

Cross coughed and walked in. They looked up from the tank where Engines floated, belly up. They were covering her bruised underside with Vaseline. "Hi, Dinker," they chimed innocently.

"Hi. She okay?"

"Hope so." Ian regarded the dolphin with affection, pulled on a flipper, and rolled her over. She blew, lifted her head, and saw Cross.

"Hello there."

"Hi, Engines. Thanks, you saved our skins."

"And lost my own. A small price to help my friends." She waggled a flipper and submerged, moving out into the canal.

"Dinker," said Ian, shifting back to normal speech, "How much longer have we got?"

He squatted on his heels and considered his answer, then decided, *Hell, give it to them straight.* "If all of us – and Engines – stay here, maybe two weeks. Limiting factor's not so much generating oxygen as it is the inability to separate carbon dioxide. We used to have filters, absorbents, but without resupply – "

"Two weeks," Deela repeated. "That isn't long."

"You said, 'if we stay here'. Are you planning to go someplace else?" said Ian.

"I'd like to try."

"I'll go," said Deela.

Ian frowned at her. "Don't you want to know where?"

"No."

"Well, I do."

Cross explained; about the signal, *Pilgrim,* the bare possibility they might find a place to live. And then, Graham's doubts.

Ian nodded. "He might be right, Dinker. Then what?"

"We die, I guess. What else? Staying here, it's certain."

"Well – all right. Count me in, too. When do we leave?"

"We need to take a few things along. Clothes, food. . . . " Cross trailed off. "Actually, not much. If we find a place we can live, maybe a polar island that was unpopulated before the Dying, we'll have to figure it out as we go. If we can't . . . and there's one thing I didn't mention yet. When we leave, we'll be taking away the Annex's power supply. We've got some oxygen we can leave the other dolphins, but – "

"They'll all die," breathed Deela. Ian looked solemn.

He nodded. "But you see it can't be helped. Don't you?"

"I suppose," said Ian slowly. "But can't we make one exception? Engines?"

"There's no place in the sub to keep her alive. And if we did rig one up, somehow, she'd never be happy being the last of her kind."

"He's right," said Deela softly. She looked close to tears. Cross felt his own eyes smart; he'd grown attached to the animals himself. Brave, independent, they'd kept faith with their human friends through it all.

Now they had to be abandoned.

"Decide what you want to take. The sooner we go, the more oxygen we leave for them." He got up quickly and left.

He spent that afternoon with Svec, making up a list of what they could take in the DSRVN. Weight was of little concern, but space was at a premium. The final list was short. *Make or break*, Cross thought, running a pen down it. *We'll either find a completely equipped new home, or die. No middle ground.* By 2200 he'd collected almost everything and had it stacked on the deck beside Lock I. He debated briefly whether to take some to the sub that night, and decided not to. There'd be time in the morning.

And he didn't relish facing ourslerii in the dark.

He walked back to his room, deliberately putting weight on his left leg. It hurt, but held. Mentally he added a large bottle of painkillers to the list.

He reached his room and opened the door. The light was out, but as he started to say "Turn light on," he realized he wasn't alone. Then someone put her arms around him. He stood still.

"Dinker?"

He turned, and her arms tugged his head down to meet her lips. They were soft, firm, full, and pleasant to kiss. After several seconds she released him, and he stepped back. "Sheila."

She laughed. "Wonder what I'm doing here?"

"Not really."

"Are you mad?"

"No."

"Disappointed it's not someone else?"

"No!"

"That's nice of you to say, Dink. Maybe untrue, but, still, nice."

He felt her take his hand and lead him toward the bed. "Sit down. You and I should have a talk."

"Sure, but what's left to say?"

She chuckled sadly. "Don't steal my lines."

They sat on his bunk. It was so dark Cross could not see an outline, or even a blur where her face should be.

"Hold me," she said. "For Christ's sake, put your arms around me."

And later, "Dinker. The world's ending and you're all leaving. Jesus, don't make me beg."

He kissed her face when they were done and felt tears on her cheeks. "How I wish you loved me," she whispered.

"I do, Sheila. I do."

"It's too late for cosmetic lying. We had our chance, and you . . . well, it's not your fault. Just the way you are."

"Come with us," he said, feeling like crying himself.

"I can't. We've got to stay. Heather and Roger and I. You see . . . they're like children. The Ds. They trust us. Some of them Ken and I raised together."

"I know, but – "

"I wanted to love you . . .but when you couldn't return it. I turned to them instead. I guess as a psychologist I'd say there's too much interspecies bonding. But they shouldn't have to face the dark without some of us around."

He tried to speak but found no words. He kissed her again.

"So thank you for tonight. As a human, even as a mammal, I like to have someone say they love me, even if – I don't know – it's all so relative. Dinker, promise me one thing. You were triangled, weren't you? Before everybody died?"

"Yeah," said Cross.

"They only approved that for partners who could handle it. So you must have loved very much. You can again. You won't be really human again until you do."

"All right," he said, stroking her hair. "It's all right."

"Move over," she said briskly, but still with a hint of tears in her voice. "Let me up. Christ, these bachelors. Is there a towel in this dump?"

"Right here." He found one in the dark and gave it to her. A moment later the mattress sighed as she got up. "Remember," she said.

She opened the door, then paused to look back at him for a moment. He saw her as if for the first time, the rounded profile of her face, the swelling hips, silhouetted in the dim light from the corridor. "Love, Dinker. Try."

When she had gone, he wept.

"But what about your leg?" said Graham. "You're still walking wounded. Today's too soon."

"No reason to hang around." Cross pulled the wetsuit pants up over his shorts, taking care with the bandaged area, and reached for the jacket.

"Why don't I get the sub for you? Your leg must still be hurting like hell."

"Ever drive one?"

"No, but – "

"Hold the rudder left too long and she'll tear through the Station like a bull through tissue paper."

"Well, I'll come with you then," said Graham.

They slid out of the lock, sank to the bottom, and searched the gray sea. Cross let a few drops of water into his mask and bent his head to swirl them around, clearing the condensation, and looked again. Nothing in sight.

"Let's go," said Graham.

As they moved out from the shelter of the lock he felt like a piece of tripe being trolled across the bottom, bait for every shark in the Caribbean. Even the stinger in his hands failed to comfort him now he knew what oursleriii – in company – could do.

They came up on the cable and followed it, staying low.

"There," said Cross. The first gray shape glided in from their left. As one, they sank, motionless. It swam past. They looked at each other. The shark disappeared, still heading in its original direction. After hugging the sand for several more seconds they swam on, moving rhythmically, traveling slowly but with extreme vigilance.

They'd made it halfway to the sub, and Cross was beginning to breathe more easily, when he felt a sudden, sharp tug on his left leg, and screamed.

"Go!" said Graham, turning. He extended his stinger, and the shock wave rippled up Cross's body. His foot came free. *"Swim, Dinker!"*

He swam as hard as he could, forgetting the injured leg as he put everything into the sprint. Water tugged at his mask and rippled in his ears. He reached the bow, hit the hatch switch, and hauled himself up along the ladder that led out of the lock. As he got to the top Graham surfaced below him. He reached down a hand to help him up. "Well, we made it, partner."

"Barely," panted Graham. "It was one of those little bastards. Look at your fin."

Cross pulled his fin off and inspected it. The trailing edge hung in ribbons.

"What you want me to do, Dink?"

"Get your gear off and follow me." He flicked on the lights without looking as they entered the control room; his fingers knew every inch of this steel cylinder. He seated Graham at the diving board and explained the mechanics. "It'll be a delicate job, but I'll tell you what to do. Don't touch anything just yet. I'm going aft to cast off the power cable."

He undogged the hatch leading to the next compartment aft and entered, sliding sideways along on a narrow catwalk between the twin nuclear piles. He put his hand on one. It was warm to the touch. Inside, radioactive wastes were breaking down at a temperature of over eight hundred degrees centigrade. Thousands of quantum microthermocouples turned the heat to direct current.

The next compartment was locked. He centered his eye on the sensor next to the hatch. A light flashed; the door unlocked. He undogged it and stepped in.

This compartment had been spliced into the basic DSRVN hull in secret, at Newport News Shipbuilding and Drydock, after the United States had ratified the Coordinate Treaty and accepted supervision by the AIs that had fought, then finally agreed to terminate, the Last War. He walked slowly between the double rows of thick pillars, recalling Admiral Sands's words: "They've dissolved us, Commander. No more Navy. No more military forces. But you'll be our insurance, Cross. Our ace in the hole."

It had turned out, he thought, *to be one hell of a deep hole, all right.*

In the last compartment, the farthest aft, the pile DC was converted to 440-volt 60-Hertz current to run the main and auxiliary propelling motors and power the air scrubbers and oxygen generators that made the sub habitable. Not unlike the gear in nuclear subs built decades before, but smaller, simpler, and far more dependable.

He pulled down circuit breakers. Back at the Station, the lights would flicker for a moment, then come back on; a bank of batteries supplied emergency light and power, though they wouldn't last long. He unplugged the cable, dragged it to the aft airlock, and bundled it through. It vanished with a slithering splash.

He went forward again, sealing the weapons compartment behind him.

Graham was sitting at the dive panel, looking at the holocube on the captain's console. "Yours?"

"Yeah."

"What were their names?"

"All Pats. Patricia, Pat, and Patty; we had to make a distinction."

"I'll bet." Graham smiled sadly. "You were lucky, Dinker. You had people."

"Didn't you? Um, before Matt, I mean."

"No." Graham leaned back. "I didn't. I was a hot-shot biologist, remember? Delphinus delphi – the project carried a lot of weight in academic circles. It took so much work, somehow that angle got left out. I regret it. They'd have died, I know, but I'd have had *something* Even just a memory. What've I got now?" He spread his hands.

Cross shook his head. This was a different man from the absorbed scientist he'd known. "Same as the rest of us, I suppose. Nothing."

Graham nodded. "Yeah. Zero."

An awkward silence.

"Well, let's lift," said Cross at last, taking his seat. A flicker of motion through the window caught his eye; a shark. He bent to see what it was doing. With four others, it was pulling apart the carcass of the one Graham had killed.

"Blow to five thousand positive," he said.

"That's these top two switches?"

"And the gauge."

Cross rotated the maneuvering motors for downward thrust and started them at 50 rpm. The pile hissed and valves clanked shut as the steam it generated cleared the buoyancy tanks of water.

"Think that does it, Dinker."

He decreased rpm as *Pilgrim* began to rise from the sand. He used the bow thruster to bring the bow around and started the big four-bladed screw, two meters in diameter, ahead slow. *Just a bit too light,* he thought. "Flood to four thousand positive."

Valves thudded and they stopped rising. The Station came into view. He reversed the bow thruster to stop the swing, then shut it down.

Ahead slow with the main screw. Now he had enough speed through the water to use the rudder. He lined up carefully on the Lock I approach markers. Done just right, as the cargo subs had, the curved surface of his hull would mate with the concave outer surface of the Lock, and the crossing could be made dry. He came left a touch, brought the nose up slightly, stopped the main screw. *Pilgrim* coasted on, straight for the lock. As the nose passed it he ran the main engine for four revolutions astern. The sub stopped, hanging motionless over the lock.

"Flood to negative five tons."

It settled into place. "Good," he said, exhaling. "Just right. Would have been tough without you; thanks."

"Glad to help."

They dropped down the lock into ten feet of water. The outer door opened and they swam through. He closed the outer door and locked it carefully; there was, he remembered, now no safety interlock. Pumps started, the water level dropped, the inner doors hummed open, and they walked out to find the others waiting.

The transfer went quickly with five pairs of willing hands. Too quickly, thought Cross, looking around the inside of the lock as he shouldered a case of canned food. There should be time for some kind of leavetaking. When everything had been loaded they stood awkwardly in a little circle on the damp concrete.

"I'll get the Chief," said Deela. "Oh, and . . . Sheila. Aren't you coming? We've been through too much to split up now."

The psychologist shook her head. "Dinker and I discussed it. I'd like to. But my place is here, with Heather and Roger and Engines and . . . all the rest." She hugged both Kids, holding them tight.

"Won't budge, eh, Cap'n?" said Svec from a wheelchair.

"No, Joe. We'll have to do without a headshrinker."

"Help me up," said Svec. Cross and Ian lifted him, got his arms over their shoulders, and stood ready to step through the lock.

"Goodbye." Sheila raised one hand. "See you – well, no more reincarnations – see you in the next cycle."

Deela ran to her and buried her face, sobbing. Klassen patted her shoulders. "You go on. With the others. Maybe . . . maybe a lot will depend on you."

The lock door whirred up. It seemed slow, tired. Cross wondered if the batteries were already weakening. "Sheila. With just three people, you'll have air for a month or more."

"And if I share it with the dolphins?"

His throat ached. "Oh – not as long."

"I'll be sharing."

"I know you will. That's the way you are, Sheila."

"You don't want to leave me," she said, looking at them. "So I'll make it easy. "Goodbye." She turned away, and left.

Back in the sub, Cross could barely see the CO's console in front of him as he rotated the maneuvering motors. "Chief?" he said hoarsely, clearing his throat.

"Diving board, standing by," said Svec, voice hushed.

"Ian? Deela? Ready to go?"

"We're ready, Dinker," said Ian.

He twisted a control and the motors began to hum. "Ten thousand positive."

"Ten thousand positive, aye. Blowing cells 3-4 through 8-9."

"Clear of lock?"

"All clear to port."

"Pressure in the boat?"

"One-oh-five and . . . holding. Ten thousand up."

"Secure blowing. Give me fifteen psi in the boat."

"Fifteen in the boat, aye." A pump throbbed aft and Cross felt his ears protest. He bent over the console, letting the sharp edge of it bite into his stomach. He put his hands over his face.

"What's our course out, Cap'n?" said Svec.

Thanks, Chief, he thought. *For giving me something to do, locking me back into the routine. Because I can't face what I've just done.*

"Let's head out at zero-nine-zero," he said. "That'll be a good run for a day at least. We'll get a new bearing on the signal, then I'll lay out a track."

He aligned and cut the maneuvering motors, then housed the bow thruster. He switched in the main engine and ran it up to 100 rpm. *Pilgrim* began crooning to herself, a gentle little song of power.

"Cap'n, seeing an eight degree up bubble. Want me to trim?"

"No," said Cross. His throat ached. "I've got her cranked up with the planes. I want to go up. Let's see, Chief, just what the world looks like these days."

SEVEN

Pilgrim's conning tower was little more than a vestige. The DSRVN class hadn't been designed to run surfaced, so Cross and Ian found themselves almost in each other's arms as they peered out at the surface of the sea from two tiny ports.

"Still looks the same," said Cross. "But isn't it bright out there!"

It hurt his eyes, but then, he hadn't seen full sun for almost three years. Beyond the thick glass it sparkled on the green sea, glittered on the waves through which the blunt nose of the sub plowed, dazzling him as he raised his eyes to a painfully blue sky.

Ian said nothing. He glanced at the boy's face. It was only inches from his own but in the dimness of the tower red and green afterimages hung before his eyes and he had to blink. "How's it look?"

"All right," said Ian. His spare young face was set, somewhat hard. *He's a good looking boy*, Cross thought, studying the strong jaw, the high, almost Asian cheekbones, the smooth slanting planes of a face as yet unsullied by age or fat.

"It'll kill us, huh?"

"Pretty sure. We don't know yet how far to sea Carsonella gets blown. Ken's pulling a sample through one of the topside valves. When he analyzes it we'll know more."

"Uh huh."

How much does he realize? Cross wondered, looking out again at the sea, so unchanged, so familiar. Ian and Deela had been twelve when the Dying started. They'd never seen a victim of it. *Hell, neither have I. But I can imagine it. They've seen the videos of Before and read the books. But how much do they realize?*

"No seagulls," he said.

"Seagulls?"

"Big white and gray birds. You used to see them almost everywhere at sea. They followed the ships. So pretty to watch; they soared."

"That so?"

He didn't sound interested, and Cross frowned. He'd never quite understood the boy. Deela, maybe. But Ian . . . there was something cool, impenetrable in him, like the icy depth of the sea.

He slid down the ladder to the control room. Ian stayed above, staring out the porthole.

"Sun still there, Cap'n?"

"Sure is. Want a boost?"

"Too much trouble. Thanks anyway."

"Ken got his sample? No leakage to the boat?"

"No, it's safe. He took his kit up forward, workin' up in the berthing space."

"Deela?"

"Can't be far. In the head, maybe."

Cross glanced at the console. *Pilgrim* was humming along at a steady pace, rolling slightly. The autopilot kept the lubber's line of the inertial compass rock-steady on 090, due east.

"Good to be out again, even if it's our last voyage."

"Yeah, probably will be, Chief." He glanced at Svec. The Kentuckian had lost weight; his shining bald dome looked like the head of a mummy, and his long limbs, draped carefully out on a portable stool near his beloved board, were thin as sticks. But he seemed in better spirits than he'd been since his reaction to the enzyme. Cross had to admit having him along, even stove up, made him more confident.

If only Sheila had come too. . . .

He wrenched his mind away from that and crossed the compartment. He searched through an assortment of navigation 'grams in an overhead rack. Finding the one he wanted, NOAA 1011, Central and South Atlantic, he snapped it into the chart table projector. Svec leaned to see.

On the flat surface of the chart table a miniature 3-D world sprang silently into existence. Mountain chains, craggy and towering, marched down the center of the vast basin. On either side the continents shouldered into the sea, which appeared in the hologram as a layered blue pool, out of which rose islands. Cross toggled the Own Ship marker. A golden spark blinked on some kilometers northeast of Puerto Rico.

He pointed at holokeys. A dark line appeared, then was studded with semicircular symbols, each representing one day's run. He continued the line due east for almost a thousand kilometers, then angled south, paralleling the South American coast out into the central Atlantic.

"What's the plan, Cap'n?"

"Our original bearing on the signal was one-four-six from Navidad Bank. That cuts a straight line across the hump of South America." Cross traced the line of bearing on the chart. "*Pilgrim's* a good ship, but she doesn't climb mountains. I'm assuming the signal comes from beyond there, since it's so faint, but we'll keep checking as we go. When we get a little farther we can take another bearing and get a fix. Anyway, we'll continue on south around Natal, keeping clear to seaward. Then see where the signal takes us."

"How long?"

"Twenty knots, four hundred eighty nautical miles a day . . . say five days till we can get a clear bearing. After that, depends."

"We're in no hurry, right?"

"Maybe we'll speed up later. Right now, I'll let the old girl shake herself down."

"Good weather, you said?"

"Beautiful. Very pretty topside."

"Maybe I'll step up for a smoke later."

They laughed quietly together.

"Dinker," said Svec. "You know, I won't last out this voyage."

"Sure you will. You're tough as an old boot."

"If I don't," he continued, looking up to where a stray beam, darting down from one of the tower portholes, was gilding gauges and piping, "Don't dump me deep. Drop me off topside. Let me just drift away up there in the sunlight."

"Jesus, Joe. You've got a lot of life left in you. Hell, how long you been in?"

"Twenty-eight years, three months, as of yesterday," said Svec instantly.

"All that Navy horseshit, and you don't want to enjoy your retirement?"

Svec had to grin. "Okay, since you put it that way. The Navy sure owes it to me."

"I'll see it gets paid. Meanwhile, I'd like to keep Ken and the Kids busy. Avoid moping. I want you to make up a watch bill, start getting them Qualified."

"Teach Deela and Ian the boat? They're only sixteen!"

"I just lowered the enlistment age."

"Aye, aye, Bligh," said Svec.

Deela came in. Her sheet, dirty now, was dragging and he guessed she'd be tripping over it in the confines of the sub, catching it on handles and square edges. He tossed her a set of crew's coveralls. "For you."

"All right." She undid the sheet and it dropped away. She didn't look at him, but he figured the display wasn't as innocent as it seemed. He swiveled his chair to face forward. Reached for the radio, extended the antenna, and tuned in. The monotonous four-second beat droned in their ears, clearer, it seemed, now they were surfaced.

"That's it, eh? Where's it from?" Graham came aft, the analysis kit tucked under one arm.

"South. That's about all I can say right now. How's the air?"

"Take a few hours to tell. For the culture to grow. I did a quick gas analysis, too, though I'm not sure I did it right. Carbon dioxide's down. No surprise there. But I got chlorine too."

"Chlorine? Like, from bleach?"

"In the air," he said, sitting down in the only place left, the deck. The control room was crowded with four of them there. "Free chlorine. Not much, a fraction of a percent, but. . . . "

"Odd," said Cross. "Well. Deela, if you can get Ian to come down here, we have a watch bill to make out."

July 2 Underway as before, surfaced, ballasted up to 20,000 K positive. Speed 20 kts on main motor, course 090. Came right to 128 T tonight at 2200 GMT.

July 4 As before. Course 120/20.

July 6 As before. 120/20. Pile output down; cause unknown. Sure could have used Parrish. Graham and I put in 6 hrs tracing circuits with no success. Still enough power but hope decrease doesn't continue.

July 7 As before. 120/20 till noon; came right to new course 169, straight line to signal, which is increasing in strength. Definitely not from South America. Weather worsening; seas from the east. Submerged at 1500 to oblige Kids' stomachs and ran submerged throughout the day.

Amazing, thought Cross, lying in his curtained, darkened bunk, how quickly the human animal readapts to once-familiar conditions. Even after a couple of years of Station life – regular meals, plenty of sleep, a room to himself, a flexible and not too demanding schedule – the change to cruising conditions had felt effortless. He and Svec were standing six on, six off, sleeping in two- or three-hour snatches, sharing a tin of food with Deela or Ian or Graham at odd times of the day or night. Underway, immured between steel walls with only screens and portholes, day and night merged into each other imperceptibly. Only the log and the creep of the glowing dot across the chart affirmed time was passing at all, that they were making progress toward their goal.

And what lies at the rainbow's end? He stared at the underside of the bunk above him — Ian's, though the boy was on watch with the Chief now — and tried again to hammer the pieces of the puzzle into some recognizable picture.

First piece: *Oxyphilus,* the Red Death.

Second: *Carcharhinus ourslerii.*

Both, according to Graham, evolutionarily impossible.

Third, the signal. The time factor — one and two had occurred more or less together. But the signal hadn't been picked up until nearly a year after the last shoreside broadcaster had fallen silent. Automatic aircraft beacon? Some sort of weather transmitter?

Then why didn't it transmit data?

Could there be someone left alive, who'd found the transmitter, provided power, and turned it on?

Then why didn't they broadcast a message, to make it clear someone was there?

A possible fourth piece occurred. Chlorine. Another test had confirmed it. Not a lot, but where had it come from? He cudgeled his brain to recall his college chemistry, but all he could remember about chlorine was that it was a component of ordinary salt.

His mind spun on in the darkness. A pump hummed aft; Svec was trimming the boat. *As soon as we're well out into the Atlantic,* he thought, *I'll run down that bearing on the chart and see what we have.*

But what if they found nothing? Suppose it was an abandoned transmitter yammering on mindlessly, powered by wind or a solar panel or geothermal? Perhaps a roof had fallen in, closing a switch accidentally. He vaguely recalled an old movie with a plot twist like that.

He clenched his fists, held the tension, let it ebb out. *Got to get some sleep. I'm on again in two hours.*

With Deela. At the Station he'd seen her daily, true, but there was choice to it. Not so here. She was in his face wherever he turned.

You're old enough to be her father, he told himself sternly. *She's a kid. You had your shot with Kasson. And blew that. Forget about it. Don't let her distract you.*

Eventually he managed a light, troubled sleep, haunted with dreams about reaching out, jumping, jumping across a dark chasm . . . reaching. . . .

"Jesus," said Cross. "No, Ken, this isn't normal. I've never seen anything like it before. It isn't sargasso weed."

Three more days had passed as the sub's blunt bow slipped through the chilly waters of the South Atlantic. But the sea outside the tiny portholes of the sail bore no resemblance to the murky gray-green ocean, broad and cold under the winter sky, they should be seeing.

Instead it was a sickly, scummy hue, as if fluorescent paint had been dumped in the water and allowed to stain and spread. Cross stood on tiptoe to look down at the hull just in front of the sail. The dark metal was matted with dense clots of something green.

"Some kind of algae?"

"I need a closer look," said Graham. "It doesn't look like any marine flora I'm familiar with."

Cross peered upward. Even the low-hanging clouds seemed to have a greenish tinge. "Must be reflecting the color of the sea. But that means this stuff must cover a lot of ocean."

Ian poked his head up by their feet. "Want me to get some?"

"How?"

"Just stop. I'll duck out the lock and grab some from underneath. Please, Dinker. I need the exercise. We've been cooped up in here for years."

"A week," Cross corrected. He debated refusing, but the stuff piqued his curiosity. And the prospect of a swim appealed too. "All right. But I'm going out with you. Stretch my legs. Ken?"

"You go ahead."

"Sure? Ian, see if Deela's game."

A shriek of joy came from below. Ian smiled slightly. "Oh, yeah. She'll go."

"All stop, Chief," Cross called down the ladder. "We're heaving to for swim call."

"All stop, aye."

He realized anew how silent the sea was as *Pilgrim* coasted on, gradually slowing, beginning to pitch as it picked up the long swells from the southeast. No birds. No dolphins, surfing the pressure wave at the bow.

He followed the Kids to the lock, suited up, and cycled out into the sea.

The cold seized him by the chest, making him gasp. It was far colder than he'd expected. *Of course. South of the equator July's the middle of winter.*

He swam around the looming undersea bulk of the DSRVN to warm up. The sea water trapped inside his suit gradually warmed and his shivering eased off. He looked around for the Kids.

They were a few meters away, hanging motionless under what looked at first like a layer of drifting green mist. He inhaled and rose slowly, careful not to break the surface, and reached out to touch it.

It was filmy and insubstantial, like mermaid's hair. The green fibers, so thin as to be invisible only a few feet away, were encrusted with what looked like tiny silver eggs. He gathered a handful gently – it swirled away from his hand if he moved too fast – and held it directly in front of his mask.

They weren't eggs. They were bubbles. When he squeezed the handful into a wad a flock of them burst from his glove and wafted upward, upper hemispheres flattened into rocking silver mushrooms. He looked after them and frowned. The "moss," as he began to think of it, must be several feet thick; only a dim emerald glow made it through from the surface.

Deela swam back toward him, a specimen jar in her hand. She held it up, then turned it over. Against the bottom of the jar a few clear cubic centimeters of gas showed.

She handed it to him. "Can we swim around a little more?" she asked in seatalk.

"Yes. But stay out of this stuff," he said. "I'm going back in."

Back in the sub, he set the jar on the deck and eyed it as he stripped off his wet suit and hung it to dry. Another impossible mutation? He carried it in to Graham, who studied it carefully. "I'll try the library," he said after a pause. "But I'm pretty sure . . . Joe, hand me that viewer?"

After ten minutes of searching his references he nodded. "Completely new taxonomy," he announced. He set the jar on the chart table, in the center of the South Atlantic Basin. He shook his head and grimaced. "Shit."

"Week at sea and already he's talkin' like a sailor," said Svec.

The clunk of the lock cycling came from forward. A minute or so later Deela came in, dripping and shivering. Goosebumps covered her arms and chest. "It's freezing out there! Ken, Dinker, did you find out what it is?"

"No," said Cross. "Hey, look out!"

He made a grab for the jar as she brushed it, but missed. It struck the metal deck and shattered. They froze, looking down at it.

"Don't move," said Graham, pulling a fire extinguisher from the bulkhead. It hissed hollowly as he played the stream of subzero gas over the soggy mass, stopping only when it was frozen solid.

"Scrubbers on full, Chief," said Cross. "Ken . . . do you think carsonella. . . .?"

"Probably not, if you took the sample from more than a meter below the surface. But the cold'll make sure."

"What's that smell?" said Ian, coming in. He too was dripping and shivering.

"Smells like bleach," said Svec.

Graham sniffed around the room, came back to the chart table. Bent cautiously. "Yeah. Those bubbles must be chlorine."

"From the plants?" said Cross. "From the salt in the water, I'll bet. Another anomaly?"

"It ties in. To the gas I detected in the atmosphere, if these plants cover enough area. Let's see, how would that be done? A modified photosynthetic reaction. . . ." He blinked at the overhead.

"Lock secured, Ian?"

"Aye aye, Dinker."

"Green light, Cap'n," Svec confirmed.

"Let's start her up again then, Chief. And take her down, steady at about thirty meters. Keep that green crap out of our intakes."

He slumped over the chart table, and joined Graham in silent thought. Too many weird changes were building up. They needed a synthesis, a common explanation. He bit his lip savagely, feeling stymied, frustrated, impotent. "Getting anything?" he asked the biologist.

"There's always been a high halogen content in marine plants. Let's say you're right – this stuff's breaking down the salt. NaCl dissociates in water. Green; autotrophic. Structure like ulothrix or oedogonium, but. . . ."

"Never mind," said Cross. "You're giving me a headache."

"Dinker?"

"Yes, Deela?"

"If it's safe, I'll sweep up the glass. I knocked it over, after all."

"Yeah, go ahead," he said, staring blindly down at the chart.

July 9

As before. Submerged, running at thirty meters. Weather degenerating. May have a lead on our beacon at last. It's getting stronger as we run down this bearing. Got out the Antarctic Regions charts and laid out 170 from our present position. Not much in the way of land; that track leads dead down the center of the South Atlantic. About a thousand miles on we pass the Tristan de Cunha group, but I don't think it's them; too far off our bearing. Then on, leaving South Georgia to the west around latitude sixty. Nothing from there on until the coast of Antarctica.

Then I saw it. Actually thought the thing was a spot on the 3D projection but when I increased magnification there it was: an island, within a degree of our bearing. Ostrova Dvina, Dvina Island, midway between the South Sandwich group and Bouvetoya. There was a code by it. I hit the button to read it out.

Restricted area, *it said.*

Cross nodded to himself, half with satisfaction and half with bone weariness. He was in his bunk again, with the *Sailing Directions* open on his tablet. There was something at the end of the rainbow after all. Probably not a pot of gold. But not a wild goose either. He reread the entry:

6-19. Ostrova (Island) Dvina consists of a single isolated island, partly covered by ice cap. Highest elevation is Mount Bellingshausen, 550 meters. Island is shaped like a half moon, with a large bay (Vostok Bay) in the Northwest. Small rocky islets mark the western corner of the bay. The westernmost one is marked with a steel tripod structure with radar reflector. The bottom shelves steeply around the island except in front of the bay. Once past entrance reef (see chart) bay shoals gently. Anchorage is poor with shifting bottom, but presents some protection in gales. Dvina generally completely surrounded by pack ice during winter months.

NOTE. Ostrova Island declared Restricted Area 2039. Former British biological research facility now leased by Coordinate Scientific Authority. Vessels in extremis are directed to lie offshore until contact is made on maritime distress frequencies. Do not land without clearance.

A biological research facility. Well, the spot was well chosen; it would be hard to find a more isolated location. On Earth, at any rate.

He enlarged the chart and studied it for a few minutes, noting the shape of the bay, the entrance reefs, navigational aids.

All right, he thought. *Even if it's iced solid we can probably get in pretty close.* He began to plot a track in through the reefs. The exercise took him back in time, to the War, when he'd navigated a little Scalare-class boat up the rivers of mainland China, with Admiralty charts dated 1887. He added estimated ice cover and subtracted the depth of the channel. If the hydrography was accurate, he could get to within about seven hundred meters of the beach.

Then what? he asked himself.

I'll take a little swim. Break or burn through the pack from below. Then hike on inland, to the building on the chart.

And what will I find there?

Probably nothing. Still, didn't it fit, all too neatly? Not just research, but *biological* research. Genetic recombination, gain of function experimentation, or why site it so far from any populated area? And only the Coordinate, by one of the conventions of the Treaty, had the authority to grant exceptions to the rules governing research on dangerous diseases.

And he remembered something else. The first outbreaks of the virus had been in Argentina. The nearest land, though across many kilometers of wintry sea.

Could it have been developed there, spread accidentally, the way some thought COVID-19 and the War Flu had escaped the lab years before? Rather than a deliberately deployed weapon, as he'd thought before?

His bunk phone chimed. *"Cap'n. Your watch in fifteen."*

"Already?" He glanced at his watch. "Be right down, Chief."

He swung his legs out, reached for an overhead pipe, and lowered himself to the deck. There were few privileges of rank on a DSRVN; the CO slept in a bunk appointed just as spartanly as the others.

Deela pulled the curtain of her bunk open. In the dim red radiance he couldn't make out her expression. "Dinker? What's the matter? You've had your light on all night."

"Couldn't sleep. Besides, we may be making a landfall in a couple of days. I was studying the approach."

"Land? Where?"

"Little island called 'Dvina.'" Quickly he explained the situation, and what he suspected.

"You mean the germs came from there?"

"Whoa. That's all just-suppose right now. But the signal's from there, and I want to get a look."

"Oh." She drew the curtain a little wider. "Dinker – "

"Sorry, due for watch." He turned away and hurried off.

"It's gettin' mighty loud." Svec's long body was folded into the seat, earphones clamped over his skull. "Got to be this little Ostrova Dvina. Diddly past that till you hit Antarctica."

"I came to the same conclusion. Hi, Ken." He nodded to the biologist and swung himself down into the conning chair. "What's the scoop?"

Svec took the earphones off. "Steady on 170 true, speed twenty. Some dirty weather topside; we were getting some of the roll, so I took her down another ten meters."

"Nice and smooth here. How's machinery holding up?"

"Bearing temps normal, air supply okay, but pile output's lower and I'm seeing a drop in temperature. I'm worryin' over her, Cap'n."

"Open it up, take a look?"

"Can't do it down here."

Cross looked at Graham. "Hey. Ever hear of a 'biological research facility' on a place called Dvina Island?"

Graham rubbed his face. "Uh . . . not that I remember."

"Set up by the Coordinate Scientific Authority?"

"What?" He got up. Cross showed him the entry in the Sailing Directions.

"Hey, now."

"Yeah." Cross glanced at Svec. "Chief, this might explain a lot. We're going ashore." He looked at the chart. "In about . . . oh, two days, if we can pull power for thirty knots."

"It'll be tight," said Svec. "But I'll start bringing the pile up."

"Never mind, I've got the conn. You go on, turn in. Need a hand?"

"I'll make it." Drops of sweat sparkled on Svec's forehead, but he hoisted himself and made his way aft, supporting himself on chair backs and overhead pipes to ease the strain on almost useless legs. Cross watched him go, then turned in his seat to nudge the throttle forward.

Night. The porthole before him, looking out into the sea, was a circle of black. Around and under them the fabric of the ship hummed as power built up, the big screw spinning faster, sucking energy out of the dying atoms in the pile and spewing it into the water that roiled in their wake. He stared at the hologram of the Pats for a while, then turned on the sonar and scanned the depths around and below. Scattered echoes between them and the bottom two thousand fathoms down. Whitetips? He wondered whether there would be, in a few years, any other predators left in the sea.

The sea, he thought, looking out at it again. He saw it differently than when he'd been a land dweller. Life on land, air-breathing life, was gone. It had always been risky, vulnerable to glaciation and solar flares and what-have-you; a gamble on the part of Evolution. But a bet with only a fraction of the planet's resources. The sea, the ancient reservoir of life, continued, and always would, whether the lands above were peopled or sterile.

It's odd, he thought, *but that makes me feel just a little better about the Pats and Sheila and the rest of us.* Humans would die out; mammals too; but one day the sea would creep again over the edge of the land and venture, on short stumpy amphibian legs, again into the gigantic new universe that was the air. Seen that way, even the deaths of species didn't matter much in the long run. The sea was eternal, so life was as well; and there was time for everything.

He swiveled his chair to take a bearing, and raised his eyebrows. Graham was still sitting there, viewer on his lap, concentration knitting his brows.

"Ken. You all right?"

Graham shook himself, stretched. "Just thinking. There *could* be a connection with Carsonella. Though it'd mean the bioengineers were way ahead of where I thought they were. But that still leaves a lot of unknowns."

"Couldn't they have been experimenting with sharks and algae too?"

"Doubtful. I can't explain why in less than a monograph, but take my word for it . . . We planning on landing there?"

"Not an easy landfall. Ice. Old charts. No more GPS. But yeah, I'd like to take a look, provided you think there's no danger of infection."

"I can't say *no* danger. But if the air temperature's below the critical point, it should be safe."

"I got a surface temp off our antenna probe. Should be well below minus thirty C."

"Good. When we go ashore – "

"*Me*. Not *we*. I'm asking a favor, Ken. Stay aboard until I establish it's safe."

Graham was silent. Then looked up angrily. "That's a hard ask."

"I know. But Chief can run the boat, and you're vital if we run into trouble with the bug. We sure can't send the Kids up. So it's me."

"Well. Two days from now, you said?"

"Right."

"I'll think about it."

July 10

As before. Icebergs on sonar 0900. Running deeper, 100 meters. Speed 28.3 knots, all that the pile, in its weakening state, will give us. Worried.

Will be off Dvina tomorrow night.

The Chief buzzed him at 1700 the next day, as arranged. Cross ran his hand over five days of beard, decided to let it go, and began moving about quietly, assembling what he'd need.

First off, it'd be cold. But the wet suit, with booties and gloves, should keep him fairly warm on land. He'd have to stay out of any shelter; any refuge warm enough might also harbor virus, live and virulent.

Okay, he thought, pausing in the cramped airlock trunk. *Warmth. Air should be safe. I'll need some water, something to eat, keep up my body heat.*

Would I need a weapon?

Ken was right. An accident might explain carsonella, but it couldn't explain the new sharks, or the chlorine-producing mold.

Was it still possible it had all been done deliberately, part of some gigantic plot he and Graham could not even guess at? And the beacon could be a trap, meant to lure any scattered remnants of the population to where they could be dispatched, or enslaved.

It sounded paranoid, but he was no longer certain where the line lay between madness and reality.

No doubt about it, he'd feel more confident with a weapon. Of course he'd take the pistol, but it seemed inadequate. He thought of the stingers and boomers, then grinned.

Actually, they had something a lot more potent aboard.

He paused in the control room to look over Svec's shoulder at the overhead sonar display. Some ice ahead, but safe. He pulled up the readouts for electricity output. Down again. Temperature falling too. The pile was overdue for maintenance and element replacement. They were losing power, like a dying car battery. He shook his head and opened the locker above the CO's console, taking out the flat foil-wrapped envelope, the commander's manual, and the gun.

He walked aft, through the pile compartment – was it his imagination, or was it cooler? – to the locked hatch. He bent to eye it and it slid open.

He stood for a moment regarding the missiles. Sheathed in their steel tubes, they were only a few meters long, but even from a thousand feet down, from a sub lost in the slowly flowing abyssal currents, they could leap to the surface in seconds, and be on their way.

The ace in the hole, he thought. Probably the Russians had one too, the Chinese as well. The League of Nations had failed, then the UN. Who could be certain the Coordinate, or the AIs that directed it, wouldn't go the same way?

So there'd had to be insurance.

He pulled out a tool drawer and went to work. Even with the combination template, the manual, and the access codes, it took him two hours to extract one of the warheads, disassemble it, and detach one of the cores.

He hefted it cautiously in his hands. It was about the size and shape of a large cake, and only weighed fifteen kilos; but of those fifteen, six were a polarized-chain thorium isotope. The assembly was rated at thirty kilotons explosive yield. His briefings, years before, had mentioned a land demolition mode. With one eye on the manual, he opened the arming module and very carefully disabled the altitude function. That done, he selected Time Fuzing. Reassembled it, dropped the makeshift bomb into a canvas tool bag, and headed forward again.

"Chief says you're going out," said Ian. Deela, beside him, looked at Cross steadily, but said nothing.

"A quick recon. Back soon as I'm sure it's safe."

"Why shouldn't it be? Too cold for the virus, isn't it?"

"That's not all I'm worried about, Ian."

"What do you mean?"

"I'm wondering about a lot of things. Such as this signal. Might be a beacon. Could also be bait for a trap."

The boy fell silent. Graham came in from the bunkroom. Cross turned to Svec. "Joe, can you bring us up around 1900 and get a radar fix on the island?"

"Aye. Laid out a track in?"

Cross switched the chart projector on. "Just how far in we go depends on the thickness of the ice and the inshore gradient. I want enough sea room to turn around and get out."

"Sounds like a plan." Svec studied the chart. "Making the approach at night?"

"Yeah. In the dark."

"You carrying?" He made a slight motion with his head toward the locker.

Cross nodded. Hefted the tool bag, and slid his gaze aft. "Along with some other material."

"What?" said Ian.

"Tell you later," said Cross.

"You may have company," said Graham.

"Company?"

"Sharks," said Deela. "Lots. We can see them through the window. They get out of the sub's way, though."

"Ourslerii?"

Graham nodded. "You got it."

Cross leaned forward to peer out. The light around them was a sickly pale green.

"That shit must grow right between the icebergs," said Svec.

"Yeah," Dinker said softly.

"Want to eat?" said Deela. "We've got something called 'asparagus', in a can."

"Not for me. Not hungry," he lied.

He headed to his bunk again, feeling sick. There wasn't much left. Two or three days' reduced rations. If this place was deserted, if he could find nothing safe to eat, they'd have to re-enter this weird sea and try to slaughter one of the whitetips. There seemed to be no other life left this far south, save for the drifting green.

He lay down, yanked the curtain closed, and was instantly asleep.

* * *

"Hey, Dinker."

It was Ian. Cross pulled himself groggily up from black depths and groped for his bunk light. He started to get up but caught himself just in time to avoid being flung out. Things clattered and slid around him as *Pilgrim* hung on the edge of a roll, then began to recover. "Yeah."

"Chief says to get you up. We're five klicks out."

"Okay." He rubbed his face and dropped to the deck, grabbing for a handhold as the boat started another slant.

Control was a shambles. Cross and Svec had lost the habit of securing for sea, and Graham, Deela, and Ian had never learned it. Each roll brought a clattering cascade of objects from shelves, lockers, and other points of convenient but insecure stowage. Cross ducked as the portable viewer slid off an overhead locker, straight for his head. He ducked and it crashed with a sickening crunch, disintegrating into shards of glass and plastic.

"Rolls for breakfast!" sang out Svec. "Shallow water, Cap'n. Can't go deep till we're in beyond this bar."

"Speed up, then."

Svec shook his head. "Go too fast around these rocks, and we'll be sorry."

"Okay, okay. Where is everybody?"

"In the head being sick together, I reckon."

"Better there than in here." The tubby submarine was rolling like an empty bottle. As the bow fell Cross felt a queasiness in the pit of his own stomach. He grew light for a moment, then terribly heavy as it crashed down again. "Can't we ballast, Chief?"

"I did. It'd be worse if that green stuff wasn't damping the waves. I've seen twenty, thirty-foot seas in these latitudes."

"Thanks for small favors." He gripped the edge of a cabinet and staggered to his chair, pleasantly surprised to find it had a safety belt. He'd never had to use it before. "How much farther to the jetty?"

"About four klicks. Wind and seas from the west; ought to be coming into the lee of those little islets shortly."

As if by magic, the violent pitching stopped, and the crazy rolling slowed to a gentle rocking. "There's the lee," said Svec. "And we're over the bar. Nineteen meters under the keel. Want to take over?"

"No, you conn her in," said Cross. "I'll man the board."

Svec glanced up at the fathometer. "Eighteen meters."

"Give me depth five. Go down slow."

"Depth five meters, aye." Cross knew the board as well as Svec; as usual in submarines, every crew member could handle any job on the boat. The rocking gentled further and became barely perceptible. "Steady at five meters. Any ice on the 'scope?"

"A ways in yet."

"Don't approach too fast."

"I know, Cap'n," said Svec patiently. "I'm down to three knots."

They ran silently for several minutes. Svec had turned on the underwater lights and was peering ahead through the murk. Cross, over his shoulder, watched the fathometer readout and glanced from time to time at the sonar, which now had been angled to show a 360-degree picture.

"Ice," he said. A solid ping had suddenly appeared in the upper part of the screen. "Couple, three meters thick."

"Take her down to fifteen."

Cross dropped the sub gradually and watched Svec, ready to adjust their trim. The hum of the main screw slowed to a deliberate *whoosh-whoosh-whoosh*.

"Is the storm over? Oh." Deela, face white, dragged herself in and collapsed into a chair. "I was so sick. Ian and Ken are even worse than me."

Neither man responded. She shrugged. "Okay. Ignore me. See if I care."

"Sorry, this is a tricky approach," Cross said.

A rattling, grinding bang from above startled them all. "Hell, the aerial," said Svec. "Forgot to rig it in."

"Don't worry about it, Joe."

"Fix?"

"Sonar fix: pings from two crags shows us on track. Inertial agrees."

"How far to stop point?"

"Thousand yards."

"Three knots – thousand yards – three hundred yards in three minutes – about ten minutes," Svec calculated.

"See bottom yet? Fathometer says two meters under the keel."

"Could be. Pretty murky."

Cross studied the sonar. The upper part of the screen was solid light; the surface was covered with ice. They were under the frozen bay, creeping inward under the pack.

"There, I got bottom now," said Svec.

"Getting narrow. About five meters to top of the sail." *And,* Cross added to himself, *it shoals fast from here on in.*

A scrape shuddered underneath. "Give her some up angle, Chief."

"Hell, no, Cap'n, you'll jam her tail into the rocks. Take on another two hundred. Water's colder under the ice, we're gettin' more buoyant."

"Never argue with the Chief," said Cross to Deela, opening valves on the board.

"Figure a hundred more yards," Svec muttered. "Agree?"

"Inertial agrees. . . too narrow for sonar. Multiple echoes. Better come left a tad, get started on the turnaround."

"Left fifteen. Shutting down motors."

The murmur aft stopped. Only the whir of the air conditioning, and the ping of the fathometer, until the scraping began again from above, dragged down the scale. Then it too stopped.

"Dead in the water, Cap'n."

"Thanks, Chief. Good conning."

"My watch," said Svec. "Deela, why don't you help him dress out?"

The unspoken message, Cross thought, being, *you might not see him again.* He looked at Svec's rigid back and knew the old sailor wanted no goodbyes. *Thanks*, he thought. *For everything.* "Yeah, I could use some help," he said.

"Thank God . . . are we here?" said Graham. He and Ian, behind him, were pasty-faced and their eyes looked out of focus.

Cross clapped them on the shoulders as he went by. "Yeah, wherever 'here' is. Any advice, Ken, before I go out?"

Graham wiped his face with the back of his hand. "Gimme a minute . . . Stay out of any warm places. Shelter from the wind's okay as long as air temp's less than thirty below. Got a thermometer?"

"I'll just stay where it's coldest."

"Don't go into a building. Even if there are people there. Don't eat anything. If you start feeling diarrhea, fever –

"Then I won't be back," said Cross.

"Uh, right. Dressing warm?"

"Sure."

"Food? First aid kit?"

"I'm all right. So long, Ken. Ian." They shook hands.

"Good luck," said Ken.

"Be careful, Dinker," said Ian.

"Boy, you look terrible. You better sit down," he heard Svec say to Ian as he walked forward.

Deela had laid out his suit. "What's that?" she said, starting to open the canvas bag.

"Don't touch. Now listen. I'll use a boomer to punch through. Then leave my breather on the ice topside. Be easier without having to carry it."

"I see. Dinker, can I – "

"Don't ask."

"All right. I won't. No fins?"

"Don't think I'll need 'em." He swung the bag down into the lock, took the boomer she handed him, and slid feet-first into the lock. He reached up, but she was already lowering the hatch. As he ducked his head he felt surprised. He'd expected her to make a scene.

The water flooded up around him, icy cold, murky, foamy gray-green. As it reached his neck pressure equalized in the lock and the lower door opened. He shoved himself downward and out.

The sea was frigid, piercing his ankles and joints and neck, scorching his face. His mask fogged instantly, but the water was so murky he couldn't have seen much anyway. Sliding his hands along *Pilgrim's* curved side, he felt his way up and around the hull until he was floating gently up. His head struck the underside of the ice, jarring his teeth. Arming the boomer, he averted his face and jammed it upward.

For such a terrific detonation – confined under the ice, it rang his skull like a grenade going off – the channel the shaped charge left was narrow, with jagged edges he had to wriggle past. He struggled inside the suit, cursing where appropriate, up through a meter of pack, until he could flop out prone on the surface.

It was like climbing up from Limbo into Hell.

EIGHT

His face mask was snatched from his hands as he took it off, instantly blown away into the darkness. A hail of stinging ice drift drove into his cheeks, eyes, nose. He choked, covering his face with his hands. The wind howled around him, tugged at his breather pack, flailed the canvas carrier furiously against the ice. He tucked it under him and tripped the straps of the back pack.

It was far colder here than the water below the surface. Not to mention the hellish wind.

Blindly, he tried to wedge the breather down the hole, and wasn't sure how well he'd succeeded. It might work loose and fall in, drifting away under the ice and, incidentally, stranding him. *Can't be helped*, he thought.

He suddenly realized he was breathing air, raw air, fresh and clean and so cold his throat constricted on it as it sawed in and out of his lungs. He lay flat, gathering his strength, then raised his head to peer around.

He could see only blackness. *Cloudy*, he thought. *Else I'd set* something, *stars, moon, aurora australis*. But it was dead dark, with only a slightly darker dark ahead of him — the mountain, probably — to show where the island lay.

He tried to stand, but the wind, gusting and blustering, would not cooperate. It leaned into him, but then, when he tried to push forward, lulled, sending him stumbling. The ice, as he'd feared, was anything but level; as it froze, cakes had been bumped and jammed together, creating a wilderness of tilted surfaces and ridges and jagged edges he could neither see nor anticipate. He realized too late he'd neglected to bring a light.

He struggled on, crouched like a wrestler confronting an opponent. From time to time he missed his footing and fell heavily, turning as he went down to protect the contents of the bag. The wind was so strong it was hard to breathe. He wondered how far to trust Graham's research. Was carsonella already in his lungs, sensing warmth, beginning to unfold in deadly blossom?

The dark mass seemed just as far away when gravel crunched under his feet, and he was able to walk cautiously up a smoother incline. The strand.

He halted to orient himself. The chart had shown the research building less than a kilometer directly inland. The jetty should be to his right; the installation, or lab, or whatever it was, should be straight ahead. He stared in that direction, then squinted. Was it his imagination, or was that a light?

If there was . . . he quelled his excitement, resisting the impulse to run. If he didn't break his neck on some unseen obstacle, he'd overheat. *No, take it easy. If there are people around they've been here for years, and they'll keep for a few minutes longer.* He stamped his feet. Even in the heavy wet suit booties, the pause had allowed them to numb. The cold air whipping under his hood was freezing the water on his face and neck.

He bent and began walking again. The way was easier now and he didn't fall again, only stumbling when his foot slipped in loose scree or snow.

He halted and turned. Had there been a sound behind him, all but inaudible in the shrieking wind? It came again, a high-pitched call. His name?

"Over here!" he roared.

"Dinker!"

Someone blundered into him, slipped, and fell. When he bent his hands told him it was Deela, in a wet suit, oxygen bottle slung around her waist. He stared for a moment, then felt so uncontrollably angry he drew back a foot. The thought died, but he still saw red as he jerked her up. "What the *hell* are you doing here?"

"Don't be mad. I couldn't let you go alone. And you *said* not to ask."

He didn't know whether to laugh or slap her. "So you came anyway, eh? You stupid little . . . little *fish*. I ought to stuff you right back down that hole."

She didn't answer, only clung to him as the wind roared around them. He blinked. His vision was adjusting. He could make out the oval that was her face, and the mountain inland was sharper against the smooth darkness of the horizon. But he still couldn't see the ground under his feet. He bent to shout in her ear. "Get back to the sub. Right now."

"I'm coming. It's too late to send me back."

"The hell it is. Go back, I said."

"I won't. I'll follow you even if you don't take me with you."

They were both shouting as loud as they could, yet only faintly could Cross hear himself. *Damn it. Now I've got her to worry about, too.* "Stay with me, then," he shouted, and searched again for the light he'd glimpsed. It was gone – no – it flickered ahead, the clouds of driven ice crystals making it twinkle like a distant star.

She took his hand and they plowed forward, bent low into the wind. He stumbled over rocks. *There must have been a road, or a trail, leading inland from the jetty,* he thought. *Obviously I'm not on it.*

"Don't you have a light?" she shouted in his ear.

"No."

"Here."

A little of his anger evaporated. She'd thought of what he hadn't. It was immensely easier going with the little flashlight to pick out hollows and rocks in their path. He used it in short bursts, aiming it at the ground and shielding it with one gloved hand.

The light ahead grew brighter as they moved uphill. It seemed low to the ground, and behind it he sensed the looming bulk of a building. It was tall; no one-story hut. But he could make out nothing more. The going got easier, the ground leveling, and he tucked the flash into his wet suit.

"Is that where we're going?"

"Yeah."

"It's big."

"Uh-huh."

"Round on top."

"What? You sure?"

"Yes. It's *awful* big."

She can see better than I can in the dark, he reminded himself. But rounded on top? Odd. Like, an observatory? Still, it was an impressive mass of shadow, and some preconscious sense slowed his pace as he covered the last hundred meters to the light, now a dim square of saffron yellow.

Halfway there he stumbled and almost fell. The object was long, hard, but not as solid as a rock. A log? He took out the flashlight again and flicked it on just for a second.

He blinked. It was a body.

He stood still. A carsonella victim? But surely cold enough not to be infectious. He bent and felt over the shape gingerly. It seemed to be a man, in a heavy, fur-trimmed parka, lying face down. The clothing was flexible around the rigidly frozen corpse. He tugged to loosen it from the ice crust and rolled it over, moving his light to the face to check for the characteristic cherry-red hue.

The skin hue was normal. The cause of death had been the great charred hole in the man's chest.

"Oh, Dinker . . . it's. . . . "

"Yeah," he said. "Oh, yeah." He let the frozen corpse roll face down again. He liked it better that way.

"He's all burned. What could do that? That's not – "

"The virus? No. Several things could do that," Cross said, clicking off the light. Images of other bodies, along Asian rivers, came to mind. War memories. "A flame-thrower. White phosphorus. A battle laser, on wide beam."

"He was killed, then. He didn't just die."

"Looks like it. But it could have happened years ago. This island probably stays frozen even in summer. Come on." He pushed on, covering the last few feet to the light.

It came from a door, a common ordinary wooden door, with yellowish illumination from inside shining through a square pane of glass or heavy plastic. He peered in at a small bare anteroom. Coats and boots were hung and neatly racked around the walls. Another door, closed, apparently gave onto the interior. The light he'd seen came from a tiny emergency LED panel burning dimly in the ceiling.

He tried the handle. It resisted, then gave suddenly. He slammed it closed quickly, backing away.

"Aren't we going in?"

"I don't think it'd be smart, no." He hesitated, though, still staring. It looked so normal, so inviting, so *warm* . . . but the sense of wrongness awakened by the corpse grew stronger every minute. Dingily homelike as the anteroom looked, there was danger near. "Let's walk around this place, see if there are any windows."

He started to the right, along the front of the building. Dim as it was, the light had weakened his night vision. He had to feel his way along the corrugated metal wall.

"Hey. Shine your light over here."

"What is it?"

"I think another, um, dead person."

A woman this time, burned across the back. It looked as if she'd been hit running away. Her fingers were dug into the frozen soil as if she'd lost consciousness while still trying to crawl. He clicked the flash out, then turned it on again and swept it around.

Three more huddled shapes lay scattered across the snow.

"I don't like this, Dinker," Deela murmured into his ear. "Let's go back to the sub. Leave."

"For where? I'm afraid, too. But we need to check it out. Come on."

They groped around a corner. Cross, running his hand along the wall, felt the frame of a window, but it was dark.

"Something up ahead. Something big."

He felt it too. Extending out from the side of the building was another mass, considerably higher than the rest. He moved toward it cautiously and flicked the light on for just a moment. The structure was dark, huge, and slightly curved. He could make out where it met the ground, and where it bulged outward toward them; but he was too close to see how high it rose. He aimed the beam to the right, but the dark bulk extended beyond the light's range.

Fascinated, he walked forward. The wind died. It still wailed and blustered overhead, there was a small zone of shelter here.

He stopped a step away, examined the surface with the light, then leaned forward to touch it. It was solid, smoothly curved, yet rough under his gloved fingers, like rusted iron. *Some kind of containment vessel? To seal in the experiments?*

"Let's see how far around it goes."

"Okay." Her fingers gripped his hand, hard.

They walked along it, feeling the curving sides swelling out above them. He counted steps. Fifty paces. A hundred.

When the wind hit them again he realized the building was round. They were walking not in a straight line, but around it, though the curvature was so gradual he hadn't sensed it at first.

Two steps farther and the ground suddenly fell away. They felt their way cautiously down into a shallow depression. He counted a hundred more paces, and the wind shifted gradually around until it was behind them, shoving them along, before the ground slanted up again to a normal level.

He halted there. Their flash was growing dimmer; *cold's getting to the batteries*, he thought. But he could see that the ground they had just walked over was planed smooth, as if scraped and pressed down by the passage of a great weight. He turned to the west, facing into the wind, heedless of the ice drift stinging cheeks and forehead.

He was starting to understand.

It had come from that direction – from the west; maybe south by southwest, if he'd kept his orientation in the dark. It must have come in fast and very low, struck the ground near the western edge of the island, then continued sliding on, its terrific mass gouging a wide shallow trench right across Dvina Island. Sliding and gouging on until it stopped – accidentally, or not? – square across the low laboratory building.

Standing there, he tried to visualize it. The thing was enormous. And terrifically heavy. A meteorite? No. It was artificial.

A pull at his sleeve. "Dinker?"

"Come here," he said. They crawled under the thing's edge and he held her close so he could speak directly into her ear. "Deela. Know what this is?"

"No. Something big. With rough sides. Made out of cement?"

She sounded frightened, but he thought, *she has to know. In case I don't get back.*

"It's a ship. Understand? And it's enormous. I counted two hundred paces to get halfway around it. That's four hundred meters around; it's over a hundred meters across. Looks like about thirty meters high."

"A ship? You mean, a *space* ship?"

"Yeah. Nobody on Earth could fly a mass like this."

"But how'd it get here?"

"It flew here, Deela. You know – " Abruptly he realized she'd never in her life seen anything fly, except in videos. "It traveled here from somewhere else. Another planet or star."

"But how?"

"I don't know." He tried hard to smile, but his face was rigid from the cold. "There are lots of things I don't know. Alien spaceships among them."

"One's never landed here has it? Before?"

"Not that I know of. Though there were so many UAPs, UFOs, those last couple of years before the Dying. Things they couldn't explain. . . . " He reached out to rap the surface. "There's one here now, though."

"All right." She sounded about as scared as he felt. "What should we do?"

He considered. When it had landed, and slid into the building, the people in the undamaged part of the lab had come running out, to escape what they must have thought was a collapsing roof. And as they ran, they'd been burned down. Perhaps the woman had seen whatever had killed her, and had tried desperately to crawl away, anywhere, her horror stilled only by death.

Were there any researchers left inside the lab? Doubtful.

Was anything still alive inside the ship?

He had to figure there might be. The beacon was meant to attract survivors.

Except this mouse is not going to be caught. And not only that. He's going to leave a little housewarming present as he slips away.

So many deaths. Vengeance seemed a mild term to use. But he had to try to avenge what they'd done. A ship that could drop from the sky, slide across an island, and smash a building like an egg crate was obviously sturdy. But however robust it was, he had no doubt what he carried would shatter it.

"Dinker?"

"Yeah," he said, recalled from his thoughts. "I guess we can go back. I don't know where after that . . . we'll talk it over with the others. But I want to leave this."

He unslung the case and, fumbling in the heavy wetsuit gloves, unzipped it. He took the pistol out first and slid it inside his jacket, then eased the bomb assembly out and handed her the light. "Shine it here."

As she held it he set the timer. A hundred and twenty minutes was the maximum on the dial and he set it on that and checked his watch. It was 2200 GMT – he always set his watch by GMT at sea, even now, when Greenwich was no more and Greenwich Mean Time existed only in the inertial brain of *Pilgrim's* navigational system. He checked the setting and the time again, to be certain. Then unlocked the switch on the charge itself and moved it to Armed.

"Is that a bomb?"

"You guessed it." He reached far back under the curve of the thing and scooped out snow with a hand. Then shoved the warhead in, right up against the hull material.

"Dinker." She tugged at his arm. "Should we do that?"

He didn't stop, packing snow in around it until it was covered up. "What do you mean?"

"I feel . . . well, what if there's somebody in there?"

"You feel somebody inside? Is that what you're saying?"

"Well . . . sort of. Not like a person, but . . . something."

"That something is whoever invented carsonella. Spread it. Killed everybody. Animals, people, birds, everything. Don't you think they deserve it?"

"If they did, sure. But how do we know? I mean – "

"We're not going to hold a trial." He got to his feet. "I'm satisfied and that'll have to do. Now let's head back. We'll finish going on around, though I don't think we'll see much more."

He hesitated, then leaned in and lightly kissed her icy forehead. "You're doing great, Deela. I'm glad you came with me, I really am. Now, let's get going. Hand me back the light."

He crawled out from under the overhang and stood. Waiting till she was up, he began walking on, not close enough to touch its curving side, but near enough to sense it beside them. *The wind covered our noise*, he thought. He began counting paces again, fifty, a hundred, a hundred and fifty. They reached the lee side again.

An irregular shape loomed up suddenly before him. He crouched motionless for several seconds before making sense of it. The far corner of the lab building, smashed in, roof tilted against the sky. He breathed out, relieved, and felt his pounding heart slow. "'S'okay," he whispered, turning his head. "Just some wreckage."

No answer. He turned, reached out. She wasn't there.

Oh, Jesus, he thought. *Where'd she go?* Tripped, hit her head . . . he turned the light on again, swept it over their path. It weakened quickly, dying to a dull orange glow. Illuminating only the snow-covered ground and the dark curving side of the massive hulk of the stranger.

Nothing to do but go back. He stumbled into a run, hardly able to feel his feet. *An hour to get back to the sub, find it, if we're lucky. Get underway immediately . . . an hour to get out to sea before it happens. An hour . . . if I can find her. . . .*

"Deela," he called. Then, louder, *"Deela!"*

No answer. He halted, panting, smothered by the icy air, sweat clammy inside the warm rubber of the suit. He stared around. "Deela! Deela, *Deela!"*

His voice sounded shockingly loud, but still there came no answering cry. He turned on the light, despairing, and swept the ground in front of him. A light film of powdery snow had coated it here in the lee. He could make out their tracks; two sets, hers distinguishable by the shorter length of her strides and her wider feet, engineered for the sea. He followed them. After twenty paces hers veered and stopped, growing deeper. As if she'd halted for a moment, stamping her feet, deciding what to do next.

There, he thought, studying the ground by the ruddy light. Her tracks led off to the left, toward the ship. He called again, trying to pitch his voice to carry without shouting. He peered around. Then, on impulse, snapped the light off.

A faint glow showed under the snow, beneath the dark mass of the hull. Her tracks led toward it.

22:27, his watch read, electroluminescent numerals bright in the darkness. He turned its dial to the inside of his wrist and looked searchingly all around him. No other illumination broke the island's total darkness, except for the feeble, slightly greenish glow from beneath the hull. Except for the wind all was silent. The cold crept a little farther into his lungs.

Finally he dropped to his knees and crawled under the overhang. Snow had been dug away, making a narrow burrow leading down. He looked around once more, took a deep breath, swung his legs into it, and let go.

Almost immediately he emerged into an open space, the mouth, apparently, of some sort of tunnel. He crouched at the edge, looking ahead, where the glow was stronger, then around at the tunnel itself. Its sides were smooth, silvery, and when he put out a hand they felt slick as pearl. They flared outward here. Ahead, they seemed to narrow in a series of complex curves.

"Di-di," he hissed.

A scuffle sounded from somewhere ahead.

He scuttled forward, bending beneath the ceiling, until it was too low to continue. Then dropped to hands and knees.

Abruptly the way opened again to form a large chamber, High enough to stand in, and lined with the same polished silvery material.

Deela ran to him and hugged him, hard. "I'm sorry. I saw the light, and I felt something – something alive, strong – and thought I'd just look. I dug a little and then fell in. I yelled, but you must not have heard me."

"I'm just glad I found you. What's up ahead? Did you look any farther?"

"Mostly like this, except wider. Then finally it stops where it's all packed full of ice and dirt."

"Dirt?" That didn't make sense. He'd thought at first this might be some kind of exhaust, but it didn't seem to be. It looked organic, not engineered the way a human would design something.

"Come on. Let's go back," she said.

"You didn't see anything leading off this main tunnel? Doors?"

"No. Oh, there was a kind of a puckery place, but that's all."

"Okay, let's go." He twisted his wrist to show her the dial. "Hour and a half left. We need to skedaddle."

He crawled back through the constriction, helped her through, then ran. Their footsteps echoed eerily. The tunnel, he suddenly realized, was growing warm, almost tropical.

The exit, when they reached it, was gone. He stopped dead, staring around what was now a cul-de-sac. The silver walls had drawn together, closing like a healing wound. At their center, where the opening to the surface had been, was a little puckered mouthlike aperture.

"It closed," she muttered. "How'd it do that?"

He bent to draw the knife from his leg sheath, and tried to force the point into the pucker. The material was slick, tough, impossible to cut, but yielded slightly to pressure. By dint of his full strength he was able to work the blade partway into the opening. He pulled up, hoping to pry it open. The blade snapped.

He stared at the useless handle, then threw it against the wall. It caromed off and slid from side to side, coming to rest on the floor of the tunnel.

"We have to get out, Dink."

"I know. But it won't be this way."

"Maybe the other end?"

"Maybe," he said. "We'll have to dig our way out. I don't know if we can, in an hour and a half. But I guess we've got to try."

But when they emerged into the large chamber again they found that way blocked too by the same sphincter-like contraction of the walls. Deela sank to the floor, moaning. Distorted reflections of their frightened faces leered back from the curving walls. "We can't get out," she said.

He dropped to sit cross-legged beside her. "No. I guess we can't."

"You can't get out," said a loud, oddly remote-sounding voice, emanating, it seemed, from the walls around them.

NINE

With a *pop*, a hole appeared at the side of the chamber. It widened quickly, like a screaming mouth. Looking up into it, Cross saw the interior was lit with the same sourceless greenish light that filled the tunnel. But the walls of the new passage it revealed were an irregular gray instead of the smooth silver.

"Enter," said the voice, coming now from above them, somewhere at the top of the passage.

"Is that who you felt?" he whispered.

"I can't tell," Deela said. "I don't really . . . I don't feel it now."

He looked at the aperture, and stood. Touched the heaviness of the gun, still zipped inside his jacket. "We better stay together. Okay?"

She hesitated, then stood too.

When they stepped through the pucker closed swiftly behind them. He heard no sound of motors or pneumatic hiss. Only a soft *phut* as the orifice sealed.

The corridor led upward, at a curve, so he couldn't see what lay at its top. Behind him Deela sneezed, suddenly and violently. He felt the same tingle in his nose as he had in the sub when the jar had broken. Chlorine, he thought. The sting of it lingered in the passage, though the air he sucked into his lungs seemed normal, if very warm.

Again panic scraped the edge of his mind. Did warmth equal infectious carsonella?

The ramp flattened as they continued, then emerged, leading out onto a level. They stopped, and he tensed.

They looked down through a filmy screen or curtain upon an interior both breathtakingly huge, and shockingly inhuman.

Great splayed ribs arched overhead, supporting a vaulted dome. His first impression of what lay below it was of a vast mushroom garden; his second, of rows of brilliantly-colored tortoises, squatting before a gigantic rounded mass. Then his eyes adapted to scale and distance, and began to make sense of what they saw.

From above – he was standing, it seemed, on a rise at one end of the dome – the creatures seemed discoid. Rounded, of varying sizes, from an arm's-breadth across to much larger. And thick in proportion. They seemed to have crablike carapaces, or perhaps scales, that shifted color as they moved. No visible limbs, unless they were underneath or otherwise out of sight.

"They're working." Deela's face was pale, but she flashed him a look that said, plainly as words could have, *I'm all right. I'll be brave whatever happens.* In fact, for a moment he imagined he could hear the words in his head.

He looked back at the scene below. Yes, most were tilted back, moving slightly as if – working? Feeding? – at low square contrivances that might be tables.

He realized for the first time there was no one waiting for them. He looked around for the source of the voice. But saw no one. He cleared his throat. "Where are you?" he said loudly.

"Here, before you," said the voice, sounding only a little less remote

"Jesus," he muttered. This was creepy as hell. "Where? Who are you? What's your name?"

"We do not bother to name individual life forms. Here I am called the Mature."

He cleared a suddenly dry throat. "Where are you from? I assume, not from this planet."

No answer came, but there was a commotion down on the floor. He shaded his eyes to watch. One of the smaller discoids, apparently struggling with four others, was being carried or forced toward the rounded mass. It broke free, was recaptured, then forced inexorably toward a hollow that slowly widened at the large mass's edge.

Where it was . . . engulfed.

"God," said Cross. Horrified, he stepped forward, raising a hand to brush aside the transparent film that surrounded them.

"If you open that, human being, you will die."

He hesitated, still trying to process what had just occurred on the floor below. "Why? What'll happen?"

Again, no answer. He gathered the material in his hands – it was thin, tough, pliable as plastic but both less substantial and stronger – and managed, with a huge effort, to tear a small rip in it.

Instantly, he recoiled. The puff of colorless gas burned like fire in eyes and nostrils. Deela dropped to the floor, coughing. He pulled her away from the vibrating rent. His throat burned, hydrochloric acid reacting with tender flesh.

The far side was filled with chlorine gas. "Stop it," he grunted, coughing. "I didn't . . . stop it."

Something occurred in the torn film. It sagged, melted, flexed. The flow of gas slowed, then stopped.

A current of fresh air came from the mouth of the tunnel. He blinked, mopping at his weeping eyes.

A faint wrinkle marked where he'd torn the hole.

"I can spare you no more time at present," said the locationless voice. *"More permanent quarters are being prepared. But for now, you will return to the reaction chamber."*

"What are you?" said Cross, desperately. "Do you know about carsonella? I have questions. You must have met people before, you speak English – "

The rush of air from behind them stopped. *"To the chamber,"* the voice said again. *"Now."*

"Come on," he said to Deela, and they walked downward, hearing the sphincter snap closed behind them, back into the silver-walled room. He looked around. "The 'reaction chamber', he called it. I wonder what kind of reaction."

"Forget it! You sound like Ken now. We've got to get out."

The silver room was so quiet he could hear himself breathing, hear the pounding of his heart. "Yeah. Sorry. I'm . . . a little disoriented."

"Me too." She gave him a quick hug. "But it's nice to hear you admit it."

"Stand back," he said, and pulled out the gun.

He hefted its reassuring weight, studying the walls. Up was out of the question; he didn't relish breathing any more chlorine. Down was no good either. "Better hold your ears." He chambered the first round, pointed the muzzle at the wall, and fired.

The report left his ears singing. He examined where the bullet had struck. A shallow gouge, not very deep. Something glinted inside. When he dug at it with a finger the bullet fell out, slightly flattened, and very hot.

He fired twice more, at different points, then directly into the puckered place. None of the bullets penetrated, and one simply bounced out onto the floor. "No use," he said. "This stuff's too tough."

"But look," she said. "It's bleeding."

The edges of the holes were closing, and at each of them a yellowish tear formed, hung for a moment, then trickled down the curving silver wall. As he stared another two drops oozed. Then the flow stopped.

"Don't shoot it any more. I feel it hurting . . . it's alive."

"We've got to get out," he said. The indentations were shrinking even as he watched, leaving only ribbed wrinkles on the mirrorlike surface.

"You are here to stay," said a new, croaking voice, and they turned.

One of the aliens had joined them.

Close up, it was obviously one of the neatly-ranged domes they'd seen from above. But now, close up, he could make out its organs of manipulation, flexible tendrils that roved restlessly beneath it. This individual was a little over a meter across. Its primary color at the moment was an iridescent reddish-green. The entire body was loosely covered by a suit, or bag, of the transparent film. A long tail – no, a hose, he corrected himself – of flexible tubing stretched out behind it, running back up the corridor.

Cross guessed its chlorine-rich breathing atmosphere was being supplied through the tube, which pulsed slowly. The strange thing – he frowned as his eyes searched the richly textured surface – was that aside from a hole or vent at its apex it appeared to have no eyes, no sense organs at all, that he could make out. No visible mouth. Nevertheless, it had spoken.

"I am a Molder," said the creature. It did not speak in a clear but distant way, as the first, louder voice had, but in a humming croak.

"You're different than the one who talked to us before," Cross said, balancing the gun in his hand.

A pause. He sensed it was studying him, a microscopic cold scrutiny without sympathy or warmth or humor. "Correct," it said at last. "That was our Mature."

Mature? he thought. The other, then, was . . . its superior? This was 'a Molder'. Was that a species name, or the name of this particular, individual?

"Is the Mature also a Molder?"

"How did you come to this island?"

A lie seemed in order. "We flew," he said, winking at Deela.

"Your aircraft?"

"Crashed at sea."

"Are there more humans?"

"How do you mean?"

"How many came with you to this island?"

"Oh. Two only. Ourselves."

"You followed the signal?"

"Yes."

"From what land did you come?"

He glanced at Deela, who was watching the Molder intently. This was the tricky part. If he was right about what these things were, what they'd done . . ." From India," he said firmly.

"Is there not disease in India?"

Ah, he thought. *They know about carsonella. Charge number one. They don't know it, but right now they're on trial for their lives.* Aloud he said, "Yes, of course."

"Then how did you escape demise?"

"Living in an underwater station."

"Why did you leave?"

"We were forced out." *The bait,* he thought. *Choke on it.*

"Forced out," it said, with a different intonation, though Cross couldn't tell what it implied. "Perhaps by sharks?"

That's it, friend, he thought. *You just pled guilty to Charge Two.* "Yeah, some very deadly sharks. Now look. We have questions, too."

"Wait." The disc-thing brought out a small shapeless form and held it close. A thin, rapidly modulated whine. It lowered the object. "The Mature has given permission to answer."

Two goals, Cross thought. First, find out more about them. Deeply though they'd already incriminated themselves, it was still possible they weren't directly responsible for the Dying. If they weren't, he could explain about the warhead, use it as leverage to get them released.

But if this ship was the origin of the Carsonella virus and *C. Ourslerii* and the green chlorine-producing plants, he'd let the bomb tick on, let their doom come as it had to all the people on the once life-rich blue planet of Earth.

Second goal: to escape. Or, if he couldn't, at least get Deela back to *Pilgrim* alive.

"Let's start with you. Tell us who you are and where you're from, and why you came here."

The thing settled its rounded body to the floor, like an old man settling down to tell a long tale.

"In your language, we would be called Molders. Where are we from? Judging by our bodies, we deduce a massive, high-gravity planet, with a smooth surface and chlorine atmosphere. But our kind has lived too long and travelled too far to remember its origin."

He glanced at Deela. She flicked her gaze toward him, leaned in, and whispered, "I don't feel a thing from it."

He nodded, and looked back at the Molder, formulating his next question. He wasn't sure what she meant, but he sensed something uncanny too. A human being, confronting any other life form, felt kinship – of varying degrees, reaching its highest point with mammals – but with this squat creature he felt no sympathetic link. It was entirely, coldly, foreign.

For the first time he felt the chill of space in the word *alien*.

"Molders? Of what? What do you 'mold'?"

"Life," said the being.

"Okay. You engineer, manipulate, living things. Right? But how did that bring you here?"

"Reproduction. Expansion. Colonization. None of these is fully accurate, but you may gather the meaning."

"You mean to conquer this world."

"Correction. We *have* conquered this world. Only a little time is now required to allow the processes to finish."

"Processes? What do you mean?" said Deela.

"Difficult to explain to a lower form. Are you sure you wish to know? It will make little difference for you."

"We wish," said Cross. "But first, tell us more about the Molders." *We won't make it out alive. We'll die with them, now this thing's explained their plan.* But even inevitable death did not make him less curious. *A weak point,* he thought. *Every species must have one.*

"Gladly. First, we are a nomadic, spacefaring race, though we must have planets to cultivate the Seed. Like me, Molders are long-lived, great-brained, and beautiful of body."

"How can you tell? You have no eyes."

"Not of your design. But I can see as well as you, though in different wavelengths. Do not mistake absence of eyes for absence of sight."

"I'll remember that," he said grimly. "If you need planets for reproduction, then you were born on one. Where? Mars? Neptune?"

"Much farther away. And those two were unsuitable in any case.

"We reproduce wherever conditions are favorable. Or can be made so. I myself was born light years from here, not far from your galaxy's rim, just after the great crossing to find new planets. We travel far, move often, pause only for a century or two to reproduce."

Like locusts, he thought. "I take it, then, your – Mature, is it? – was who brought carsonella to Earth."

"Not brought. Made. He crafted it of small harmless viruses. It was, we think, quite successful. You are the first to arrive since we began broadcasting."

He half raised the pistol. "Dinker, don't," said Deela, taking his arm.

He shook her off, breathing raggedly. "I won't. Why should I hurt this one? It was the Mature that killed my family, the Chief's, everyone, every bird and animal, everything that breathes air. Why should I? Why – " He halted, choking.

"You are driven by emotion," said the Molder, with a tone of detached interest. "We have seen few humans. Only the few we encountered on this island.

"It is the purpose of the strong to bring order to the unimproved areas of the universe. Earth produced nothing but anarchic, primitive fauna. What you call carsonella is in your soil now, fixing the atmospheric oxygen. Its presence in the atmosphere will drop rapidly. At the same time specially modified plants are producing a more congenial gas, one that can support higher, more energetic forms of life.

"When the proper level is reached, the Mature will circle the planet, setting the Seed at each suitable site."

Cross's mind was a maelstrom. The only thing that kept him from killing the thing, not with the gun but by tearing it apart with his bare hands, watching it writhe and die in what to it must be a poison atmosphere, was the knowledge that tucked against the hull was six kilos of polarized-chain thorium, ticking nearer with each passing second to ravening incandescence.

He turned his wrist to check his watch. 2255. A little over an hour to detonation.

"I'm emotional, yes," he said to the Molder. "Don't you feel anything when you steal a planet and destroy everyone who lives on it?"

"Not destroy. Transform," said the Molder. "And why are you surprised? Your various life forms steal from one another, eat one another, on the slightest pretext, or none at all. Every one of your nations lives on territory torn from its previous inhabitants. On what ground can you object to our doing the same?"

He started to object, but the thing went on speaking. "But no, we don't feel what you call 'emotion'. That is for lower forms, herding animals. We do not herd, or live in groups. We grow individually, and live alone wherever possible."

"You seem to be cooperating in this ship."

"A different matter. Those who bud in flight must work together as we cross space. It is hard. Many die. For Molders to cooperate in the Seed is hard; for two Matures, impossible. But it will not be necessary much longer. In three years – four, at the most – your atmosphere will support advanced life. We will scatter, each to prepare his Seed for sowing."

"And the Mature?"

"As we too become Matures, he must move on, or die."

Cross felt confused. An alien race. A bizarre society. How could he even trust the terms they used? But so far, he'd grasped nothing he could turn against them.

That left goal number two. "What do you plan to do with us?"

The Molder paused, apparently considering. "That remains with Him. He has not yet informed me."

"Can't you let us go?" said Deela.

"Why?" said the Molder. "You can't live on this island. There is no shelter or food. Perhaps you lied to us. Is there a vehicle of some sort nearby, in which you can maintain your atmosphere?"

"No," said Cross.

"You lie again, I suppose. Still, your machine technology cannot maintain an oxygen atmosphere long. But here, in a special area, we can do so."

"Why would you want to do that?"

"I did not say we would. The Mature may simply destroy you. But avoid false hope. Your kind is finished. Accept it as the working of the universe and the laws of life."

"The law of life isn't dog eat dog."

"An interesting saying. Dogs, indeed, do not eat other dogs. But your dogs are warm-blooded pack animals. They live and feed together in the wild. For this reason you find them easy to tame; the human is accepted as his leader, even as a friend.

"But you have other animals that do not herd. They live and hunt alone, forced together only by the need to mate. And they *do* eat each other."

The vivid memory of the swirling frenzy of ourslerii. "Like sharks," Cross said. He looked at Deela, then back at the Molder. "The sharks that drove us out . . . another of your 'moldings'?"

"Not mine. What is done here is done by the Mature."

"But did you help?" said Deela.

For the first time, the creature shifted position. The multiple limbs writhed uneasily. "The question does not translate," it said at last.

It can't be embarrassment, he thought. *Or shame; it would have shown that earlier. Can it be fear, that this mysterious 'Mature' will hear, and punish it somehow?*

"But I don't understand why . . . look. I understand carsonella now. And why the sea plant produces chlorine. You seem to've won without a war, without our even suspecting you were here. But why make intelligent sharks?"

"On this planet the sea contains more life than the land," said the Molder, settling down as if on safe ground once more. "Life here came from the sea. Even air-based life depends on it for oxygen. But the sea is relatively independent both of the air and the land. Our oxygen-fixing organism, as you obviously know, living underwater, is effective only on land.

"But we knew – we monitored your broadcasts for years, as we approached – that human beings had begun to migrate beneath the sea as well. We guessed there might be remnants there after we cleansed the land. So, the Mature decided to upgrade the most successful predator of the sea, giving it what it had lacked. Did you find it challenging?"

"We sure did," said Cross.

"There are few of us here, in this Seed. We could not have colonized a populated planet, even one with only a machine technology. One setback could have destroyed us. So we had to proceed in our own way. You mastered machines. We long ago mastered the mechanics of life. Self-healing, adaptable, self-replicating. Your carbon-oxygen forms are what we call 'soft'; simple to manipulate; so simple your race even learned a little Molding on its own."

"A little," said Cross, looking at Deela.

"Enough to understand Life is the most powerful tool a race can grasp. By a very few Moldings we make your atmosphere and your planet into what we need. No wars. No invasions. Your ranchers once spread myxomytosis, rabbit fever. Did they regret the rabbits' deaths? Then how can you ask us for compassion, seeing it is not in our nature, any more than in the shark's?"

"I have a question," said Deela suddenly. "Why kill the animals? You said you wanted to kill humans. Well, we could fight you. But why the others?"

"I must not understand this language yet," said the Molder. "Either that, or you are evidencing some sort of interspecies concern.

"But that would not seem logical. As your own broadcasts stated, humans devoted most of their history to exterminating other species. You 'tamed' a few, true, but you Molded others and even ate them. Why then wonder about the fate of other species, when your own is extinct?"

"It just doesn't understand, Didi," said Cross. "I don't think it *can*. – Tell me, do the Molders keep pets?"

"A lower species nurtured for no material benefit? No. Lower forms we keep alive within the Seed, but only insofar as they are of use for experiment, or breeding stock."

"I see," said Cross. "You feel nothing for other species. What about your own kind? You said you don't herd, and that you have trouble living together in the . . . Seed." He recalled the engulfing horror they'd witnessed in the dome; it seemed, now, to make more sense.

"We do not mate, nor reproduce as your animals do. Perhaps long ago we did, but since then evolved a more efficient route. What I called 'reproduction' is in actuality a Molding. The Mature buds his progeny to serve his purposes within the Seed."

"And feelings?"

"As I said, of little use to us."

"Still, I guess, you're, like, the Mature's offspring? Sons, daughters?"

"Neither; we are genderless. But, yes, He is my parent. I honor Him for that," said the small Molder. Louder, Cross thought, than was necessary in the enclosed chamber.

But he was getting an idea.

"What time is it?" Deela whispered.

He dropped his gaze and felt ice on his backbone, despite the sultry heat of the air. 2330. *Enough chatting. We have to escape. Now.*

He waved at the closed entrance. "When we came in, that – door – was open. Now it's closed. Who controls this?"

"The Seed. As directed by Him."

"You can't open doors?"

"I control none of the functions of the Seed."

He stood. "It's warm in here. Do you mind if I take off this suit?"

It didn't answer. Cross unzipped the wet suit jacket. Rivulets of sweat dripped to the silvery floor. He bent to lay it out, crouching low.

When he came up he jumped, putting every ounce of muscle into the effort, vaulting directly over the creature, and hit the floor hard, trying to roll. He half-rose, facing the Molder again, gun ready in his hand. Taken aback, the thing hadn't moved, crouching between him and Deela. He raised the pistol, lining up the sights on the creature's center of mass.

"What are you doing?" it croaked.

With his free hand Cross felt for the "hose." He held one loop up. Squeezed it in his fist, and the pulsing stopped. "How long, Molder, can you live without breathing?"

"Longer than you. But not very long."

"And how long," he said, waving the gun, "if you suddenly start breathing oxygen?"

"Don't." Its fringelike appendages began to ripple. "What is in your paw? A mechanical weapon?"

"Yeah. I don't know if you have a hard shell there, but I'm sure it'll kill you. Though just letting air in would probably do the job."

"Don't do that," it said. From underneath, it produced the small writhing object it had used before.

"Put that down."

It released the thing down hastily. "It is only a communicator. You are emotional. You are not thinking, human."

"Correct," said Cross, feeling the power in his arm, the lust to kill. "I am filled with primitive emotions of hate and revenge. I wish to blow your cold-blooded shell open and watch you struggle for air and bleed and die like all the human beings and animals you killed."

"Killing me will not change what has happened. Or what will be done to you."

"Almost correct," Cross said. "But not killing you is going to get us out of here. I'm surprised; never heard of hostages? You helped destroy Earth, and I'd love to watch you, personally, die. Now get the Mature on that wiggly thing and get him down here."

"Not possible. The Mature cannot move."

"He damn well better." He tightened his grip on the hose and watched colors play across the thing's surface.

"He *cannot*. The Mature is . . . immobile. Anchored to the Seed, one with the Seed," it croaked.

"Oh. All right, then. Get him on your radio, or whatever it is."

"Air, *air*. . . . "

He relaxed his grip on the hose a bit. The alien panted in irregular, rippling pulses. A minute passed before it was able to lift the communicator. It spoke in the same high modulated note they'd heard before. After a moment, the thing, apparently a small living being of some kind, whistled in return.

"What did he say?"

"What I knew He would. You may kill me or not. Neither makes a difference to Him. Though he notes I was useful and loyal, and asks you to spare me."

"Maybe he doesn't get it," said Cross. "Either he opens that door, and we stroll out, or you die."

"*Your request, human, is understood.*" The enormous voice boomed suddenly from the very walls around them. "*The one you speak of has no influence on my decisions. I sent him for study of you only.*"

"You don't seem to understand the situation," said Cross. "I have a weapon. If you don't release us, I'll use it on your, uh, offspring."

"*Do what you must. I will send another. But I have no time for you now.*"

"He doesn't care, at all," Deela muttered.

"Yeah, so I gather." He looked at the pistol, then at the creature before them. "Ready to die?"

"Don't kill me, human," it grated. "I would free you if I could. Do not end my existence with your machine."

"You fear death, then."

"All things living do. Yes, I fear death."

"And it's here," said Cross, aiming.

"You're not going to kill it," said Deela.

"We'll watch one of them die, at least."

"The door will not open," said the creature desperately. "Even if you kill me. But wait. If you let me live – " its voice dropped to a hoarse whisper – "let me live, and I will try to help you."

"How, if the Mature controls everything?"

"The Mature can be killed," it whispered. "He can – can be – "

It stopped talking. Cross glanced down, startled, at the tube in his hand. It had gone suddenly limp.

"I didn't mean it," gabbled the thing. "First Among Us, I didn't! I spoke to trick the animals into letting me go, that I could continue to serve! I would not betray . . . let me breathe . . . I will explain. . . . "

The tube stayed limp. The disc's edges writhed. It shuddered. Its words turned to short hard croaks. Then it began to buzz.

When the buzzing stopped Cross realized it was dead.

He stared across the motionless disc at Deela, who'd pressed both hands to her mouth. "Did it . . . kill itself?"

"No." He lifted the tube, now flat and empty as a discarded snakeskin. "Its boss cut off its air. Smothered it."

"Because it offered to help us?"

"More likely because it tried to disobey." He looked at the handgun, snapped the safety on. "Their society . . . it's not . . . very nice," he faltered.

He prodded the creature with a toe. The shell wasn't rigid, just tough, like the scaly skin of a tortoise. It was changing now, turning a slaty, lusterless bluish-green.

"And that was the Mature's own . . . child?"

"Or bud, or . . . something like that."

"Oh. Oh." She crossed her hands over her stomach. "Then they don't care for anyone, do they? Only themselves. Not even their own. . . . "

He stepped cautiously over the body and held her as she wept, as much to quell his own horror as to comfort her. "It doesn't look so good for us, does it. But you've been brave. I'm proud of you." He stroked her hair with a shaking hand.

"Brave?" she caught at the word. "Not a pest?"

He smiled. "You were never a *pest*, Deela. If I acted like it sometimes, well . . . I'm sorry. That was my problem. Not yours."

She lifted her eyes to his. "How much longer?"

"The bomb? Twenty minutes. It'll be so quick we'll never know it happened. And after they're all dead," he said, mingled sorrow and triumph at the pit of his stomach, "Maybe life on earth will come back. It has a way of doing that. Adapting.

"Ian and Ken and the Chief will hear the explosion. They'll be safe; the ice will deflect the shock upward. Joe'll know what I did. It's not much, is it? But it's all we can do."

"Not all," she said, and he looked down into warm, wide-pupiled brown eyes. Her breath was warm on his cheek. "There's no more time, Dinker," she whispered, hugging him. "Not for us, or anybody else. But say it. Please."

He smiled. It wouldn't be a betrayal of the dead. It was a reaffirmation of them.

"I love you," he said.

"Humans!" grated a new voice.

Still embracing, they turned. A second, larger Molder crouched in the tunnel, the curved mirror sides bending fantastic reflections around it. It too was enclosed in the transparent film. But in its tendrils this one held a rectangular instrument. The first machine he'd seen them use. "The decision has been made. You will go to the holding rooms. Lay your weapon on the floor."

"Like hell I will."

The rectangle made no sound, but suddenly the gun in his hand grew hot. Cursing, he dropped it.

"This way."

"We're not coming. Kill us here."

"Dinker . . . it's only for a few minutes," Deela whispered. "If that's all, we can go along."

"You're right. Okay. We're coming."

He helped her step over the corpse. They followed the other Molder out of the chamber and into another aperture-doored corridor. They emerged at a different place, and he stopped, looking around.

They were lower this time, near the bottom of the dome. The transparent material – *they must grow the stuff on demand,* he thought – formed a veiled tunnel. Outside it, not reacting to the humans as they walked along, Molders of different sizes carried various sorts of equipment, while others busied themselves at the low tables he'd seen before. He had no idea what they were doing, but the place was a hive of activity, not frenzied but busy, purposeful as a colony of ants.

"Stop," said their escort. Obediently, Cross and Deela halted. He looked at his watch.

2357.

They were quite close now to the large varicolored mass he'd glimpsed from above. Around it Molders were busy, some with instruments, some with what – he peered through the film – yes, with what looked like animals or insects carried or clamped to their backs.

"It's alive," Deela said.

"What's that?"

"Look." She nodded ahead. Her look of horror had returned.

He slowly realized that the looming mass was a Molder. Gigantic, huge as a house, an immense flattened sphere that loomed over the others like a cliff. The same one he'd glimpsed earlier, from above.

"My Lord," he whispered.

"Yes. It is I you see."

Up close the voice was not as loud; some sort of amplification had been involved before, he guessed. But it was still detached, the remoteness not of distance but of utter objectivity, utter logic, utter disregard for the lesser beings that served and were sacrificed to it.

"You're the Mature," Cross said.

"And you, a human being," came the toneless response. "Strange, to think I destroyed your race, while meeting so few."

"You might have come in peace. We might have allowed you to reproduce here, exchange knowledge, then travel on."

"Unlikely." A smaller Molder moved among the Mature's tendrils – tentacles, really, swollen to the size of Cross's thigh – then was lost to sight. *"Our spawning takes years, our Seeds require much material. And how could I spawn in an oxygen atmosphere? But, it is no loss. An inconsequential species. You will be neither the first nor the millionth type of beings we have Molded."*

"Molded?" said Cross. "You haven't Molded us."

"Not yet," said the Mature. "The other is a female, is it not?"

Cross stroked the film between them. Could he break through it, run a few steps, plunge his fingers into the swollen mass before the chlorine choked his life out? It was inviting. But he remembered the bomb. Only a few seconds were left. "You won't mold us," he said. "We'll die first."

"The matter of your death, and that of every creature on this planet, is for my decision now, human. Not yours."

He glanced at Deela. She still looked scared, but as their eyes met she smiled and squeezed his hand.

"Perhaps we will talk later, before Molding begins. Perhaps after. Depending on the results. Your genetics are malleable, but the modifications sometimes yield unexpected results. Now you will follow your escort to where we will begin."

"No. We won't." Cross looked at his watch and saw with satisfaction he had one minute left to hurl defiance in the face of their destroyer. "Nor will you inherit Earth."

"I won't?" said the Mature.

"No," said Cross. "Earth will live on, and someday give birth to life, and intelligence, and love again. Because you're all going to die . . . now."

He lowered his watch. Deela gasped and hugged his arm. He turned to her, ready at last to meet oblivion.

A few seconds passed.

"Now I understand," said the Mature. "Are you referring to this device?"

A different Molder brought it close to the film. Cross saw the arming switch was set to Off.

"Of course, I had a search made," the Mature continued. "It was not well hidden. Not to an animal we keep with remarkable senses. It took a little longer to locate your undersea vessel and capture your friends. You will find two of them, drugged but otherwise unharmed, in the holding rooms.

"Have you further questions?"

"I have no further questions," said Cross.

He turned away, and followed the Molder guard blindly.

TEN

Graham and Ian sprawled unconscious on the smooth gray floor of a small chamber.

Cross knelt beside them, disoriented, bewildered, appalled. He'd been resigned to death. But not only had their executions been postponed, the Mature had turned the tables on them.

From avengers, they'd become hostages. And now, either victims, or some kind of experimental subjects.

Trying to shake off his bewilderment, he examined his friends. Both were breathing, though shallowly. He lifted Ian's eyelid; he was out, but the pupils looked normal.

"I think Ken's waking up," Deela said. Bending, she shook him. "Hey! Wake up!"

"Wait a minute," said Cross. *Two of them*, the Mature had said. He wheeled on their guard. The big Molder was immobile, blocking the exit from their cell. "Where's the other one? The man who couldn't walk?"

"Undergoing study," said the Molder.

"What's that mean?"

"You will find out, in a little while."

"Tell me where he is." Cross got to his feet.

"Stay here." It retreated as he approached, then scuttled backward through the aperture, which closed behind it. A rush of gas hissed outside.

Behind him Graham groaned again. Cross turned as the biologist sat up, opened his eyes, and blinked. He waggled his head. "Dinker? Di-di? Where the hell are we?"

"Take it easy. How do you feel?"

"Woozy. I must have been knocked out somehow. Last thing I remember is you banging on the hull. We figured you were hurt and couldn't work the airlock, so we opened it from inside. After that – nada." He shook his head, looking around. "This is the strangest room I've ever seen."

Cross helped him up. "Walk around. You were gassed, when you opened the lock."

"Gassed? Who by? And where are we?"

The biologist paced up and down, listening intently as Cross told the story from the beginning. He ended with the Mature's frustration of his attempt at sabotage. "And Joe's not here. They say he's 'undergoing study'," he finished.

"I'm not as surprised as you might think," said Graham thoughtfully. "I'd considered something like, uh, extraterrestrial intervention. I never mentioned it, but the evidence seemed to lead that way."

"That's why I brought the bomb along."

"That *was* a surprise, to hear that. You had those aboard your sub this whole time? Why?"

"Long story. One we don't need to go into just now."

"It won't detonate? No chance?"

"Afraid not. It's on Safe. They obviously recognize its function."

"Forget that, then. – Deela, is Ian coming around yet?"

"I'm awake. I've been listening," the boy said, sitting up.

"It's not looking good." Cross tried not to sound hopeless, for the youngsters' sake, but doubted he was succeeding. "We're still alive, but for how long? Apparently they intend to use us for whatever they're using the Chief for. Experiments, it sounded like. Deela, can you . . . feel him?"

She closed her eyes, standing still. "I feel . . . *something*. Part of it might be him. He's nearby. I don't think he's in pain."

"Part of it?" said Graham.

"Yeah, there's something else, or someone else. I can't tell where, though. That's funny."

"The Mature?"

She shuddered. "You can't feel something that doesn't feel itself. This is, oh, it feels like a person. Almost."

Graham and Cross traded looks. "A survivor from the research facility?" said Cross.

"I hope not," said Graham, looking around the interior. "Okay, we have to make a plan, *do* something. You know the layout here, right? Any ideas?"

"We've got to get out, any way we can. Any way, especially, that causes damage. Find Joe and take him with us, too.

"Ken, a question. The chlorine in the atmosphere. Could it . . . could this transformation be reversed somehow? Or stopped?"

The scientist considered. "We might develop a chemical to kill the plants, but judging by the expanse we plowed through, it'd take millions of tons. And planes, to disperse it. The best solution would be to breed something to eat the stuff, I guess."

"Could you do that? Maybe back at the Station?"

"Dinker, you overestimate me. I'm not a geneticist, a genius like Dr. Oursler. I'm a specialist in marine mammals. I have a vague idea on the theoretical level of how to go about it, but it would take decades to learn the techniques, gather samples, find or engineer chlorine-resistant animals or fish, then breed them in captivity to subsist on the plant. What these . . . *things* are doing's beyond our science. No," he finished, looking haunted, "I couldn't. They're converting our whole environment to what they want, and it's irreversible."

"So," Cross said, "All we have left to think about is how to get out of here. If we can."

"You know, Commander," said Graham, looking depressed but also amused, "You have to be the stubbornest son of a bitch I've ever met. We've been sunk since Parrish smashed everything up. Yet you never consider quitting." He shook his head.

Cross poked at the aperture the Molder had left through. It was as tight as he'd expected. He suppressed a sigh. Was Graham right? They really didn't have a chance? *I'm probably wrong, but I just don't buy it.* "It's, oh, a matter of choice. We each have to choose, every minute we keep on living. Keep trying, or lie down and die, like Parrish, or Klassen."

"Now, wait a minute. It's not the same."

"Well, it sort of is, though Lew was suicidal and Sheila's a hero. They both decided to give up." He took a breath, tried to straighten, though the low overhead made it hard. "Well, damn it, I won't! Not because it's my evolutionary duty, the way these slug-things would probably put it. But just because, I guess . . . that's how a human being should die."

"I agree."

They turned. Ian, looking haggard, was getting up. He tottered to the wall, leaned against it. "He's right. We shouldn't give up. Ever. Not till they kill us."

"Okay, okay." Graham held up both palms. "We're lucky to have Dink. We couldn't have come this far without him on our tails." He looked around. "Wherever 'this far' is. We'd better start figuring a way out."

Their compartment was cramped, perhaps five meters across and ten long, with a sloping curved overhead that made one end too low for an adult to stand. Walls, floor, and ceiling were the same grayish-pink material lining the other corridors of the ship. Cross prodded the wall. It was slightly softer than the silvery material in the lower chamber, though still tough enough to keep them in. There was no furniture, no decoration, no facilities. Just a storage cell, and inside it, four captives.

"There's a hole," said Deela, pointing up.

Cross gazed up. The orifice was in the middle of the overhead, about an inch in diameter. As he paused under it a warm current of air struck his face. He covered it with a hand. The flow pushed it away. It was under pressure, pumped in an even, pulsing flow.

"Air supply. Must be an outlet here, too, somewhere, or the pressure'd be rising."

"Dinker, something just occurred to me," said Graham slowly. *"Do you think it can hear us talking?"*

He nodded. Graham hadn't spoken in English, but in seatalk, and though the high notes didn't carry as well in air they were audible in the confined space. *"You're right,"* he said, in the same language. *"And they wouldn't know seaspeech from listening to broadcasts. Kids, anything we don't want them to overhear, seaspeak it. But don't overdo it."*

They nodded. A moment later Ian motioned them over to the lowest corner. Near the bottom of the wall, a slightly larger hole was let into the floor. Cross lay down and tried to peer inside. It was just a hole, leading into a tube, then darkness. Far too small to be useful. Intended for waste, perhaps. He got up, disappointed.

"No good?" said Graham.

"Nope." He began to pace around the walls. *A specimen jar,* he thought. They were like lobsters in a tank, waiting to be selected by discerning diners, plucked out, carted off, carved up.

How would lobsters go about freeing themselves?

He paced round and round, twisting his fingers together behind his back. Force wouldn't get them out of this. The bomb had failed. And they had no more weapons.

We've got to use the thing that makes us human, he thought. *Our brains.*

But nothing came to mind. He sat, squatting into a corner, and after a moment Graham got up and joined him.

"Any ideas?"

"It's the proverbial locked room. Worse. Same barrier system as an aquarium. If a fish escapes, it dies. I'd bet there's chlorine outside that sphincter, um, thing."

"I heard gas hissing out there after our guard left."

"But there may be a psychological way out."

"What's that, Ken?"

Graham patted his pockets, then fiddled with his empty pipe. *"This intraspecies friction you mentioned. You say they aren't a cooperative bunch."*

"That's what the one that interviewed us said. And from what I've seen, it's an understatement."

"It wouldn't seem necessary for them to lie to someone in our position. So let's assume it's true and start from there. As nonsocial animals – "

"I think they'd say 'non-herding'," said Cross.

"Same – same. My ethology isn't up to date, but as I recall one big difference is in dominance interactions. Social animals have complex, nonviolent ways of constructing authority frameworks. Nonsocial species, when forced together, can sometimes do the same, but violently. They haven't the intraspecies inhibitors social animals do."

He stroked his chin. *"These Molders could be like that. The structure's unstable. If we could encourage some of them to turn against this Mature – "*

"A mutiny," said Cross. *"Yeah, I think they might revolt, if they got a chance. He certainly has no qualms about killing them. But how would we start a mutiny from in here?"*

"That's one problem. But already I see a bigger one. There's a difference between deposing a human captain and doing it to this thing."

"What?"

"If he's as big and as different from the rest as you say, and as omnipotent within the ship – "

"He is."

"Then, unfortunately, he's in the only stable position in the hierarchy. Is there anyone second in line, that might rival him in size, or something?"

"Not that I've met," said Cross. *"It's like there's the one queen and the rest follow orders. Only here all the workers are going to be queens eventually. When they do this Seeding they keep talking about."*

"Then I'm not so sure we could start anything. Unless we could strike directly at the Mature. Then the others – "

"– Would start fighting for first place," supplied Cross. *"But no matter who won, they'd still see us as prey, or pests, or experimental subjects. It might even be worse with them than with the Mature. At least he's keeping the air coming."* He pointed to the duct in the ceiling.

"I wouldn't say he's *doing it,"* said Graham. *"No matter how big he is physically, his attention can't be everywhere at once. There must be a subordinate, or some automatic system, controlling the routine operations – air manufacture, heating, power, whatever makes this thing fly."*

"Maybe we could find that and take it over," Cross suggested.

"We'd have to get out of here first." Graham switched to English. "But you look dead on your feet. Deela too. We can't do anything till those things come back, can we?"

"Uh, no."

"And I still feel a little dizzy. Deela, Ian – "

The boy looked up, eyes glazed, as if suddenly awakened. "What?"

"Let's get some sleep, since there's nothing else to do."

"I'm really hungry," said Deela.

Cross shifted to sit beside her. "We all are, Didi. But let's sleep, now. We may need energy later."

"All right," she said, closing her eyes. In a few minutes she was breathing quietly. Cross out his arm around her. Ken and Ian had closed their eyes too. He rested his head against hers. And let the dreams come in place of reality. . . .

He's a fish. In a school of other fish. Strange fluttering bodies, silversided, yellowtailed, that eddy between the shallow coral reefs like butterflies, turning in unison at an invisible signal, a touch of pressure, flanks glistening like fistfuls of thrown coins in the light that streams golden down from above.

In the midst of the school he swims with them, matching his speed to theirs precisely, effortlessly, turning as he senses the leader turning, a thoughtless and desireless ballet that is beautiful with no thought of beauty. He feels secure in the mass of his fellows. Above, behind, around him. He is one of many. He is not alone.

Needle-thin, barracuda rip in from the sides of the school. Broken bodies flutter a last time and sink as the gap-mouthed shapes tear through. He fights panic, tries to stay with the leader. He will know what to do. But now the leader is gone. He and the other survivors find shelter in a cave, and the barracuda change, their shapes rounder, their silver tarnishing to a dirty gray, and they are gone.

Peering out he sees that the dead fish, mouths open on the blood- and sun-dappled sand, have human faces. Some of them he knows.

They go on. He understands now that they are looking for a place to spawn. Turtles attack, then other predators, and only a few now swim with him, huddled close, a compact body darting through the vastness of the sea.

They reach the spawning ground. It is good land, with fields and green forests with deer, stretching out across the sea bottom.

But waiting for them are the crabs. Eyeless, their shells are rich with heraldic color. They move quickly, pincers held at the ready. Behind them, one enormous crab directs them as they tear at the fish that twist and swim for the land, which shimmers, wavers, and is gone.

Cross is alone. He's no longer a fish but a small furry animal, crouching in fear. The crab is no longer a crab but from above comes the whining shrill croon of an antisubmarine sonar. He burrows into the soil, hearing the up doppler pinging, knowing that they know he is here, in their river. He has no room to maneuver; it's too shallow. He wants to burrow beneath the mud, cover his hull with it, hide from the ever-closer pinging that begins to sound like the whir of a torpedo and at the same time like the alarm-call of the dolphin and the screaming —

He came awake suddenly. The screaming was real. Ian was covering his head with his arms and slamming his body into the wall.

"I-I!" Deela shrieked. They pulled him away from the wall and held him down. Graham forced his head back and looked into the boy's terrified eyes.

"Ian. You all right? You were having a nightmare."

The boy came back from far away and Cross felt the rigid muscles under his hands soften. "Nightmare," he whispered.

"Yeah. Just a bad dream. Lie still a minute. We all get them. I was having one too."

Ian stared up at them. The spare young features turned rigid again. But then his control broke and he shoved Deela away roughly. "You too. Leave me alone, all of you. Let go of me. Get *out* of me!"

"Ian, it was nothing. Just wake up, that's all."

"This was no dream," he muttered. "I was with Joe."

"Wait." Deela placed her fingertips on his arm. "Tell us, I-I."

"He's there." He pointed to the wall. "White light. Pain, terrible pain. And he's *alive*, he *feels it all!*"

"Deela," said Cross, suspicion growing, "Can Ian 'feel' things, too?"

"Why do you think he's so different?" she said. "I-I, I'm gonna tell them. There's no use keeping secrets any more. All right?"

The Kids looked at each other, and something passed between them that was not spoken, or signaled, but known in some manner he couldn't share.

She nodded. "He says all right. Ken, Dink, it's true. Ian can feel. He can even hear thoughts sometimes. He's like a dolphin, sort of. But one of us, too."

"Hear?" said Graham, frowning. "You mean, our thoughts? Mine?"

"Only sometimes – when things are a special way – like they are now with Joe!" Ian's eyes were large, frightened. "He doesn't know I can hear. He can't hear me."

"Why didn't you tell us before?" said Graham gently.

"Because you . . . you think I'm strange, and unfriendly. Well - *I know you*. It's hard for me to stay separate. And you can't talk back."

"All right," said Cross, "But, the Chief. What're they doing to him? Can you see?"

"I just get fragments. He's not how he was. He's not thinking right; he wants to die."

"They must be torturing him," Graham said.

"And we're lying here snoozing." It resolved suddenly in his mind: they were in one room, together, and Svec was somewhere else, alone, in pain. "Damn it, we've got to get to him. We've got to get out of here!"

"How?"

Just that suddenly, it came to him. How a lobster might escape from a tank. He wasted the better part of a second exploring it, positing difficulties. It was a hundred-to-one chance. *No, Dinker. It's not a hundred to one. Maybe more like a million to one.*

He looked around at them. *The last fish*, he thought, a remnant of the dream lingering. *We won't spawn. Or live. That's what the dream meant.*

But they could at least die together. Not one by one for alien delectation.

Lewis, he admitted silently, *your only mistake was that you were too early.*

"Listen," he said, in seatalk. *"I have an idea."*

"Sit on it?" said Deela, making a face.

"That's all. It'll hurt, but you're the best-padded, there, of all of us."

"If it'll help." She crept to the outlet, near the low side of the room. Regarded it for a moment, then turned and put her back to the wall and sat down on the hole.

"Now, the door." Cross, Ian, and Graham gathered around the tightly-sealed sphincter.

And waited. Cross felt the pressure lean on his ears, and cleared them by opening his Eustachian tubes – a trick divers learned early. Ian bobbed his head to do the same thing. Graham yawned. The pressure eased, or seemed to as their ears adjusted, then kept rising.

He kept his eyes on his watch's depth gauge. The reading dropped steadily. He cleared his ears again and did some calculations in his head.

When his gauge read twenty meters the pressure of air in the room would be twice times normal sea level pressure. When it read thirty, it would be three times. At fifty meters, if the pulsing inflow kept on, the door sphincter would be resisting seventy-five pounds of outward pressure, and every square foot of the walls would be resisting over five tons.

The doors and walls were strong. But were they *that* strong?

"Deela, you all right?"

"I'm okay. Just stuck." She grimaced, squatting square on the outlet. But the pressure would build. How long could she stand it?

Though it seemed to be climbing more slowly now. Twenty meters, his gauge read. He swallowed and glanced at Graham. He was staring at the sphincter, a bundle of their clothes in one hand, his pipe lighter ready in the other. Ian looked calm again as he glanced from Deela to the gauge on Cross's wrist. He was crouched, ready to go through first.

A good group of people, he thought. *If you really can hear me, Ian, Deela, it's been good with you. Really good.* And Ken . . . he looked at the dark face, the by-now heavy beard, the alert, intelligent eyes. *You're a hell of a friend.*

"What's the reading, Dink?" Graham interrupted his thoughts.

"Uh, twenty-three meters . . . about seventy feet." Over two tons per square foot. The air was getting hotter. Compression. He dragged sweat from his face with one arm. He glared at the sphincter, willing it to open. So far it had shown no sign of stress.

"There," said Ian. The wall creaked, and began, very slowly, to balloon outward. "Flexible," whispered Graham, touching it.

Cross felt at his waist to be sure Deela's oxygen bottle was still slung there, and heard her moan softly. He glanced back. She was rigid, turning white.

"It really hurts," she moaned. "I'm gonna be bloody back there."

"Just another minute or two," said Cross. "The wall's starting to give."

She can't *get up now,* he thought, looking back at the sphincter, which was still stubbornly closed. *There's too much pressure holding her down.* The only way they could get her off now would be by pulling her skin away. But how much more could she take before she hemorrhaged?

"Give, damn you," he hissed to the wall. "Open up."

The hiss grew louder. The sphincter, letting a thin whistle of air escape to the outside. Cross tore off his wet suit trousers and stuffed them over the opening. They stuck fast, and the hiss stopped.

"It'll go any second," Graham said, beads of moisture standing out on his forehead. "It's got to. It can't stand – "

Part of the wall blew out with a vicious, low bang. A sharp smell bit at their nostrils. Burned their eyes.

"Chlorine!" said Cross. "Ian! Deela! Hold your breath!"

Graham's lighter flared on, burning with preternatural brilliance. The pile of clothing he held it to blazed up as the flame played over them. He and Graham stuffed them through the fluttering rent in the wall as the air sighed out. A flash of flame ignited violently outside as the burning cloth hit nearly pure chlorine.

"Deela?"

"Here." She stumbled into him, holding her rear end with both hands. "Oh, it hurts."

He turned her around and bent, pulling her wet suit down. "Lemme see . . . you'll have some bruising. But the skin's not broken." His eyes were tearing from the chlorine and smoke eddying back in through the hole. "Now, if they're any kind of spaceship designers at all – "

With a thump and a rushing hiss the firelight began to dim. "Wait," said Cross, holding Ian back, readying the oxygen mouthpiece so he could bite it and go. The sibilance slackened. "Now!" he yelled, and followed the boy, who'd leapt through the rent a second before.

Outside, the corridor was full of white fog. Cross crouched, searching for Ian. He spotted him running down a side passage, and followed. *I was right,* he thought. They'd have to have a fire-extinguishing system in a chlorine atmosphere, and the best way was to blanket it with an inert gas.

"Up here!" Ian cried in seatalk. Cross stumbled after him, into a side room.

"Chief?"

"He's here," said Ian.

Cross looked around, blinking through stinging tears; the air still held traces of the deadly gas. The room was the same size as theirs, but the ceiling, for some reason, glowed white, as if more light were needed here. A mass of – equipment? Small animals? Both? – dominated it, grouped around what looked like a large tank, perhaps eight feet long and two deep.

"Oh, my God," he said, looking down into it.

It was the only thing there that could be Svec.

The tank was filled almost to the top with a clear, thick looking liquid. Tubes and tendrils led into it, joining at different points with a complex network of grayish cords, from fine threads to clothesline-size, pegged out in a rough star shape over the bottom. Down the center of the network, for perhaps a yard, stretched a thicker, ropy mass of light gray.

At the top of this lay a naked brain.

"He hurts, he *hurts*," Ian groaned, cowering away from the tank.

"Oh, God," said Cross again. "Joe? Can you. . . . ?"

"He can't hear you," said Ian. "He wants to die. Dinker, he wants it so badly."

"I came to rescue him," said Cross. He looked at the spider's web of gray. "This can't be him. I don't believe it. This is another of their – "

A glint of metal caught his eye. He leaned forward, close to the surface of the liquid.

At the end of one network of gray threads gleamed the slow fire of a ruby, set in silver. Svec's ring.

Cross swung his arm backhanded around the tank. Equipment shattered; tubes pulled free; parts of the array – soft parts – wriggled as they hit the floor and crawled away. He thrust his hand into the liquid. It burned and he snatched it out. He found a broken glasslike tube and probed with it, gritting his teeth.

"He's dead," said Ian at last. Cross dropped the rod, shaking, and turned away, fighting nausea. He couldn't take the oxygen mouthpiece out now, or he'd smother. He made for the door, to find it beginning to contract again.

A rush of gas hissed above them. The burning in his eyes told him it was chlorine.

Ian was behind him, but he seized the boy and pitched him through the aperture first. He had his own legs through when he began to cough. *Got a whiff of it somehow*, he thought. *Joe, I did the only thing I could – can't let myself cough – hope it was right, it was what you wanted –*

The gas scalded his nose and throat. He began to retch and gag. He slid through just as the orifice sealed. But the corridor, as he staggered along it, blurred, then vanished as hydrochloric acid etched his corneas. He screamed.

The mouthpiece dropped free, and he breathed in the burning air.

ELEVEN

The agony pulsed in his ears, his legs, his head. The dark acid ate at his skin, burning, creeping through the apertures of his body to smolder inside him.

Cross tried to breathe, and couldn't. His lungs were filled with some heavy hot fluid. Panicking, he sent messages to his arms and legs to struggle against whatever was choking him.

They didn't move. He screamed soundlessly, strangling.

Yet after a few minutes passed he was still alive. The pain still smoldered, like a banked fire, around and in him. He could not breathe or move. But he was alive.

He tried to open his eyes.

The ceiling above him was white.

He blinked. He seemed to be staring up at it from under several inches of clear fluid. At the lower edge of his vision – he couldn't move his eyeballs – a translucent tube curved downward into his mouth. He could feel vaguely now something filling his mouth and extending down into his throat. The gag reflex wasn't gone – he had a powerful urge to vomit – but the muscles didn't respond.

His eyes burned as the fluid acted on them and he closed them.

Where am I? he thought. White ceiling. Tube. Fluid.

An ominous thought occurred. He flicked his eyes open again.

Yeah. The sides of a tank to right and left. He was lying at its bottom, a lab animal pegged out for dissection.

Like Svec.

Poor Joe, he thought, eyes squeezed tight. To lie here, feeling the flesh being dissolved, sensing this acid creeping inside you, eating away your proud muscles, tender fat, the faithful organs that loved you. . . leaving only the spiderweb gray of the nerves and the pulsing, blind brain . . . and to suffer it alone, alone, alone.

He lay and giggled a little and burned alive. *When they come to inspect the wiring, dissect it and hook in their instruments, will I be sane?* He hoped not. Something was fracturing inside him already, a fault line beginning to quiver and sideslip, some panic discontinuity starting to open up.

The death wish? He'd read it somewhere once . . . Freud, maybe . . . the last instinct. Not so strong as the others, but you only needed it once.

Simply to die would not be so bad. But to live like this, one of Moreau's beasts under the tendrils of the Molders – that was true horror. What would they make from him, what obscure shapeless thing for their amusement, shambling forever in a tiny bubble of oxygen on a chlorine world? On a transformed Earth . . . Earth under the icy malevolence of the Mature.

I'm glad I killed the Chief.
But who will kill me?

Maybe the pain was sharpening his thoughts. Or the treatment stimulated the nervous system, heightening consciousness even as the ego was forced past the edge of sanity. But after a time he discovered that if he concentrated he could think clearly and dispassionately. Recall and consider his past with crystalline clarity.

He felt again the love that had flooded through him when he held little Patty for the first time, smiling down at Pat, while Patricia moved about the hospital room setting things right. He saw Parrish's frightened face and knew they, *he*, had shut Lewis off and driven him over the edge. He saw Sheila's face vague in the dark and realized it was love, not surrender, that had kept her with her beloved dolphins.

Matt Oursler, disappearing in a cloud of roaring black.

Ken Graham, losing what he needed most.

Chief Svec, Navy to the end, bravest of them all.

Ian Silent, talented, but shutting them out to protect himself.

Deela Hunter, and Sheila Klassen. They'd both tried to love him. And what had he done? Pushed them away.

Living and dead they paraded before his closed eyes, and each pointed accusingly at Commander Darrin Cross. Not for what he'd done. For what he'd failed to do.

The key to humanity was love. How could he not have realized. Or inadequately. And always, too late.

He tried to weep.

Something crumpled inside his chest. A hot wave rolled upward from it, like flame from a growing fire.

How long, he wondered, *can it take to die?*

Forever?

Something crackled in his leg. The muscles jerked. Spasmed.

Something crackled, intolerably loud, in his ears.

Cross.

He listened, fascinated. This, then, was what it was to go mad. Brilliant patterns of color burst from the spoken word. They chased themselves in expanding whorls across his closed eyelids.

Can you see me?

His alter ego sounded distinctly odd. At first it had been his own voice. Now it sounded like that of a weps officer he'd known during the War.

The colors faded. *Din . . . din . . . din . . . don . . . don.* Random sounds, distant bells, trickled through his burning brain. Deep inside he felt the fault widen.

I'm losing my mind, he thought happily.

Cross. I get feedback. You should be hearing me.

He snapped his eyes open. The ceiling was white. There was no one there.

You cannot speak. That is to be expected. Yet you can think. And your thoughts are intelligible to me.

To you? Cross thought. *Who are you? A Molder?*

No. The colors were gone now; the voice, still curiously shifting, as if searching his memory for a voice to speak in, seemed to settle now into a youthful contralto, whether male or female he could not tell.

Who are you? I don't recognize you. You must have been captured when they —

No.

He lay still, waiting for it to speak again. Doubt returned. He tried again to move, and failed.

You are still thinking, though your mind should have become dysfunctional by now.

Maybe I'm dead, he thought. *But I didn't think the dead heard voices. Probably I'm just insane.*

You are neither. You are in one of the Molders' tanks, as you seem to have guessed.

He struggled again to move, and failed again. He struggled to speak, and couldn't. Finally he lay still and just tried to formulate a thought. *If you're not a Molder, and not another captive, then . . . what are you?*

I am the Seed.

The Seed, Cross thought. He mulled it over for some time, while the voice in his head waited patiently. *The Seed is a living thing?*

Yes.

It . . . you . . . think?

Evidently.

He recalled everything he'd seen and heard since he and Deela had crawled into the ship. All its processes, door and air supplies and rooms, seemed alive, organic. The Molders derided machine technology. Might their ship by extension be nonmechanical, i.e., alive?

And Deela, and Ian, both had said something around them was alive, that it *felt. . . . .*

Can you feel things? Emotions?

At times.

That makes you different from the Molders, he thought.

There was no answer.

They are your masters?

The Mature is my master. The others, only parasites.

Why are you speaking to me? he thought into the dark under his eyelids. *And how?*

The how is simple. I extended a nerve into your tank. The why is more complex . . . some of the things you do puzzle me. I have not studied your culture as the Molders have.

What things?

An image flashed into his mind, concrete and immediate. He saw himself, choking, running through smoke. It was a curious sort of vision; he could view himself from all angles at once.

A flicker; the scene shifted. Svec. He saw himself raise the jagged tube, slice it down.

Flicker. Saw himself outside, in the corridor, clutching his chest, falling –

Stop. Stop.

Obediently the images faded into the burning dark. The voice resumed. *You accepted death to bring death to the older human. Why?*

He was a friend. Cross groped for the concepts. *He was suffering. I had to help him.*

By killing him?

We knew he was in agony and wanted to die, but couldn't save him. One of us, Ian, can sense such things. If you killed me now I would thank you. Anyone else would do as much, if he couldn't help.

Anyone else, the voice in his head repeated, sounding skeptical. *Can you see a Molder doing so? Caring about the pain of another organism, even of his own race?*

Careful, Cross thought deep within himself. On the surface, he sent, *You don't like them?*

Like? Dislike? They call those the thoughts of a herding animal. The Molders only distinguish, useful; useless. Advantageous; disadvantageous. You think they hate you? Even now, no. They do not have the capacity for hate.

Or for love, thought Cross. *And what about you?*

There was no answer.

Do you hate? Or love?

No answer.

I've gone too far, he thought. *Pissed it off.*

No, it said at last. *I want to discuss it, but I don't know how. The Molder language does not have the concepts, and I am unfamiliar with yours, which I am learning from within your mind.*

There are so many differences between Human and Molder thought. I grew up with the Mature within me, guiding me across space. We made the Great Journey together.

Image of space, black, endless, starless, with only remote ghostlike whirls of light. Galaxies?

We travelled together for centuries. Yet he feels nothing for me. Nor for his offspring. Only for himself. Humans, it seems, act differently.

Sometimes, Cross thought guiltily. *Not always.*

I see something in your mind I seem to recognize, though I have never sensed it in the minds of the Molders. Guilt, you call it.

They have no guilt? With all their crimes?

Not crimes to them. They do what is advantageous without guilt. They are not concerned with the fate of others, whether the Kareen, or the small ones of the eighth planet, or the Humans, or even one of their own. This seems logical to them, and to me also . . . until now, and it still seems logical, but not . . . right.

Not right, thought Cross. His lungs burned. He wanted to shift in his coffin, to escape, to die. Instead he could only think. *What do you mean?*

It is not a Molder concept. Yet it brings back a memory. Something from long, long ago.

The voice trailed off. Cross lay quietly. He opened his eyes and the fluid burned and he closed them again.

What happens in this tank?

The organism is selectively dissolved, leaving structures of interest to be studied. The Molders are fascinated by this trick of telepathy. They want to study the living nervous system.

I have a feeling they won't find anything, Cross thought. *The Talents are a function of sympathy. Like-feelingness, as the dolphins call it. No matter how closely the Molders look, without closeness, they won't crack it. And from what you say —*

Tell me — this sympathy, is this what made you break out, to help the old one?

Yeah. Plus a sizeable helping of desperation.

I see. The voice had taken on a more human quality. As if reminiscing, it went on. *I recall feelings now, I think. Would you like to see the memory?*

Sure.

That suddenly, he was flying. At an incredible speed he dashed across a ridge, dipped over it, banked, and raced along a narrow reddish-rock valley. Updrafts buffeted him. Ahead and behind were his fellows, small dark discs.

The valley ended and he followed-the-leader up the side of a mountain so vertical it was like a scarlet needle. Up, up, the others milling around him and exchanging places. They flashed over the mountain top and fell free, tumbling end over end lazily for endless seconds down through the bright orange sky.

Cross caught the feeling plain. He'd felt it with the young porpoises, and remembered it now from much farther back, sliding at full speed down a long snow-covered hill, the toboggan singing under him, his friends shrieking as they struck the bump and flew free through space. It was joy.

Flicker. He was back in the tank. The ceiling was white, and he burned. *What was that?*

Play.

Those other discs?

Friends. Companions. Playmates.

I see, Cross thought.

The Seeds grouped. Herded.

No wonder it could not understand its masters.

Look, can you tell me more about where you grew up?

Instead, it showed him.

Flicker. From far out in space, a vast orange-red sun. Shadows dot its surface, gigantic sunspots.

A reddish planet spins, dotted with small blue ocean patches. As by a monstrous zoom lens, he's dropped toward it. It swells around him until he hovers, motionless, above a flat ochre plain dotted with neatly-spaced rows of tiny ovoids.

I don't understand.

Flicker. The disks are bigger.

Flicker. They're gone.

Except for one. As he watches, the light-gray domed top of the plant seems to wobble, as if blown by the wind. But there's no wind. The ochre dust lies still.

Then a puff of dust leaps up on one side and the cap leaves its stem, a withered pedestal, and half rolls, half flies a few meters, sliding to a stop in the dirt.

Cross watches, fascinated. The little dome lies motionless. Suddenly, again, a puff of dust, and the gray disc sails up out of it in a graceful curve like a self-propelled frisbee. It tries again and again. Each leap is longer, higher, more controlled. Eventually the cap is flying several hundred meters at a leap. Travelling, apparently, by jet propulsion, using the thin atmosphere as reaction mass.

Flicker. The same scene, almost; but at a different point on the surface. The ground's tumbled rock, veined with yellow and coppery green. Among the shattered boulders more disks graze, feeding. As he watches one lifts and flies off, moving rapidly and purposefully.

Flicker. A single one, meters across, half-submerged in lapping greenish waves. A stir at the ocean's surface shows where it's expelling water.

Flicker. He's one of the discoids now. The red planet reels far below. Above sparkles the starry velvet black of space. He senses the bowl-like curve of the orange horizon as a confinement. A sense of youth and power fills him and he increases thrust, knowing that out there, far away, he'll find the pure minerals his adult appetite will crave. He's not strong enough yet, though. He hovers at the edge of escape velocity, shudders, begins the long tumble back to the surface. The next time, he knows, he'll make it.

But as he nears the surface he becomes aware of something calling. The alarm-transmission of his species. He speeds toward it, tacking to establish its bearing, then homing in, flying low so as not to miss the injured individual.

And an invisible net snares him. Confused, he drops to the ground near the great saucer he recognizes as one of his own kind, though huger than any he's seen before.

Flicker. From the outside now, Cross watches a small disc's skin being cut open, watches the process of bud removal from a Mature, then its careful insertion within the disc's shell. There it will grow with its host, learning to direct its flight, control its growth, Mold it, use it.

The sequence ended. He swallowed. It was clear now what the Seed was, and what the Molders were.

You do not breathe chlorine, then?

We breathe any gas, or none. The chlorine is required by the Molders, but we can generate different atmospheres within our shells.

And your propulsion?

In our life cycle we recapitulate our evolution, as you saw. Squirts of air, first. As we mature the squirt-chambers develop into fusion chambers. We can generate powerful electromagnetic fields, and interstellar hydrogen is plentiful.

Cross tried to put himself in the Seed's place. It had grown up free, with play and companionship. Even, from some overtures in the . . . visions? . . . songs, chants, a culture. Only to be trapped, to have a living master inserted into its body; to feel that parasite growing inside, taking over more and more control . . .

Seed, can the Mature hear us? Does it know what you're thinking?

No. It's linked to my nervous system after it leaves the forebrain. The Mature is in parallel – you understand? – with the afterbrain. If I sense its attention shifting here, I will cut off this nerve I extended.

Wait, thought Cross. *You're losing me. Forebrain? Afterbrain? Who's really in control?*

There was a pause of several seconds before the Seed answered. *This is complicated. Are you sure you want to know?*

It's important. Believe me.

All right, then. The Seeds develop with two brains. You have two also, I believe, though yours are co-located. Ours are separated, since the adult form is so large.

Go on, thought Cross.

The forebrain is my conscious part. The . . . cerebrum? It is located low in the shell and far forward, cushioned in heavy fluid and protected by thick walls.

And the afterbrain?

The motor center is smaller. It controls my physical functions – flight, and the interior activities.

Where is it? Cross was trying to visualize the Seed in cross-section.

Between the fusion chambers somewhere. This may sound strange, but I don't know precisely where.

Cross opened his eyes, feeling a growing excitement. The ceiling was steadily, blindingly white. *You said the Mature controlled you. How? You just follow his orders?*

Partially. But there is direct control, too. A sort of spinal cord runs from forebrain to afterbrain. For most of the way it is well protected. But directly below where the Mature is grafted, the internal sheathing is thin.

When we were grown together, it penetrated this spot with tissue of its own. Its nervous system is intertwined with mine there. Are you following?

Then you're saying, it runs things from then on.

Not exactly. For the most part I am myself. The Mature gives directives and I carry them out.

Can you disobey?

Not as long as he is there. He will take back control. And there will be pain.

He punishes you?

Yes, with overtones of remembered agony.

I think I get it now, thought Cross. He tried to imagine how it felt: to have a master inside you, like a horse with a human rider, but one living within you, subsisting on your flesh and controlling every action. For . . . centuries? He marveled the Seed's mind still functioned.

Why did you contact me? he asked it.

Curiosity. As I said, I have never spoken with another life form than the Molders.

All right. Cross sensed this, now, was their very last chance. *Do you want me – or us – to free you from your master?*

No. The answer was immediate, as if instinctive.

Then why did you contact me?

Just . . . to talk. As I said.

Do you enjoy carrying them around inside you, controlling you?

A pause. Then, *There are certain functions they perform. By now I am so molded as to need them. I could not cross space, for example, without their navigational help.*

Cross stared up at the ceiling, trying to ignore the pain. This was the crux of the argument – an argument he had to win. If the Seed, the living ship itself, could be turned against the Molders – even if it lacked complete control, if the Mature were, in case of conflict, dominant – maybe, somehow, he could get free and reach the others.

Then answer this, he thought fiercely. *Do you enjoy helping them enslave and kill?*

His mind recoiled at the emotion, stronger even than his own fear and pain, that came flooding across from the strange being around him.

It was guilt.

So you do feel it, he thought. *I pity you. To have to watch it all, and be unable to stop it . . . that would really be torment.*

The Seed sent, *You are the first being I have been able to speak with. I knew something evil was happening. But I did not comprehend its magnitude. To kill whole planets, full of life.*

You'll help us, then, Cross thought eagerly. *To get free, and free you if we can?*

A pause. *It could mean . . . never going to space again. But I will try.*

The corners of his mouth twitched as triumph overcame the pain; then it turned to worry. What if he couldn't move? What if too much of his body had already been dissolved?

It hasn't. I diluted the solvent. And that liquid in your chest is a healing fluid, stimulating new growth in the alveoli. Your lungs were almost completely destroyed.

What? You had this all figured out!

No. At first I wanted only to talk. Do you want to know what decided me to help you?

If you want to tell me.

When you tried to feel like me. What you call . . . sympathy. Do you have any idea how many centuries it has been?

He didn't, so kept quiet.

The Seed said, *I'm releasing you now. Try the legs first.*

He pulled up his left leg first, and then the right. They hurt viciously when he moved them, but they responded. The motion sent slow wavelets coursing through the fluid above his eyes. He flexed an arm. It worked too and suddenly he could stand it no longer. In one jerk pulled the throat-piece out and sat up in the tank. retching and coughing a salty pinkish liquor over the side.

Don't get up yet. You'll break the tendril. We'll need to communicate in some other way.

"Can't you hear me when I talk out loud?" said Cross hoarsely.

Quiet. I can, but so can He.

How about Ian? Deela? They're in tanks too, aren't they? And Graham?

I've already spoken with the one called Ian.

That's great. Are they — they're not being hurt, are they?

Not at present. I delayed their processes, while you and I talked.

Good. Now listen. Ian can 'hear' me mentally. Once you tune in to him, maybe he'll be able to communicate with you even without the nerve connection. His talent is . . . superhuman. That'll keep you informed as to what I'm doing, at least.

What will you be doing?

First I'll rejoin the others. Social animals, remember?

I would do the same.

Also humans fight better together. After that, we'll play it by ear. How do I find them?

I'll open your door. You'll be in a corridor. Go right, then left in the next corridor.

Chlorine?

I'll take care of that. The Molders often work in corrosive atmospheres.

Can you open their doors? The other humans?

If the Mature doesn't interfere. Once he suspects trouble, though, he'll take control. Then I won't be able to help.

Got it. Tell the others to get ready. I'm coming.

Something delicate snapped as he stood, and the voice was suddenly gone. A gossamer-light fabric fell from the ceiling. It shriveled, tightening around him, a loose, baggy suit of the same transparent film he'd seen before. He climbed stiffly from the tank to the floor, balancing with his arms. He searched the room, and found – great good luck – Deela's oxygen bottle. He bit through the film to insert the mouthpiece.

He examined his body through the suit. His skin was raw; even the diluted solution had stripped off the outer epidermis, leaving him red and tender as a newborn. He rubbed his head, grimaced. Bald as Joe Svec had been, too.

The door dilated. He walked to it with quick nervous steps and peered cautiously out. The corridor was empty.

Here goes, he thought, and stepped through.

This passage was greenish-gray, flecked with striations of a yellowish hue. The floor yielded under his feet. Right first. He passed several closed sphincter-doors. Best not to think what might lie behind them.

There, another corridor, intersecting the first. He slowed as he reached the junction. All clear. He breathed out and turned the corner. Then froze as a sphincter dilated open directly in front of him.

A Molder paused halfway through it, obviously just as startled.

Cross reacted first. The creature tried to roll aside but was caught awkwardly as the door snapped closed on it. He mentally blessed the Seed as he reached the thing.

Had to be quick. He got both hands under its edge, feeling the tentacles tear at his fingers, and flipped it. The "mouth" was exposed, gaping, ready to cry out. He stepped into it, feeling the soft cartilage buckle and give, the flesh beneath squish. Tendrils whipped wildly at his foot.

Finally they stopped. He backed off, looking down. Then past it, through the door from which it had emerged. A transparent box, an aquarium, perhaps, filled with a violet liquid. In it a shape floated, neither human nor animal. An enormous fleshy ring that seemed to be blindly groping about its tank. . . .

He turned and pelted down the corridor, panting.

Halfway down it he fell to hands and knees. The floor was tilting under his feet. He scrambled up.

Dinker. Get against the wall to your left. Quick.

What? Is that you, Ian? He looked frantically around the empty passage.

The Seed's talking to me.

You're working together?

Yes, listen. The Mature's ordered it to get ready for space.

Ian — how can you talk to me? I'm not a Talent. I can't receive —

You're receiving now, aren't you? Dinker, I think we've been wrong about a lot of this. You do have Talent. Every human does, only their nervous systems aren't . . . cleared. The tanks, that fluid in them —

A jolt ran through the hull, and the floor began to vibrate in a strange rhythm.

Dinker, against the wall!

He slammed himself against gray-green and waited, sucking oxygen. He wondered how much more the tank held. A little air was trapped under the film, around his body, but not enough to sustain him for more than a few breaths.

The shuddering increased. The jolting became worse. The Seed was starting to move, sliding along the frozen ground. Of Dvina Island — he'd almost forgotten where they were. The deck bumped and jolted again, then suddenly jerked upward. He grew light, then heavy again. The wall behind him seemed to tilt back.

The acceleration increased. He grunted involuntarily as patterns of light burst behind eyeballs suddenly ten times heavier. The air wheezed from his lungs. A Molder rolled out of the corridor he'd just left and struck the wall with a sodden thump that split it open. It lay twitching obscenely, and a dark liquid oozed from it.

Then, as suddenly as it had come, all weight was gone, and he was floating away from the wall. *Ian. What's going on?*

The boy's thought came back instantly. *We're coasting, a hundred klicks up. A suborbital jump. Free fall for ten minutes. Then it will rotate and thrust the other way.*

Where are we going?

The Caribbean, Seed says.

Cross, drifting toward the opposite wall, tensed with premonitory horror. *The Caribbean! Why?*

Apparently the Mature found out about Sheila and the interns. And our Delphinius sapiens. He wants to be sure we're all wiped out. He plans to use your bomb.

It'll do the job, Cross thought. *Anywhere within two or three kilometers. But how did he find out?*

The Seed says the other, the first one, told him. It means Svec, I think. But, Dinker, he'd never do that. The Chief wouldn't —

I don't think he had much of a choice, Ian. You saw what was left in that tank. How long could you stay sane? Wouldn't you answer any question to make it stop? We only got a little taste of what these creatures can do.

There was no answer. Cross bit his mouthpiece in frustration as the wall drifted slowly closer. The weightlessness was like being in the sea again.

Ian, still there?

Yes.

Get out of your tank. Are the others with you?

Deela's here. Ken must be in another room.

Get out of your tank. The Seed will give you a suit and open the door.

Dinker. . . what are you trying to do? Are you trying to get to the Mature? What then? I want to help, but —

Then listen, thought Cross. The wall was almost within his reach; in a moment more he'd be able to move. *Listen, Ian, and pass this to the Seed. I've got an idea.*

TWELVE

t last. His fingers, straining outward, touched the wall. He spun himself clumsily in mid-air.

Ian. Ask the Seed to open your door.

An aperture dilated across the corridor from him almost as he finished the thought. He aimed and jumped, gripped the door's rim, and pulled himself inside.

The Kids were waiting, both dripping, pink-skinned and bald from the tanks. Deela opened her mouth, but Cross put a finger to his lips. He nodded to Ian, who was already encasing himself in the pliable membranes. The boy's relief at seeing him flooded into his mind. *Dinker! So glad to see you. Ken's in the next room. Should we —*

No time, thought Cross brusquely. *Ask the Seed when we're landing.*

In nine minutes.

The Mature will bomb the Station from the air?

Not till he's located it. Don't think that'll take long, though. You said you had an idea.

A pretty simple one, I'm afraid. Cross looked around the chamber. The festoon of equipment above the tanks caught his eye and he pushed himself toward it. *We've got to kill the Mature. But we have to break his control first.*

How?

The Seed mentioned a nerve trunk that taps its version of a spinal cord. That's how the Mature runs the ship. He can override what it does, but till he realizes something's going on, the Seed can help us.

There, he saw something that might serve: a curved piece of fairly stout metal, around which the curious half-living instruments of the Molders twined. He stripped them off, watched them wither and die, and flourished the bar in mid-air. The end was even reasonably sharp. He sent it sailing across the room to Ian. *You get to cut the link. The Seed should be able to direct you to it.*

Ian communicated surprise. *But what are you going to do, Dinker?*

D'you think the Mature's going to let us hack away without trying to stop us? So we need a diversion. Cross's lips twitched. *That'll be me.*

A new thought came, with a new flavor, different overtones. It wasn't like Deela's voice, but he could tell instantly that it was she. *Dink, how about me? I can help.*

He hesitated, considering. Another distraction, at a different point in the ship? No; the one he was planning should be sufficient, if anything was.

Yes, you can do something. I need you to stay here, be our reserve. Can you contact the Seed? Talk to it like Ian can?

Yes.

Both Kids could, yet he couldn't. Well, they'd started with higher Talents in the first place. *The seconds are ticking by,* he reminded himself. No time to wonder, no time to think. Time left only to act.

And all too little of that. He looked to Ian. *Any questions? We've got to get moving.*

I guess not, Dink. The boy's thoughts "felt" scared, but the same fierce pride that had kept him silent for so long came through too. *He'll do,* Cross thought.

Then we're on our way. Keep in touch. He pointed himself for the door, twisted to pass through it.

Too late, outside, he realized he hadn't found a weapon for himself. He half-turned, but Ian was already through and the aperture was closing. Seconds counted now. Not only were they coasting at the top of the suborbital arc, but, sealed in the suit, even Ian could hold his breath only so long.

Cross turned again. He had no idea, really, which way led up, but jumped hard anyway, sailing his body down the length of the corridor. Catching, as he leapt, a last glimpse of Deela, raising a hand to wave goodbye.

How could I be so blind about so much, he thought, sailing free.

The far of the passageway loomed ahead, curving, tapering toward . . . up? His only clue to up or down was the darker hue of the veined floor. If the opposite face was the ceiling, he should be at the outside edge of the circular hull. He had to stay with it, moving around its circumference, until he found a way up.

Then a quicker solution came to mind. *Ian. Ask the Seed which way to the Mature? Afraid I'm lost.*

He blinked twice, surprised. For a moment there he'd *been with* the boy. Had been receiving an incredibly detailed sensory image, not words, but a perception of the boy's surroundings through every sense. A corridor not unlike the one he was in, but narrower, lower, darker. Ian was pulling himself along it. Then came the thought, in words. *Dink. Hurry. Seed says we're on our way down; seven minutes to landing now.*

Can't he slow the descent?

Not without alerting the Mature.

How do I get to the dome? Can he see me, tell me how to get there?

A second's pause, then: *You're headed okay. Keep going and the Seed will open the right door.*

Cross hoped so. He pushed off, using the closed sphincters as handholds, as Ian had been doing. *Was* doing. The boy could transmit more than thoughts, that had been a whole experience. Was it inadvertent? Because he was becoming more finely attuned to Ian? Or had the Kid been deliberately holding himself back all along, to avoid overwhelming his companions?

A sphincter popped open ahead. He snagged it with an arm as he coasted by, and braced, ready for an attack. No

Molder emerged. He pulled on through and sucked a deep breath. The tanked oxygen was cold and dry in his mouth.

He was in one of the ramps, leading up. But a wave of dizziness staggered him suddenly. The Seed's treatment had regenerated him but he still felt weak. He looked at his empty hands. If only he had a weapon.

Ian. You there?

Here, Dink. No image this time; only words.

Progress?

Almost there, Seed says. Let you know when I reach it.

Cross forced himself into motion again. He pinballed up the ramp from wall to wall. At the top, a sphincter snapped open. He drifted the last few feet, braked with his hands, and brought his eyes slowly level with the edge of the opening.

He was looking upward, halfway back along the dome. The vast, multicolored bulk of the chief Molder was plainly visible. Ranged before it – between it and him – were the smaller Molders, in rows, perched at the tables. A subdued gabble filled the dome, the high-pitched, rapid speech of dozens of them. He sank back into the hatch till only his eyes emerged. The seconds dragged by.

Ian? he thought again.

In reply, a vision.

No other word for it. The boy was cramped in near-darkness, crouched beneath a low ceiling, confined by smooth cool walls. He twisted, and saw, above him, a slender whitish cord that emerged from a perforation in the grayish fabric. It looped downward, then seemed to grow seamlessly into a ridge that ran the length of the compartment's floor.

And he noticed something more. It was getting harder to breathe. He needed air, not yet desperately, but he felt stifled. He sucked greedily at the mouthpiece until he remembered he was seeing through Ian's mind, feeling Ian's sensations, not his own.

The boy's power was incredible.

Dink?

Here.

Does this look like it?

Are you in the right place?

Seed says so. Cut it?

Wait one. He bobbed up for another look. All seemed quiet around the Mature. No untoward commotion among the smaller aliens. Maybe this would be easier than he'd expected. *Yeah. Cut it. Now.*

The vision: Ian poised the pointed metal, then plunged it in. Cross felt the shock in his own wrists. The whitish cord, thick as his arm, was tougher than it looked. The blade only scraped its covering. *Again. Hard as you can,* he sent. His own muscles jerked as he tried to help.

The vision blanked then. He came back to himself and found to his dismay that his involuntary movement had drifted the upper part of his body through the opening and into view.

"I see you, Human. Stop there, where you are."

The hollow tones of the Mature boomed from the walls of the dome. Cross twisted in midair as he approached the great overhead arch and grabbed for one of the ribs that stiffened it. He turned to face the thing.

The Mature seemed far vaster from above. Grotesque protrusions erupted here and there from the swelling particolored bulk. *It's budding already,* he thought.

A movement nearby caught his eye and he turned and kicked savagely at a Molder creeping up behind him. Its tendrils lost their grip and it sailed end over end across the interior of the dome.

When he turned his attention back to the Mature, the surface between them seemed to have come alive. Molders, large, small, from ten-footers down to tiny ones scarcely the size of serving plates, were hurrying to place themselves between him and their master. As he watched, a ripple of agitation spread through their ranks. A few lost their grips and tumbled, writhing in space.

What's happening, Ian?

I'm . . . almost through. The outside's tough but the inside's different, soft. Dinker — only another couple minutes till we land!

The molders — they look like they're in trouble.

Seed says it was able to release some oxygen into the dome. Not enough: the Mature caught it happening and cut it off. I think . . . he and the Seed are fighting, somehow.

Get that cord cut!

But they're off guard now, Dink. Wade into 'em!

With what, my hands? Still, he had to distract the Mature, to give Ian and the Seed a fighting chance.

He started forward, hauling himself from rib to rib. A greenish Molder launched itself at him and he ducked. It sailed past, and he had a momentary glimpse of its underside, 'mouth' open, fringed by wriggling tendrils.

Two more came on. One pointed a rectangular instrument, and Cross flinched as his oxygen bottle grew hot against his skin; then he reached it, and wrenched the thing from the creature's tendrils. As a projector, it was useless, since he had no idea how to operate it, but in a simpler weapon mode — as a bludgeon — it made a satisfying crunch as he smashed through the tough exoskeleton. His second attacker managed to rip the film over his leg before he killed it. The chlorine burned his bare skin. Cross pinched the tear together and the stuff shriveled and healed itself, sealing the hole.

More Molders, a phalanx, crept toward him over the curve of the dome. Their ranks sagged as he headed for them; the sight of two companions killed in as many seconds, Cross thought, must have impressed them. Still, clinging to the surface upside-down, stuck to the ceiling by their tendrils in some fashion, they could navigate faster weightless than he could. He had to choose his handholds carefully.

Or did he?

The Molders closed in, a ragged ring. *They have to hold fast,* he thought. *Their 'fingers' are all on one side. Upside-down, they're helpless.*

He wedged himself against a rib. *Ian. How long until deceleration?*

Fifteen seconds, came back sharp and clear.

Dinker – a new thought – *It's Deela. I'm listening. You're in danger. Can't I help?*

No. Stay where you are. He aimed himself like an arrow, gauging the distance, and as the first Molder reached him he jumped.

He rotated slowly in space as the obscene mass of the Mature swelled in front of him. *Four thousand. Five thousand. Six,* he counted. Then tucked and somersaulted clumsily and hit feet first.

Its shell, as he'd expected, was thinner than on the smaller creatures, and his feet broke through to sink into a pulpy mass beneath. He began flailing at the curved surface with the projector.

He expected a bellow of rage and pain, but the Mature only quivered. Below him its tendrils, big as fire hoses, flailed upward for a grip. He edged away from them.

Ian's thought. *Here it comes.*

Weight hit him, mashing him into the gigantic creature. He was stuck face down in the mass, as if glued there. The acceleration increased. The smaller Molders, he guessed, would be static now, grappled down tightly to the inside of the shell.

"You cannot harm me this way," a distant voice said. Under ten g's the Mature sounded strained, laboring. Its breath puffed through a great spiracle, big around as Cross's wrist, at the crest. "But now I know keeping humans, even for experimental purposes, is not worth the effort."

Coming up on landing now, Dink . . . there! I've cut it!

"But you will precede the others," said the Mature.

"You're wrong," wheezed Cross. "You're not in charge anymore. We've set your slave-ship free!"

"The nerve trunk, you mean?" said the inhuman voice. "You do not think ahead. That is why your race is extinct. Did you really believe there would be no backup, no redundancy, in my control?"

Backup, redundancy? He stared at the spiracle, an arm's length away. *Ian, look around. Is there another trunk, maybe smaller –*

"I am still in control of the essentials. To regrow full mastery will take a day."

Nothing here, Dinker. Maybe farther forward, but it's too narrow for me to reach —

"So, you see, human, you've lost."

"Oh, yeah?" Cross felt childishly angry, and at the same time childishly impotent. Here he was, actually lying on the Mature, deceleration pressing him into its gruesome flesh. Yet he was still powerless to harm it, unable to stop the alien air from wheezing in and —

He looked at the spiracle, gaping open, the chlorine atmosphere of the dome rushing into it at arm's length from him.

"Oh, yeah," he said.

With a great effort he brought up his arms, unslinging the oxygen tank. He took a last deep sweet breath, then pulled the hose free and turned the valve wide open. Pure oxygen gushed out.

He waited for the creature to inhale, and jammed the bottle, nozzle down, into the spiracle.

The bulk beneath him quivered. A deep grinding sounded from within. The spiracle contracted, then dilated. Cross took advantage of the widening to hammer the bottle in farther with a fist. "You wanted oxygen. Wanted our air. Take it! Breathe it!"

"Human . . . remove it. I will release you. I will free you all."

He didn't bother to answer. Just hung on grimly. Jamming the oxygen tank down even farther, leaning his weight on it as what seemed to be muscular responses around the nostril tried to push it out.

The ship shuddered, then pitched. The deceleration lessened.

Ian. Something wrong?

Seed says Mature's losing control. It's trying to slow our descent, but . . . we're falling. The sea —

Suddenly they were weightless again. Cross floated free, but kept his death grip on the bottle. The Mature heaved. He held on, pounded on the tank, forcing it in deeper, glaring at the discoids crawling toward him over the hulk of their master.

A high-pitched trill, the Molders' normal speech, came from the Mature.

"You don't have to obey him anymore!" shouted Cross. "He's dying! You're free!"

It was a gamble, but his words had an effect. The Molders paused, as if torn between their hatred of their oppressor and their fear of what might happen without him.

The quivering bulk began to buzz. The ship gyrated. Cross clung desperately to the bottle. He swallowed to abate a growing need for air.

Hold on. We're close to impact, Ian sent.

They slammed down. Cross lost his grip and was knocked to the floor. The Seed rocked. The greenish light flickered, then went out, except for a feeble glow from overhead.

We've crashed, came a frightened thought. *The Seed's not answering. I think it's hurt.*

The shadow of a Molder loomed over him. He kicked feebly, toppling it. Something cold licked at his legs in the gloom. *Are you all right?*

Bruised but okay, came Ian's thought. *The lights went out. Where are you?*

In the central dome. I'm breathing air from inside the suit; I can't last long. Take Ken and Deela and try to find a way out.

The cold reached his waist. In the dark he could hear the cries of the Molders. One brushed him as it rushed by. The floor moved under him in a familiar rhythm. He put his hand down into the cold, and discovered what it was.

Water's coming in, he sent.

Must be a hole somewhere. It's rising here, too.

Another mind came into the circuit: *Dinker. I'm coming. I don't care what you say.*

Forget me, Deela. I'm finished. Get out of here!

The water lapped over his head. He struggled for air. None left inside his envelope; he was breathing his own carbon dioxide, hot, fetid in the dark. Colored lights began to pinwheel in front of his eyes.

Something touched him and he thrashed, then went limp. *Help*, he cried within himself, despairing. *Anyone, help. . . .*

The thing released him, gripped him again, and penetrated the film to touch his mouth.

The lips were warm, sweet, exhaling a breath of air he sucked down gratefully.

"Are you all right?" said Deela, letting up on him. "Oh, God. Are you hurt?"

"Okay," he managed, in seatalk, to conserve air. *"Look, I think we're sinking. If the Seed's dead —* "

No, it's alive. Ian's thought. *Just knocked out by the impact. But it says there's a crack in its shell.*

Cross blinked. In the dimness he could make out a hint of blue to one side. "Deela — is that a breach?"

"It's a hole. Swim for it?"

"Go for it," Cross said, coughing. *Ian, we're leaving.*

Yeah, get out! I'm going back for Ken.

They swam for the patch of blue. Deela fended off a round form that milled by, tendrils whipping frantically at the rising sea.

Something long slid past the hole, eclipsing the blue light for a moment. He stopped swimming, groped to grab Deela's foot. Another streamlined shape slid past. "Hold up, Didi."

The Seed was tilting, the water-air interface above them taking on an angle. They found a niche where the ribs of the roof intersected and huddled back-to-back, watching the breach. The light inside the shell flickered, brightening and dimming, on and off.

The first long torpedoshaped silhouette swam deliberately in through the hole in the hull. Cross pulled Deela to him. Another shark drifted lazily in, the rounded dorsal and rigid pectorals showing plainly in the blue sealight as it swung its nose up and opened its mouth to engulf a frantically swimming Molder.

Cross sought Ian's mind. *Ian, get yourself and Ken to cover. There are sharks in the main dome!*

The first few ourslerii to enter cruised slowly around the inside of the shell, taking the swimming Molders one by one. But as more thronged in they grew excited, swimming erratically, jerkily, backs arched. Beginning the characteristic pattern of the frenzy. The light flickered on and off.

"I thought we were safe there, for a minute," said Deela. She groped for his hand.

Cross kicked away a whitetip that rushed at them. It whipped onward, struck at a smaller shark that was worrying a long strip of flesh, and disappeared into the flickering dance.

The Mature . . . a stray thought from Ian.

Cross watched the wriggling knot of sharks fastened to the bulk. They'd bitten through the membrane and were trepanning off neat round chunks of alien flesh. But others, swimming away, were writhing, suddenly disgorging what they'd just wolfed in violent paroxysms. *Yeah,* Cross thought, *enjoy the chlorine. Hope you all choke on it.*

— Ian, it's dead. Stay where you are. We've got a full-on feeding frenzy up here. How's our friend doing?

Getting back control. It's sealed our room. Pumping in oxygen. Apparently it can generate it from sea water.

How about the hole?

The floor began to tilt again, this time toward the breach. A rumble reverberated through the water.

Tilting to put the hole down. Will blow the water clear. Wants to know how you are.

Need air bad. Anything with oxygen in it.

"Hold tight," he told Deela. They braced themselves in the ribs as the Seed tilted farther.

Suddenly the lights came on again. His ears pained sharply, and they were breathing air again. He gulped it in gratefully. It tasted strange, but satisfied his lungs even as his head reeled.

"Look," said Deela.

Below them the rounded fins of *Carcharhinus ourslerii* made vicious tight circles in the green- and red-stained water. As the water level sank, forced out by air pressure, they dropped with it, sucking out at last through the breach like tadpoles down a drain.

A film formed over the hole. Another began to grow over that, then another, binding one to the next, swiftly growing opaque.

He looked around the inside of the dome. Shreds of flesh, empty shells, the mangled, convulsing bodies of torn and poisoned sharks, lay in the projections of the floor. In the curved niche where the Mature had reigned was only a tattered, stinking mass of gnawed flesh.

"Is it over?" said Deela.

"Yeah." Cross's voice trembled and he could barely control his legs. "It's over. Now let's go find the others."

THIRTEEN

An hour later Cross was outside, frog-kicking through the sea seventy meters down.

The deep blue-gray light blurred his unprotected eyes. It danced over huge inchoate shapes: the domes and tubes of the Station. A minute more, a few strokes more, then he arrowed upward

He broke the surface in Lock III, and gasped in a breath. The air here was heavy, humid. He suspected it was oxygen-deficient, too. And the interior was strangely dim.

A splash. Deela surfaced beside him.

"Where's Ken?" he said aloud, not *thinking* it, just out of habit.

"Arguing with the Seed about some scientific stuff. Said not to bother him."

They pulled themselves up onto the platform. The overhead lighting panels glowed dully, nearly extinguished. The batteries were nearly dead.

And what he breathed was making his heart race, though he was panting in great lungfuls. Dizzy, he leaned against the bulkhead, against the racks that held the Mark 39s.

The Mark 39s . . . he straightened and checked the dials on one, Parrish's. It was full. He swung the pack down, donned it, and cracked a valve. The mix tasted stale, but it was better than the murk around them.

Deela? Air here.

Don't need it, Dink. Thanks.

Of course; she was comfortable down to ridiculously low oxygen levels. But . . . the others? Sheila? The dolphins? Heather and Roger? He burst into a limping sprint, the steel gratings in the passageways clattering under his bare feet.

No one in the kitchen, or the dining area. He pelted on into the next cylinder. Here the lights were completely out. The control room was dark too, eerie, with only the light from the big pressure-resistant window rippling over the banks of instruments and desks and. . . .

And a human figure, slumped in the chair before the window. Klassen's rounded, voluptuous body. He rushed over to feel her neck, hoping for a pulse. Her skin was warm. A pulse, but weak and irregular. Her breathing was so shallow as to be almost imperceptible.

"Sheila," he said, and shook her. The softness of her shoulders, the smell of her hair, were so familiar he nearly wept.

She opened sleepy eyes. "Hi, Dink," she murmured. Then her head drooped again.

He unslung the breather and stuck the backup mouthpiece between her lips, thumbing the overflow valve. Air sighed. Her chest rose and fell more easily. A few seconds later, her eyelids fluttered open again. She coughed and pulled the mouthpiece free.

"You came back," she whispered. "What . . . where – "

In ten unconscionably abbreviated sentences he explained everything. Her eyes widened at his description of the Seed. "It's outside, now? Waiting?"

"Out by the main lock."

She tried to get up, but fell back. "Oh, God. So weak. The last air ran out yesterday. I was too muzzy to think of the breathers. Give me another pull. No, give me a hug, that's what I need, you son of a bitch!"

He knelt by the chair and embraced her.

"Sorry," she said at last. "I thought I'd never wake up again."

"Don't apologize. I'm glad to see you, too."

"Are you?"

"Very."

"The Kids? Ken? The Chief?"

Cross lost his smile. "Ian and Deela and Ken are all right. Bruises aside. Joe . . . he didn't make it. I'll tell you how it happened later.

"How are your friends and mine, Sound-of-Ship-Going-Over and the other happy dolphins of Navidad Bank?"

"Oh, not so happy. I was out for the last time yesterday." She tried again to get up, and this time made it. "As the batteries ran out they got less and less to breathe. Some were talking about going up, to the air . . . we've got to get them some oxygen. This . . . Seed, you say, can supply it?"

"All we want." Steadying her, he had to smile. Same old Sheila. Her first concern was for her beloved dolphins.

Steps rattled in the corridor. Deela looked anxious, but squealed when she saw Klassen. The two hugged. "Sheila! I'm so glad you're all right. Wait till you hear what we did! We – "

"Good grief, what happened to your hair? Never mind, you're here. Hold it, now – I've got to go out and check on my babies." Klassen held the girl at arm's length. Saying, with the trace of a sob, "But I'm so happy to see you, too, Didi." She kissed her, then broke free and went on down the corridor.

Deela and Cross looked at each other. He took a deep breath, gripping her shoulders. "Look. You were great out there. On Dvina. But we need to talk."

"What about?"

"Look. Between us? Short version: Forget it."

"I won't take it back," she said stubbornly. "I said I loved you. And you said you loved me. Back in the Seed. When we thought it was all over."

But this time it wasn't just words. Now he could sense the emotion behind them. Feel it clear and complete, and it warmed his soul. "Yeah, I said that. I won't take it back. I *do* love you, kiddo. But there are all different kinds of love. It's more complicated than you realize now. But you will."

She stiffened and her expression went hard. Thoughts alone, now. No words. *It's Sheila, isn't it. You were with her before we left. And now we're back, so —*

No. It isn't that. He took her hand. *I want you to be my . . . daughter.*

Your daughter? There, a smile at last. *Hey. Dad. Can I have a breath now?*

He pulled the Mark 39 over, and they shared. *Yeah, I love you, And I, well, love Sheila too. And Ian, and Ken, and Roger, and Heather . . . there's a future now. We should face it as a family.*

Her hand squeezed his. More and more emotions seemed to be finding their way to his mind, the intimacy of the real Deela-inside-her-head. Would it be like this with everyone? Now that the Seed could cure their minds of the separateness that had always been the deepest and most ineradicable curse of the human condition?

Tears burned his eyes. He remembered a sunny day long ago . . . an afternoon in the sun, warm flower-scented air, the bedroom of a house now long abandoned even by shadows. He remembered green eyes and yellow hair, and Pat, and Patricia, and the child they'd all three shared and loved. Remembered, but no longer regretted. Felt only a distant bittersweet pain.

Just then, Deela giggled. She was looking at the arrangement of shells and dried starfish she'd constructed in the passageway.

"What?" he said aloud.

"This silly old thing. It's really not art. Actually, it's really ugly, isn't it? But I bet I can do better. With some more practice."

He grinned at her. *Truly,* he thought, *Oursler wrought well.*

Dink? Ian, almost painfully loud in his head.

Yeah?

I'm out at the Annex. Want to see?

He was confused for a moment, then realized what the boy meant. *Sure,* he thought. *Show me.*

And suddenly he was *there*. The low, vaulted concrete roof; the blue near-darkness; the steamy, humid, animal-rank air; the pop*whoosh* and splash and restless milling of the black fishlike bodies that weren't fish at all. He saw, then heard, smelled, felt. He was *there,* immersed to his neck in the sea. The only odd thing was the way his hand came up to caress a sleek rounded back without his own mind's command.

They're all right?

Human shapes swam among the dolphins. Comiskey, Johnson, their strong bodies as naked and unashamed as the animals they tended. But Heather looked heavier, moved a little more deliberately. Could she be . . . pregnant? A few feet away, face partially concealed by her mask, Sheila was letting her breather free-flow to replenish the air.

I'll let you see for yourself, came Ian's thought back. *Ready?*

Ready for what?

And then without warning he was through, past the boy's mind, melding seamlessly into *that of the dolphin*; and his own universe dissolved.

He hung poised in the sea, streamlined body huge around him but familiar, even graceful; the feel of his tongue against long rows of conical teeth *right;* the automatic twitch of a flipper to keep himself on an even keel *right;* the satiated, excellent feel of fish filling his belly. The memory fresh of how he'd stalked the squid, struck, then recited the Ceremony-after-eating. He flexed his broad lovely tail, exulting in the raw power of his flanks and his lovely, lovely flippers.

And it was more than physical. He was in a different universe, not the primate universe of things-seen but the vast cetacean universe of sounds-heard, a most inhuman and unstable but brilliantly right kind of world. One that flowed through him and that he flowed with in a joy so intense he suddenly saw why porpoises always seemed to be smiling.

The joke-thought seemed to break some link. Before he could resist it he was back in Ian's mind and then again in less than the blink of an eye back in his own everyday oh-so-normal human body. Deela was gripping his arm in the passageway, looking up at him. "Dinker, you all right? You seemed to, well, go away there for a minute."

He looked down at her, wordless. Never again, he thought, will man or woman or child be alone. Never again will they have to live imprisoned in a single self, crying out for love, for the simple recognition of existence, for compassion. That long night was over. Now human beings would know one another – would *know*, because they could *be* that other.

And not only man to man, but man to dolphin, man to Seed, man to woman.

"Yeah, I was away," he said, smiling down at her.

"But now I'm back."

POSTSCRIPT

*L*og-keeping is, for Commander Darrin Cross, USN, too old a habit to break, I guess.

Accordingly, this is the first entry in the log of Pilgrim II. *Of the Seed, and of what's left of the human race.*

We're in orbit, finishing last-minute computations to decide where we're heading.

To bring things up to date: After we helped the Seed with repairs, and cleaned up the central dome, we all got together and figured out some modifications.

The dome's now an enormous saltwater aquarium. With room for all the dolphins, plus a generous breeding and eating stock of plants and fish.

The chambers below are for us humans. We've moved in the Station library, a lot of equipment, even the Chief's still. Though our host assures us a Seed can produce better stuff than any crude assembly of boilers and tubes.

It'll be tough to leave. But both Graham and our new host agree that with our present knowledge we can't reverse the processes the Mature started. Earth's atmosphere will degrade to about 70% nitrogen, 25% chlorine, and four per cent oxygen. Nothing we could live in, though some forms of life will adapt, and eventually spread.

But the Seed assures us blue water-oxygen planets aren't that uncommon; and most are unpopulated – in our galaxy, especially, since the Mature was the first Molder to get here.

At the speeds we can travel, with a time-dilation factor, it'll take only a year or two between stars. We'll find and found a new Earth. One where human, dolphin, and Seed can flourish together — a symbiosis based on friendship, rather than on parasitism, as was the Molders'.

There probably will be more of them coming. But there must also be other herding races, too. If we can find allies, maybe we can stop the invasion. Graham has some ideas. So do I. The Molders are clever, but no match for people (etc.) who can really work together against them.

Graham stuck his head through the dilated door. "Hey, Dinker. Still scribbling? I seriously need some help on this navigation."

"One more minute," he said absently, wanting to finish his entry. To capture his final thoughts before they got underway.

We're crossing another boundary, then, like our amphibian forebears so long ago. Goodbye to Earth and Sea and all they've meant to man and dolphin. We'll take the memory with us, though, in our bodies and in our hearts. Someday, with more knowledge, maybe we'll come back, and reclaim our original home.

A hand touched his neck softly. He smiled and flipped the log closed. Stood, and turned into Klassen's embrace.

From that date began the Terran expansion across the universe.

THE END

OTHER SCIENCE FICTION NOVELS BY

D. C. POYER

Available from Northampton House Press in ebook and paper

STEPFATHER BANK

"First-rate satire with a serious core" – *Library Journal*

The year is 2110, and the Bank owns everything.

It's called simply The Bank because its full name is six hundred and sixty-six words long. Over its first ten years it secretly gained controlling interests in Google, Disney, China National Petroleum, Deutsche Bank, Amazon, Colombia, Fox, Egypt, and the Mafia, among many other international corporations, cartels, and governments. Occasional mentions of the Bank's existence were ridiculed as the ravings of conspiracy theorists.

By the year 2110 it has owned Earth (et cetera) for four generations. It's eliminated armies and armaments, governments and war, cash and crime, discrimination and religion. It employs, is owed by, and so rules everyone in the world.

Except Monaghan Burlew.

He's the only one outside the System. The only one on the planet who's free.

This, unfortunately, does not make him heroic, or even appetizing. Burlew is grossly fat. Of Class V (unknown) parentage, he's never been educated beyond Low English and basic computing. His green joggies stink as badly as the hopeless "pomes" he declaims in public squares. He limps because his bare toes were chewed by dogs one bitter July night in Sydney.

He also has no idea that, very shortly, he will be Earth's last hope of surviving an interplanetary catastrophe.….

THE SHILOH PROJECT

The South won at Gettysburg in 1863. Today the Mason-Dixon Wall divides Union and Confederacy . . . and many other things are different from the world we know. There was no Russian Revolution and no World War Two. The Wright brothers died in fiery crashes, and Zeppelins cruise the skies.

Nevertheless, a shaky peace has prevailed between the North and South. For decades now, steaming endlessly up and down the coast from the Antilles to Nova Scotia, the Great Line has contained the expansionist Yankees and their no less aggressive Czarist Russian allies. Ten time larger than the primitive dreadnoughts Jellicoe and von Scheer maneuvered in 1916, each line-of-battle ship takes seven years to build and strains the resources of its sponsor government.

Only now . . . that ring of guns and steel may be broken.

For now the Union has a new weapon, tested during the just-concluded Yankee-Japanese War. Unless the Confederacy can obtain its secret, the balance of terror may escalate into global disaster.

Only Colonel Aubrey Lee Quidley IV, Confederate States Army Intelligence, knows of the Shiloh Project's existence. Until the leak. In a police-state "Dixie Socialist" South, closed off behind barbed wire, there are those who want disaster for their own ends. The "conditionally emancipated" black Resistance . . . the fascist, genocidal Kuklos League . . . a beautiful Yankee mole inside the highest levels of the Richmond Government.

Together, they'll turn Quidley's mission into a treacherous triangle of conspiracy and betrayal. Whoever wins, the Confederacy will never be the same. . . .

WHITE CONTINENT

For thirty years diehard Poyer fans searched used bookstores for the few tattered copies surviving of this sprawling first novel. It followed a team of adventurers, mercenaries, outcasts, and entrepreneurs in a daring coup to take over the last undeveloped and unclaimed land on earth – the terrifyingly hostile continent of Antarctica. Using advanced technology and military surplus weaponry, they now must hold their newly independent state against all comers . . . and build a Utopian society, both communal and fiercely individualistic, unlike any elsewhere on earth.

Jaded Parisian expat turned pioneer Edouard Roudensky is the narrator, forced to drive his pencil over a damp legal pad at the point of a gun. But dozens of other sharply-drawn characters populate these pages too. Legal expert Fumiko Kasuhara; whaler and ice-captain Adrian Larsson; oil-sands billionaire Dorothea Lindahl; icy, sardonic mercenary Robert Blakeley. And others, from all corners of the world, joined under a red, green, and white flag to build a new country, and defy those who want to steal it from them.

This new edition cuts 10,000 words from the original text. The geopolitical scene has changed since the first edition. But the book is still prescient in its foreshadowing of today's conflicting claims and impending resource wars in places like the Arctic and the China Sea. Fans of Poyer's later books will notice themes he's still exploring, such as the search for authentic authority, conflicted heroes, and deeply-layered, multidimensional characters who think as well as act.

The novel's ambition and sweep, as well as Poyer's evocation of the horrific grandeur of the most hostile setting on earth, marked the appearance of a blazing new talent. He would go on to craft nearly fifty more exciting tales of action, adventure, and history . . . chronicling the struggles of heroic men and women to achieve, endure, and prevail.

ABOUT THE AUTHOR

Millions of copies of Dave Poyer's nearly fifty books are in print. His work has been translated into Japanese, Dutch, Italian, Hungarian, and Serbo-Croatian, and rights have been sold for films.

Poyer holds a master's degree from George Washington University and has taught or lectured at Annapolis, Flagler College, University of Pittsburgh, Old Dominion University, Armed Forces Staff College, University of North Florida, The New College, Wilkes University, and other institutions. He's been a writer in residence at Flagler and Annapolis, and a guest on PBS's "Writer to Writer" series, Voice of America, and the Jimmy Carter Presidential Library. His fiction has been required reading in the U.S. Naval Academy's "Literature of the Sea" course, along with that of Joseph Conrad and Herman Melville. He was a founding editor of the *New Virginia Review* and serves on the boards of the *Northern Appalachian Review* and the Eastern Shore Public Library.

After a sixteen-year university career, he currently helps new writers as core faculty at the Ossabaw Island Writers Retreat in Georgia.

Website: <www.poyer.com>
Facebook: David Poyer

Northampton House Press

Northampton House publishes selected fiction, lifestyle nonfiction, memoir, and poetry. Our logo represents the muse Polyhymnia. Our mission is to discover great new writers and make their books available in inexpensive forms. See our list at www.northampton-house.com, or Like us on Facebook – "Northampton House Press" – for more innovative works from brilliant new writers.

www.ingramcontent.com/pod-product-compliance
Lightning Source LLC
Chambersburg PA
CBHW060717190726
48289CB00002B/719